USA TODAY BESTSELLING AUTHOR

DALE MAYER

A Psychic Visions Novel

TALKING BONES

TALKING BONES
Beverly Dale Mayer
Valley Publishing Ltd.

ISBN-13: 978-1-773365-02-2
Print Edition

Books in This Series:

Tuesday's Child
Hide 'n Go Seek
Maddy's Floor
Garden of Sorrow
Knock Knock…
Rare Find
Eyes to the Soul
Now You See Her
Shattered
Into the Abyss
Seeds of Malice
Eye of the Falcon
Itsy-Bitsy Spider
Unmasked
Deep Beneath
From the Ashes
Stroke of Death
Ice Maiden
Snap, Crackle…
What If…
Talking Bones
String of Tears
Inked Forever
Insanity
Soul Legacy
Coveted

Boxed Sets and Bundles
https://geni.us/Bundlepage

About This Book

Hiding out in the French Quarter of New Orleans only made sense for someone like Skylar Livingston. Owning a voodoo shop was just an added touch for fun. It also helped with her cover, plus gave space to the multitude of ghosts in her family. And her shop was close to the cemeteries, … a very necessary part of her … hobby.

Gage Hawkins was tracking his uncle's last movements before his disappearance—hunting a special set of tarot cards—which led to Skylar's shop, Talking Bones. After a bad head injury that brought weird sights into his view, Gage could see this Talking Bones place and Skylar were special. He could only hope she had answers because he had a lot of questions …

Skylar preferred the dead to the living most times, but Gage had her reconsidering. Until she realizes something is wrong in his world, and it's quickly overtaking hers.

When Gage's uncle turns up dead, more than the undead are in Skylar's world. … A killer is too …

Sign up to be notified of all Dale's releases here!
https://geni.us/DaleNews

CHAPTER 1

SKYLAR LIVINGSTON UNLOCKED the connecting door between her upstairs apartment and that of her ground-level New Orleans shop, Skylar's Heaven, and stepped inside her store that Friday morning. She walked rapidly to the back room and shut off the alarm. With that done, she entered her shop and opened the blinds to the front windows, letting light into her store. Taking off her sweater, she proceeded to the counter, where she flicked on the lights throughout, and only then did she fully open her eyes.

With the shop fully lit, the spirits were much less prevalent.

She called out, "Good morning, guys."

There was a weird wavering of the air, as multiple personalities greeted her. Every morning when she arrived, the ghostly apparitions were so bright that it was hard for Skylar to see where she walked, as she headed to the alarm system. The ghosts were an alarm system as well, but Skylar still felt the need to have a more traditional system in place.

"Going to be a crazy day today," Thomas said, by way of his greeting. He was one of many resident ghosts here.

Checking around, she noted that nothing appeared to be wrong or different with the energy or the ambience in the store. No sign of an intruder. No sign of any problems, but she hadn't fully checked in the back yet. She made a quick walk through to the rear area, where she put on a pot of coffee, relieved to see absolutely nothing new or different.

In her world, boring and normal were perfect.

With all of that in place and the coffee dripping, she headed back out to the main store area, unlocked the front door, and peered out the window. She still had fifteen minutes until opening, but the streets were already filling with tourists. That was both good and bad. She needed the income that the tourists provided, but she didn't like some of the energy that they brought with them. As a matter of fact, she didn't like anything about the commercialism or the necessity of making a living.

But she hadn't won the lottery and neither had she been born rich. So she worked.

She yawned and quickly covered her mouth with her hand, wishing she could sleep in later in the mornings. But that would mean hiring somebody to open up the store for her and giving her those extra few hours. Then again, if she didn't spend so much of her nights in the damn cemeteries, it wouldn't be as big of a problem.

Skylar brushed her long black hair off her face, noting that in her hurry she hadn't brought a clip. She looked around, found a wooden stick and a hair pin from the olden days that she had marked at two bucks, then quickly twisted her hair up and fixed it firmly in place. Noting just how quick and efficient that was, not to mention stylish, she looked at the price on the rest of them and quickly changed it to seven dollars instead. She often found that, with things for sale in the store, if she doubled the price or made it even higher, the items sometimes took on a life of their own.

Then her ghostly friends helped too.

She knew that she could count on the effect of the spirits

and their energy to set the mood inside, which was perfect for a voodoo shop, although it took a lot from Skylar to keep it energized high enough to bring in people.

Whenever she recognized that some people were looking for a spooky experience, she would quickly lower her energy shield, so that the store had the ambience of something darker. She could cheerfully blame the ghosts for that, if any tourist was so interested.

As she looked around, she saw all her regular ghostly crew.

"You know that you can go home anytime," she stated, something that she shared probably thirty to forty times a day. At least when the store was empty. The ghosts all just nodded, and not one moved.

The frustration was crippling at times. "You all do that, seemingly agreeing with me, yet you're all still here. Even though you have options."

Thomas whispered in her ear, "We are here because we want to be."

"You're not connected to me though," she murmured. "So you don't need to stand watch, although it is appreciated."

"We *are* connected to you," he argued, crossing his arms. He looked like somebody from Abraham Lincoln's era, with a top hat and a black suit. He was tall and almost gaunt.

She sighed. "Just because I rescued some bones—"

"Yes, but we're also here because we want to be," he noted, "so you can't chase us away."

She rolled her eyes at that. "My shop is getting more crowded all the time."

"That's all right," replied Dodi, a pale-faced woman on the other side of the counter. "We'll just move to your apartment then."

Immediately Skylar shook her head. "No, no, no, please don't do that."

The woman looked at her in surprise. "Why not?"

"Because it's nice to have a place that is only mine." Although it wasn't only hers. No way to explain that to this group of ghosts though.

Dodi looked at Skylar for a moment and then gave a complacent nod. "I can see that for you, it's true. I had nine children, so I wouldn't know what that is like. But I'm happy to give it to you."

"Nine children?" Skylar almost gasped at that. When she heard a noise from the front door, she turned toward it. One of the ghost kids, Chucky, called out in excitement, "They're coming."

She groaned, plastered a smile on her face, and waited, while the door opened fully. Then her smile became real. "Hey, Tomo," she greeted the tall, spare man walking toward her with a sheepish smile. "How are you doing?"

He held up a plate. "My latest offering. I'm hoping you would try some."

She looked at the plate avariciously. "More beignets?"

"More beignets," he confirmed. "You know that they have to be absolutely perfect in order to compete with everybody else around here."

"You keep trying all you want," she murmured, as she stared at the plate with three fat treats, "particularly if that will keep the samples coming my way."

He burst out laughing, his beautiful caramel-colored skin glowing, as his face split wide into a big grin. "You know that you'll get all the beignets you want from my restaurant, when I finally get there—and for free."

She shook her head. "You can't do it for free. You'll have to play the game and charge for your goods, just like the rest of us."

"I wish I could hand them out for free though," he replied in all seriousness.

"I know you do," she added gently, "but somehow we're caught up in this commercial lifestyle, where I must have people actually pay for my products, so I can turn around and pay you for beignets."

"But, if I just gave them to you," he started, "you wouldn't—"

"Then how will you pay your rent?" she asked, with an understanding smile. He really was a wonderful soul, just not the most realistic when it came to business. He wanted to believe in a world of sunshine and roses, where everybody loved everybody else and where they all took care of each other. Well, she wanted to believe in that too, but her life experiences had confirmed a whole different reality was out there.

"I wish I had enough money," he noted, "where I could just do it by donation."

"I wish you did too because I know that system does work in some places." He looked at her with interest, as she shrugged. "I've heard of pilot programs that have popped up in different areas with that structure, but I would presume that you still need to have enough income on a regular basis to pay the rent."

He winced. "I don't understand why that rent money thing keeps coming around every month." She burst out laughing, and he shot her a quick, bright grin.

Skylar continued. "See? Now that's what I love about you—that humor, with a completely deadpan face, while you crack a joke like that."

He nodded sagely. "And you're always happy to see me because I bring along the sunshine."

She gazed at him affectionately. "That is very true. The world will be a sadder place when you choose to leave it." He looked at her in surprise, but she shrugged. "Don't ask me. It's just the way the words came out."

"Are you, like, sensing anything?" There was hesitation and worry in his voice.

She stared. "Hell no," she said out loud. "You know that's not a part of what I do."

He nodded. "But I think you probably could if you tried. At least my grandma says so."

"Your grandma would accept anybody in the business if she thought she could get them to help with her clients and could make money off them," she teased.

That grin flashed again. "You do know her, don't you?"

"I know her very well," she stated, with a smile. "You guys have been very good to me since I've been here."

"Too bad you haven't been here longer," he added cheerfully. "We would have been nice to you since then."

Skylar nodded. Nothing she could really say to that, but it was such a typical comment from him, and, thinking back, she wished the same thing.

He looked around. "Well, here we go. Looks like the tourists are filling up the streets once again. You'll have a wild and crazy day, from the looks of things. Good thing I brought you some fortification," he noted, with one raised eyebrow.

"Tourists are a blessed evil." She shook her head.

"I have to admit I do like to be with them, but then, at some point, it gets very draining, and I need my own space.

That's when I go bury myself in the kitchen and come up with new recipes."

"You go do that all you want," she agreed. "I'm always happy to try out your experiments."

"Even the failures?" He groaned, with an eye roll. "That says something."

"Hey, I don't get that much to eat these days," she murmured.

"If you'd ever get some sleep," he admonished her, "you could get up earlier, in time to actually eat before you have to open."

"I *could*," she noted, "but now you've saved me from starving yet another day." When he frowned at her, she laughed. "Don't worry about it. I'm fine."

"Have you really not eaten?" he asked.

"Not yet, no, but the coffee's still dripping."

He continued to frown, tapping his fingers on the front counter, as he glared at her.

"I'm fine," she murmured. "I really am."

"I'm not so sure that you're fine, as much as you're trying to convince me that you're fine."

Again, another astute comment from him that she hadn't expected. She patted his hand. "I get it, but it's all good."

His response was stifled, as a crowd moved into her shop. She smiled at the crowd and greeted them. "Good morning."

As if sensing that he was preventing her sales, Tomo immediately left, so she could get to work.

She was sad to see him leave. He was one of the few *real* friends she had here, among all her ghostly ones. She knew perfectly well that Tomo wouldn't remain in this world much longer. Life, then death. It was the normal cycle of life, and she saw it time and time again. It was hard when they were young, and, just because she knew Tomo's fate, she had no ability to change it. Therefore, she kept him happy, doing the things that he loved. Meanwhile, maybe he'd find a new treatment for the cancer eating away in his system.

She hadn't changed fate one bit over the last twenty years and highly doubted that she could manage to do it now. Her own grandmother would have told her to stop wasting time and energy on something she can't fix or stop, stating that the spirits had their own reasons for what they were doing, and it wasn't for Skylar to know.

She'd even asked several of the ghosts in her shop for advice on how to help Tomo, but not one of her ghosts had a word of advice on how to postpone that final date with destiny.

For that reason alone, she tried to keep Tomo focused on what was happening in his world, all to make him smile. Surely smiling had to be worth something.

The smell of the beignets, still warm on her counter, tantalized her, even as she studied the customers who had just entered. "May I help you find anything?" she asked, casting another longing glance at the treats in front of her.

"We're just looking," a woman replied, her voice upbeat.

Skylar nodded and picked up a beignet, then quickly took a bite.

Almost immediately came a gasp from one of her potential customers. "Oh my," the woman told her, "we just came from that famous café down the road. Their beignets were absolutely wonderful."

Skylar immediately nodded. "Yes, they are."

"Do they deliver too?"

"A friend of mine picked these up," she explained.

"Nice friend," the woman stated jealously.

Skylar kept her voice and smile soft, as she waited for them to peruse the store to see if they wanted to buy anything. Usually the early morning crowds were heading out for long days of sightseeing and rarely bought anything right off the bat because they were carrying everything they had with them. When they all tripped out with a smile, calling out for her to have a happy day, Skylar's forecast had proven out because no one had bought a thing.

She immediately walked to the back room, then grabbed her first cup of coffee and returned to the counter, lifting a beignet and taking a big bite. As she stood here, wiping the powdered sugar off her face, her front door opened with an odd surge of air. She froze.

Only a few things would cause the wind to blow into her store like that.

With buildings across from her shop and around on all sides, the wind ran down the street. It rarely came into her store. And, sure enough, her curious gaze followed the gust of air all the way from the front to the back of her store and again to the front, as a man stepped over the threshold of her entrance. She stared at him, and her heart sank. "May I help you?" she asked, forcing a smile she didn't feel, while she studied the strong energy in front of her.

"I'm looking for Skylar," replied the man in a deep voice, his gaze intently studying her.

She nodded. "Well, you found her. What can I do for you?"

He observed her for a long moment, but she refused to give in to the uneasiness in her gut telling her to run, even though the power radiating off his frame was unbelievable.

She didn't dare make a comment or even let him know that she registered that something powerful filled him, because surely he already knew.

"I need you to help me with something."

She raised her eyebrows. "I'm sorry. I don't know what you're looking for, but I just run this little shop here."

He burst out laughing. "That's hardly all you do."

She frowned and replied in a much different tone, not liking anything about his. "I'm sorry. I don't understand what you're implying."

"I'm implying that you're very talented in many other areas," he stated, "and I don't have time for the facade."

"That's nice," she noted. "And I don't really have time for anything you have to say, with an attitude like that."

He nodded. "No? I can see that. Apparently I'm being more abrupt than usual."

"Really?" She smirked. "I hadn't noticed."

"I don't think much of anything gets by you, and I do not suffer fools either," he stated in a silky voice.

She stared at him and asked quietly, "Are you calling me a fool?"

He shook his head. "No, and I can see that your defense mechanisms are already standing at full attention. I'm really not here to harm you."

"Interesting, yet you say the darndest things."

He frowned, as he studied her again. "Can we drop the pretense?"

"Please do," she agreed patiently, not sure where he was going with this, but afraid she wouldn't like it.

"I need help finding my uncle."

"And what has that got to do with me?" she asked, a frown crossing her brows in bewilderment.

He scowled, as if finally realizing it was possible that he had the wrong person. "My uncle, I am afraid he's missing."

"Have you gone to the police?" No way would she try to find a lost uncle. What gossip had he listened to?

He sighed impatiently. "Of course I have. And, having exhausted all leads, I'm here, looking for assistance from you."

"And whatever would possess you to come to me for help?"

"Well, you're the one who talks to all these ghosts in here, aren't you?" he asked, with a negligent hand movement.

Her heart clamped down tightly, and she stared at him in shock, her breath frozen in her chest.

"I could see them when I came in, at least some of them," he explained. "I have a very general ability, not a full slate like you do."

"I don't get it," she admitted, covertly gasping for air.

"And I don't have the time or the patience for this," he snapped. "My uncle might be dying, and I need help finding him."

She frowned, her mind trying to figure out just what this was all about. She'd never had anybody come to her with that kind of a request before. "What do you mean, he's dying? I thought you said that he's missing."

"Yes, and I got a note saying that, if I didn't produce something specific, he would die."

"I still don't get it. What makes you think that, even if I could talk to ghosts, or whatever you're saying I do here, that I could find a man, who is living?" Her confusion was real. She didn't have a clue what the hell was going on here or why this guy had targeted her. "I'm afraid I'll have to ask you to leave my store."

"And how many people will you gather up in order to force me outside?" he asked in a hard tone.

She stiffened. "Are you threatening me?"

He considered her for a long moment and then seemed to relax. "No, I'm being sincere. I need your help to find my uncle."

"And yet you have not, at any point in time, explained how you've come to believe that I could help in any way," she argued.

"I was hoping that you would be more honest, but I can see that you've built a life for yourself here by keeping those abilities hidden from this world. I hadn't really expected that."

"Why wouldn't you?" she asked, shaking her head. "Even if I did have skills that you could utilize in some way, the world is not kind to anyone with abilities they don't understand."

"No," he agreed. "I just assumed that, when you relocated, you would have found a better way to make it all work to your advantage."

Her breath caught midway through his sentence. What could he possibly know about her relocating? "Stop," she snapped abruptly. "I don't know what this is all about. I don't know how to find anybody. And, if the police haven't found a way, I sure as hell can't."

"But you have to," he stated.

Her eyebrows shot up. "What makes you think I *have* to do anything?"

"Because my uncle is also a distant relative of yours—he was into genealogy as well," he added, with a crooked smile. "And, if you don't help, according to the letter I received, everything about your life will become public."

She looked at him in shock. "I don't know anything about your uncle, but I do know that you, sir, are not related to me at all." That she knew instinctively. She could tell from his energy that they shared absolutely nothing.

"That's quite true," he admitted, "blood relative of my mother's. And we've been very close all my life."

This was so far out of what she could even process that she didn't know what to say. When she found her voice, she replied, "First, blackmail never works on me. Second, lying to me, trying to spring some *surprise family* on me, doesn't work either. Since you seem to have delved into my background some, then you already realize that I have zero family, as far as I know. What game are you playing?" She stared at him, still trying to figure out what he was up to.

He nodded. "Which is also why I guess I can understand your reaction at the moment. But, if you will hear me out, I could explain."

"So far you haven't said much of anything yet, except for the thinly veiled threats and innuendos which I don't appreciate. So, pardon me if I don't look like I'm exactly thrilled about listening to anything more you have to say."

He winced. "I get it. I haven't been the most forthcoming. Put that down to being very worried about our uncle."

"*Your* uncle. Not mine. Drop the *phony family* angle. I still don't understand where you're going with this."

"So, Uncle Jonesy," he began, with a gusty sigh and an attempt at a beguiling smile, "disappeared two nights ago, and I've been frantically looking for him ever since. He was staying close by, and I found out that his last stop on Tuesday night was one of the shops on this strip. I believe it was yours."

She shrugged and shook her head.

"Then I got a note from somebody," he added, "and, yes, the police now have that note. It says, Jonesy's been taken prisoner, and, if they don't get what they want, they'll make sure that both your world and mine become public."

She focused on him for a moment. "If my world becomes public, it would be a huge inconvenience, but I would just move on. Not a whole lot I can do about it otherwise."

He nodded. "And you've done that a time or two already."

"Once really," she stated, her tone stiff. "What is it *you*'re trying to hide from?"

"Well, let's just say I have zero interest in having my world become public either," he replied.

"So what then? You expect me to help you find out where this … Jonesy of yours is?" she asked. "I don't have any skills for that, whether my family or yours."

"According to this note, you are family, and it goes back several generations."

She waved a hand. "Which means nothing. I was adopted as a baby."

"I get that. And you probably are also aware that your records are not available."

"I haven't tried to look." She stared at him. "And just how would you know that?"

"Since getting this note and working with the police, we've worked hard to try and figure out what your family connection is."

"As I've repeatedly told you, there is none."

At that, the bell on the front door rang again and in walked a police officer. She swore under her breath. Something about the police just completely changed the energy in her shop.

"Gentlemen, you do realize that I'm trying to run a business here, and, no offense, but cops and angry strangers really don't do anything for sales."

The cop grinned at her affably. "Sorry about that."

Yet he obviously didn't give a shit. She groaned and asked, "What is this all about?"

"I'm sure he's already told you. He just asked to step in here a few minutes early to talk to you privately."

"Great. However, I have no idea who this Jonesy guy is, having never met him."

"We have video camera proof, showing him coming here Tuesday at the end of the day."

She raised her eyebrows. "Do you have a picture of him?"

Immediately the cop stepped forward and held out a photo on his phone. She looked at it, then frowned. "I kind of remember him. Let me think for a minute." She focused her memory for a moment, then nodded. "Yes, he was looking for some tarot cards."

"Do you know which ones?" the nephew asked, his voice intent.

She shot him a glare. "He was looking for a very old set, but I don't have anything even close to that here at all. He did ask me if I knew of any."

"Well, whoever kidnapped him wants this particular set and appears to believe that Uncle hid them somewhere since getting them."

She stared at him. "Well, I never had them, and I certainly didn't sell that or anything else to him. I didn't do anything but speak with him briefly for a few moments," she shared. "I don't know anything about those particular tarot cards. What's the draw about them anyway?"

The cop turned her words on her. "You tell me. You said they're rare."

"I *said* they're *old*," she corrected. "Like turn of the century—and that's just according to Jonesy. I think he told me something about how they might have been involved in several murders."

"We have one other reason why we're here," the cop added, with a not-so-affable smile.

In fact, his teeth almost appeared to sharpen as he studied her.

"His jacket was found on a side street and inside was a note to see you personally."

She stared at him in shock, not liking anything happening here. "Outside of talking to him Tuesday night, and telling you all we discussed, I don't know anything about it. So what is this all about?"

"How about the term *talking bones*?" the nephew asked quietly, the powerful energy around him stronger now.

Her gaze darted his way and then back at the cop. "No, I don't understand that phrase. What are you talking about?"

The cop laughed. "It seems that the uncle thought you were capable of identifying bones."

"What does that have to do with tarot cards?" she asked, getting more puzzled by the minute. "I'm hardly a pathologist or whatever science is involved in that skill."

"He was looking for the tarot cards that he thought were involved in several murders, and he has several bones that he wanted identified," the nephew stated abruptly. "According to everything he left behind, he believed you were the person who could do it."

As she stood here, shaking her head, she recalled the

ghosts had given her a warning about her crazy day coming and also recalled Tomo's words about needing fortification for whatever was to come.

GAGE STUDIED THE woman before him. Skylar wore a short-sleeve black T-shirt, showing off myriad tattoos that only highlighted her creamy white skin and black hair, long enough to be twisted atop her head and skewered in place. For all his newfound energy abilities—granted, he was still learning—she was damn good at cloaking. He couldn't see behind her shield. He did sense more souls stuffed in her shop, almost like sardines.

Did she even know? Was she the one who collected them? Were they tied to her? Souls would tether to a human for a lot of reasons. But Gage had seen occasions where they were tethered and didn't want to be. But, even as he studied the small store as surreptitiously as possible, he couldn't see any sign of tethers. Damn, he wished he knew more—could do more.

He frowned, as he tuned out of the conversation between the cop and Skylar. Gage had wanted to come in here all on his own, so he could assess who she was. He'd seen the cracks in her shield beginning, before the cop walked in, but her fortress had immediately become indefensible again.

He understood that anything to do with law enforcement was like a blatant stab wound to her heart because they had so little belief in this stuff. Maybe in this town, more than any others, there could be a little wiggle room for voodoo and the like, but mostly probably only for the voodoo practitioners of old. Skylar here was a newcomer, and that meant she was not one of them.

Gage wondered if she even realized it.

The energy in here was interesting; it was dark, and yet he noticed it had lightened considerably. As he looked over at her, she waved her hands gently, as if brushing a spiderweb from around her. He continued to watch, fascinated, as light beams drifted from her hands, easily lightening the atmosphere of the store. Talk about an interesting trick. Did it help with sales? Or was it merely to bolster her own mood?

Although she didn't advertise it as a voodoo shop, her store was esoteric in all things. Sure, the typical kitschy tourist stuff was all around, but he highly doubted that she made much money off any of that. If she didn't, he thought with a frown, while studying the price tags on the items closest to him, how did she survive?

Caught by a question the cop was asking about her whereabouts, she gave a flat answer, her response in a weird monotone, as she stated, "I was upstairs in my apartment."

"Can anybody verify that?"

"Of course not. If you're asking if I live alone, yes, I live alone. Did I have friends over last night? No, I had no friends over. Did I go out last night? No, I didn't go out. I was watching TV."

"What did you watch?"

It was meant as a trick question, but she gave him a flat smile and named two shows that were just probably true enough that she was off the hook.

The cop wrote it down and asked, "So, you have no idea what happened to this man?"

"No, I don't."

"Good, in that case, sorry to bother you." And he stepped back. The cop looked over at Gage. "I told you it would be useless." And, with that, he walked out.

Gage turned, then looked at her and asked, "What about the bone?"

Her gaze shot upward to read his expression. "What bone?"

He pointed at the floor. She frowned and walked around the counter and looked, found a small bone, too big to have been a finger bone but nowhere near big enough to be an arm bone. She leaned closer and studied it. "I have no idea where that came from." She looked over at him suspiciously. "Did you put it here on purpose?"

"Hell no," he denied forcibly, "but it's possible that it's part of my uncle's collection."

"Why would he have a collection of bones?"

"Because he found several open graves, and, when he went back to identify the dead, only a few bones were still there and were scattered about. Unfortunately he discovered this after bringing a crowd of people with him to check it out. They all had laughed at him and had taken off."

"Your uncle does seem a little eccentric," she murmured.

"Yes, he is, but that does not make him senile or stupid."

"No, of course not," she agreed immediately. "Older, slightly rotund, with wispy white hair and a genial smile on his face?"

"That's him. He's a good man."

"He did appear to be very interested in the tarot card set."

"Yes, but that also could have just been a diversion."

"For what though?"

"I don't know." His angry frustration bled into his tone. "But what are the chances that he left that bone behind?"

"Honestly, I don't know," she stated helplessly. "I don't know anything about this."

Just then the door opened, and a large group of tourists came in. She smiled at them, nudging the bone farther underneath the counter in the display area, so it was hidden from sight. Why? Obviously she was trying to hide it or was it more that she didn't want to touch it?

Then she turned to face her customers again.

Gage stepped out of the store, separating himself from the crowd of cheerfully chattering tourists. They all looked to be about the same age. Slightly older than fifty, probably younger than seventy, all of them wearing bright clothing. Most were overweight but not horrifically. They were all in shorts and looked to be having a grand old time. Other tourists filled the street, but Gage saw no cops. His phone buzzed, a text from his brother.

Any sign?

No, he texted back immediately.

Studying his surroundings, Gage didn't know what to do next. He needed to talk to Skylar again, only that wouldn't happen as long as she had a store full of tourists. He noted the beignets that she had been trying to eat and how lean her face was. She needed another twenty pounds to fill out the hollow planes on her face.

He also noted an odd smell to the store. Whether that was her or the beignets mixed with the bone or something completely different, he had no idea. He wished he could speak to the spirits that he seemed to see milling about her store, but none had stepped forward in any shape or form recognizable as someone in particular who he could talk to. The only time he'd ever successfully talked to a spirit, they'd approached him in human form, with very clear and distinct details, and had spoken to him first.

Those in her store were just ghostly forms in all sizes and

shapes, who stood wall-to-wall inside, but he didn't understand why. He wondered if the spirits were connected to the building. He had now wandered in her store and previously in the other likely stores on this street, but no other shop was full of spirits like Skylar's was. True, he didn't see spirits all the time, but her place had been divinely attuned to them, for some reason.

Gage knew he needed to rework his game plan, as he wandered toward the river and sat on a bench. He tuned out the world around him and tried to just focus on the water, calming himself as best he could.

When his phone rang an hour later, it was his brother again, calling this time. "What now?" Gage asked abruptly.

"I don't know," Terrence replied. "You tell me. What now?"

"I'm not sure," he admitted. "I am not sure where to look next."

"Uncle did this all the time. It was his biggest hobby to go wander around town, hit a few shops, and then come home again. So what's so different now that he's disappeared?"

"I've checked along this street already today. I'm not sure where to go next. I don't really know my way around here."

"Yeah, I'm surprised you're there," his brother noted. "New Orleans is hardly your type of place, especially the French Quarter. You've never been a partier, Gage. Always so serious."

"Count yourself lucky that I lived in Portland all these years, that you had your serious older brother around all that time. Once I get this merger deal cinched, that allows me to relocate anywhere I want, probably somewhere away from people," he shared. "No telling where I'll end up."

"I know. I know," Terrence agreed carefully. "I'm just trying to figure out what happened to Uncle."

"You and me both." Gage pinched the bridge of his nose, wishing his brother hadn't called.

"At least you found the shop he went to." Terrence hesitated. "Do you think she knows anything?"

"About him? No, not at all. About a lot of other things, hell yes."

"Really?" Terrence's tone sounded interested. "Like, did you see something?"

"I saw a lot of shapes, like spirits, but none I could talk to," Gage murmured, grateful his brother knew some of his current troubles.

"That's too bad because if you could talk to them—"

"We've been over this. I can't, so it doesn't really matter."

"I get it. I get it." Terrence sighed. "But, with that note, we need to get this resolved. Uncle's got to be somewhere."

"I'll go back and talk to her, when the crowds disperse a bit."

"Well, maybe do something nice for her this time, so you don't come across so overpowering."

"Who said I was overpowering?"

"Are you kidding? You didn't build a very successful business with your charm, bro."

"You may have a point there. I might pick up lunch for her. She looks like she's starving."

A moment of silence passed on the other end, and then his brother chuckled. "You know what? That just might do it. Get some for yourself too, so you don't come across as a grizzly bear. You probably came on way too strong. Come on. Admit it."

He winced. "It's possible."

"Of course it is. You probably accused her—or at least pushed her psychic buttons all over the place. You know that's not the way to get cooperation."

"I don't know anything about this psychic stuff," he snapped. "I'm just a newbie. Remember? Only since the accident did I start seeing these apparitions, and you know that."

"I know, but still it's intriguing," he shared. "I almost want to sign up for a car accident myself."

"Right, of course you do," he scoffed. "Chances are that wouldn't go well. So hold off, okay?"

"I know. I'm all too afraid that's exactly what would happen," he murmured. "Keep me posted." And, with that, his brother hung up.

Gage looked around and wondered if 11:30 a.m. was too early to bring her food. Hoping not, he found a restaurant farther down that opened onto the street with an outdoor window, and he headed in that direction. At least if he picked something up, she could eat it whenever.

He hated the fact that he already felt like he needed to feed her. One thing he could never do was walk by and see the homeless or the elderly suffering and without food. He didn't know why, all of a sudden, she fit into that same category, but apparently she did. With that, he immediately headed to the restaurant and studied the menu, trying to imagine what she might like.

CHAPTER 2

THIS GROUP OF tourists was thankfully full of energy in abundance, so easily distracted Skylar from the tall stranger leaving her shop. With cheerful faces, they quickly purchased multiple items, including five of the hair sticks that she had just tripled the price on earlier this morning. She smiled as they all walked out, wishing them a happy day. Following on their heels came another group and, after that, still another.

By the time the store was finally empty for the first time later that morning, she smiled and headed to the back, hoping she could squeeze in a cup of coffee before the next group arrived. She cringed a moment later when the bell signaled that the door was opening yet again. Her heart sank because she was really hoping to get that coffee and maybe even rummage in the back to see if she had anything to eat besides the sweet beignets. Instead she turned to see the stranger from earlier.

He walked in, carrying a large take-out bag.

She frowned, staring at it suspiciously, but she recognized the Chinese restaurant's logo on the bag. He put it down on the counter by the cash register and started pulling out several items. She looked at him and asked, "What's all this about?"

"A peace offering," he stated. "I realized that I came on

way too strong this morning, and I was completely out of line. I'm sorry, and I hope you'll accept my apology and some lunch."

"Well, you certainly came on strong," she confirmed cautiously. Then her stomach rumbled, as she looked at the food.

"Do you happen to have any coffee to go with it?" he asked.

"Well, I was about to go check out that coffee situation, when you walked in. I could put on a fresh pot," she offered. "I didn't even get a chance to drink much this morning, so it's probably burned and bitter tasting by now."

"A fresh pot sounds great," he agreed. "I should have grabbed a couple to-go when I got the food."

She frowned, not sure she trusted him alone in her store.

He suggested, "I'll walk back with you, if you'd rather." At that, she took a step back. He stepped back himself, putting up his hands. "Or else I'll stand right here until you return. Sorry, I'm not trying to intimidate you."

Surprised at him picking up on her reluctance, but sensing no malice in his energy, she raced to the back, put on a pot of coffee, and returned to the front of the store, almost amused to see him standing in the exact same place. He looked at her, smiled, and said, "See? I promised, and I stuck to it."

"Sure, but your presence is still more than a little disturbing."

"For you?" he asked, with an eyebrow raised.

"I don't get it," she stated. "What do you even know about me?"

"Only what my uncle researched about you, and then, of course, with his disappearance, we had no choice but to delve more into your background," he admitted almost apologetically.

"Surely it's not that interesting," she noted.

"Any woman who can talk to bones has my attention."

She winced at that phrase. "Nobody talks to bones," she countered, with an airy wave of her hand, hoping he'd let it go at that. And who the hell would even know anything about talking to bones?

"What about all the spirits in here?"

She stared at him. "Are you saying that you see spirits here in my store?"

He snorted. "I can see evidence of the spirits here, but I know, for a fact, that you can talk to them."

"And how is that?"

"Because I can hear it."

"You want to explain that?" she demanded.

He hesitated, and then, as if realizing he would have to give something in order to get a little bit of trust back, he began, "Look. My name is Gage Hawkins. A friend and I were at a business dinner a while back. On the way home we were involved in a bad car accident—and, just for the record, I wasn't drinking. I ended up in a coma for a time, and, when I came out of it, I could see and hear things that nobody could explain."

At that, she nodded slowly. "It can happen like that sometimes."

"Yes," he agreed, "but I didn't know what I was seeing or hearing, and I didn't want to tell anybody because all they'd do is say I was seeing and hearing things and refer me to a shrink."

She stared. "Yeah, that's a very common response." So far, everything he said rang true.

He went on. "It took me a long time to realize that I was seeing dead people, and then, when one ghost stepped forward, in a normal-looking human form, he explained it to me. So I could hear him, even though he was a ghost."

She frowned, while nodding. "So what exactly do you see?"

"I see like glowing white shapes." He motioned to the side of him.

She looked over to where Thomas stood right beside Gage, his top hat still in place, which was normal for him. "So, what do you see right now?" she asked.

Gage put out his hand toward Thomas again. "This white form has something about ten inches tall or so above his head, and what I presume is his body is just this long skinny white form."

"His name is Thomas," she shared. "He was killed over 150 years ago. Somewhere around Lincoln's era."

"Interesting," he replied, as he studied her. "Did he tell you that?"

"Yep, he sure did. Once you open the doorway, they really like to talk," she stated. "So, when your friend the cop was asking if I was alone last night, my answer was yes, but of course it had to be no."

He nodded. "Right. I sensed that you weren't telling the truth."

"Because, to me, these guys are real," she stated cheerfully. "Of course I'm comfortable telling you this because, if you go tell the cops, they won't believe you anyway." Then she gave him the sweetest smile.

He looked at her in fascination. "You know what? You're quite right. They would think I had absolutely gone around the bend."

"And they would refer you for some psychiatric evaluation, perhaps having you committed for however long, until you convince them that it must have been a bad dream or maybe the drugs you were taking that made you say that."

He stared at her. "You've been there, haven't you?"

Her gaze widened, as she studied him. "Haven't we all?"

He nodded slowly. "No, you're right. I did go through a similar session that terrified me."

"And it should. When people think that you're off your rocker and are doing things that they don't understand, they suddenly have all kinds of power over you. You have no idea."

"I'm sorry. … I didn't mean to send you down that kind of a negative pathway."

"Maybe not," she agreed, "but you must know that you possess a tremendously powerful energy, and, when you walked in this morning, you brought the wind with you. That's because you were uncomfortable in this situation, and you were using it to try to make you look good."

He stared at her, and she saw an ever-so-slight flush going up his neck.

She nodded. "So, from one to another, don't bother trying to make a showy presence upon arrival. None of us appreciate it, and those of us in the industry already know what you're doing and why."

"Wow," he replied. "That was guaranteed to knock me off balance."

"That wasn't what I intended to do," she murmured, backing off slightly, "but it is what you intended to do to me." As the flush rose a little higher up his neck, she nodded. "Now, with that said and understood, I still don't understand what this is all about, but, first, it smells like the coffee is done."

She retreated to her little back room, where she poured two cups and returned. Her amusement grew even greater, as she noted he still hadn't moved from that one spot. She waved a hand. "You may now move."

He looked down, and, flushing even more, he asked, "Did you keep me here?"

She seemed surprised. "None of us can do to another what they don't wish to have done."

"You know what? I'd like to believe that," he stated, "but some weird shit is happening in my world, and I'm not sure that I can agree."

"Good, because there are exceptions," she noted, "and you should always be doubting everything around you."

He nodded slowly and stared at her in awe.

An awed fascination that she didn't really want. But somehow this soul—who was new to all this—was a little more broken than she had expected. Gage covered it up really well with that macho bravado, mostly out of fear when he'd walked in originally, she figured. But no way to really be sure so she couldn't trust him quite yet. Something was going on in that energy of his that he was keeping from her. But, by the same token, she was keeping a lot from him as well. She set a cup of coffee in front of him. "Here you are."

He nodded sheepishly. "Thank you."

She shrugged. "There's too much food here just for me, so I presume you intended this for both of us."

"I know my brother would certainly appreciate it if you shared a meal with me. He suggested I was in a bit of a mood."

She snorted. "I'm not known for *not* sharing. However, when people come in, asking questions about a missing uncle—who doesn't have anything to do with me—I find it a little irritating. Especially when they bring the cops, which is bad for business."

"Everybody called him Jonesy, but we called him Uncle. He was well loved by many."

"And yet you speak about him in the past tense."

He frowned. "I didn't mean to."

"But you did."

"Yes, I guess I did, but I don't know why." He looked more than a little disturbed. He picked up one of the covered dishes and said, "I think these are both the same."

"Slight variations from the looks of it, but yes." She picked up hers. "What made you think of this?"

"I like food?"

She snorted. "And I gather you're the kind who likes to feed waifs, the homeless, the starving children, unwanted pets, and the like." He looked at her, as if stunned that she had hit that out of the park. She nodded. "It's in your energy."

"What else is in my energy?" he asked worriedly.

"That you're honestly worried about your uncle," she noted. "Which is the only reason I'm talking to you right now, by the way."

He swallowed hard. "You're a little scary, you know that?"

She nodded, as she continued to study his energy. "I am. It's one of the reasons why not a whole lot of people are in my private world."

"I can see that. … Do you have any idea what happened to Uncle?"

She shook her head. "I didn't even know he was missing. I didn't know anything about him."

"And that bone?"

"I don't know," she admitted.

"But you haven't picked it up."

She looked over at him and asked, "How do you know that?"

"I can see it peeking out from under the display."

She winced. "I was trying to move it earlier, but it's been a *very* busy day."

"You can move it now," he stated helpfully.

She glared at him and then nodded. "I kind of need to." She quickly snatched up the gloves that she kept underneath the counter, put them on, then walked around the counter and picked up the bone, placing it on a side counter, out of the sight of her customers.

"Why the gloves?"

"Well, I guess it depends on the bone," she replied, looking back at him. "Have you ever tried to pick up the bone of someone who died violently?"

He stared at her, horrified, and then slowly shook his head.

"That violence is often still sitting on the bones."

"So, do you get a shock or what?"

"Well, that's one word for it." She walked behind the counter again, took off the gloves, and picked up her lunch.

"You really don't want to tell me much, do you?"

"I don't know who you are. For all I know, you're a reporter, and you're recording this," she declared calmly, even though the very thought made her sick to her stomach.

He stared at her and started to laugh. "No, I'm not. I promise. And honestly, I probably hate reporters even more than you do."

She looked at him and realized with relief that he was

telling the truth. "Well, I'm certainly glad to hear that," she noted lightly. "That is one point to your benefit."

"I guess they haven't been very nice to you, have they?" he asked.

"Nope, they sure haven't," she confirmed, trying for a smile but not succeeding.

"Am I wrong to think that a lot of people haven't been very nice to you?"

"Most people are petrified of what they don't understand," she explained. "So, that fact alone puts me in a whole different category of life."

"I'm sorry. That must be kind of lonely."

She shrugged, scooped up the last of her lunch. "Why? It's not your fault."

"No, but I think I added to your upset today, and that wasn't fair. Especially since I did it badly."

"It's lucky that you're very powerful at something in the normal world out there. I don't know what it is because I don't know you, but you've taken that same can-do attitude, and you've applied it to something that has absolutely nothing to do with your original specialty. So, you come across forceful, as if you know exactly what you're talking about. Which probably works very well in your world. Not in mine though, because those of us who can see and can read energies know exactly where you're at on this pathway. You're a newbie. So, a word to the wise, don't try it."

"You said something like that earlier."

"Yeah, and you almost listened, but then you started to dismiss it."

He winced. "Am I that easy to read?"

"No, not that easy to read necessarily, but, for somebody like me, yeah, you're an open book."

"And yet you say you don't know anything about me. If I'm an open book—"

"I'd have to look," she replied, "and that's something I don't do." She turned and put her empty carton in the garbage can behind her. As she turned back, he stared at her in fascination.

She sighed. "Look. I'm not trying to shock you or to impress you or anything like that. But just imagine what my world would be like if, every time I met somebody, I delved right into their souls. Most people's lives are not all that great, and some are downright boring." Then she glared at him. "And then a few are downright scary on the inside. Once you've tapped into one of them, you aren't so quick to tap into anybody else, and you naturally start putting up blocks."

"I haven't had that experience."

"*Yet*. If you keep pushing people in the wrong way, you'll find it pretty fast."

"Do you find that these people have abilities?"

"You can't expect that nobody has any," she stated, "but you can expect that some of them will. It's often people you have no idea about, and honesty, they often don't know about their abilities either. They found that life went their way smoothly, and they haven't had too many problems. The girlfriend left before he broke up with her, saving him the drama, or the parents died suddenly, leaving him a ton of money. There are all kinds of ways that energy manifests and not necessarily by their conscious hand. But life has moved in their direction, in the way they wanted and at the rate they wanted. It's all a little too complacent for me to want to get close to them."

"Meaning?"

"Meaning that, sometimes people can cause things to happen, even though they don't really realize what they're doing."

"Okay, now that definitely sounds far too esoteric."

"The human will has an enormous capacity," she noted, slowly looking at him. "And, in your case, you have an edge of danger that is always around you."

He shook his head.

She nodded. "Don't argue. Like I said, some of us can see what you don't want us to see."

"You also said you weren't looking."

"No, I wasn't, but I am now," she snapped, glaring at him. "And I really don't want anything to do with whatever is going on in your world."

"What do you mean?"

She replied, "You're involved in some kind of a business deal. It's huge, and it's got the capacity to set your life on the path where you want it to go, but there's no guarantee it'll go through. And you have a traitor in your world. Somebody close to you."

He stared, his jaw slowly dropping.

She nodded. "Now I don't have any more time for this. Please leave."

GAGE STARED AT Skylar in shock. That he had been dismissed was undeniable. Something that he had never experienced before. And, almost on cue, causing him to wonder whether or not she too had the ability to make things happen, another crowd of tourists walked in. She was all smiles, and it felt like the atmosphere in the room had immediately warmed yet again. He watched as she chatted cheerfully with several of them, as if nothing had happened.

Whereas, his whole world had shifted.

He didn't like it; he didn't like anybody knowing anything about him. She was right about that, and he was also involved in a business deal that did scare him because it was something he wasn't terribly comfortable with. The figures involved had him nervous, but the whole thing did have the ability to set up his life exactly as he wanted. Then he could get out of this business and live someplace where he really wanted to be.

He would still do investments of course. It was just that this one deal was particularly big and could change his world. This feeling in the pit in his stomach had been there right from the beginning, the thought that something about it was wrong or tainted somehow. That she could sense it, that she sensed a traitor somewhere in the midst of it, was enough to make the hairs on the back of Gage's neck stand straight up. The fact that she had dismissed him, without giving him any more information, was equally hard.

Noting he was getting odd looks from the other tourists, and she was trying to cover it up, he turned on his heel and headed outside onto the main street. Out here, he found a bench and collapsed on it. He was more thunderstruck than anything else. When his brother phoned a few minutes later, Gage wasn't at all surprised. He answered, adding strength to his voice. "What?"

"Well?"

"Well, what?" he asked, striving for calm.

"Does she know anything?"

"Yeah. How about too damn much in too many areas," he snapped.

There was silence on the other end. "Is she the real

thing?"

"I think so," he stated, still feeling shaky. "And she recognized me for what I can do or not do as well."

"Wow," Terrence replied, "I can't even do that."

Such a note of humor filled his brother's voice that Gage closed his eyes and relaxed a little more.

"Boy, she's really got you rattled, doesn't she?"

"She does," he murmured, "and I'm not even sure why." Of course he couldn't tell his brother very much about what she had said about this deal because his brother was in it with him—though Terrence had come to it kicking and screaming, not wanting to sell the business, whining that he'd make more if Gage stayed on board. So, if this deal was all going south, Terrence would lose his share of the sale, which was the only logic for selling that seemed to get Terrence on board.

They also really needed Jonesy to come home so everybody could focus back on the business at hand.

"I'm sorry, bro, that sounds like a really shit deal for you right now."

"Wouldn't be so bad if Jonesy hadn't decided to take off."

"Could she tell if he was dead?"

"I didn't ask her, but I kept using the past tense when talking about him, and she brought that up to me."

"Wow, so you think he's dead then?"

"I have no idea. I don't know what to think."

"Easy, take it easy. Maybe it's time to hit one of those outdoor pubs and just have a drink or something. It's happy hour right now."

"I'll head back to the hotel," he replied.

"And you're staying in the same hotel room that Uncle

was in, right?"

"Yes, I am."

"Have you checked the room?"

"Of course I have," he replied a little curtly, "but I haven't found anything."

"Maybe get her to take a walk through the room."

"I don't think she's too interested in talking to me right now."

"Well, be there with breakfast tomorrow morning then," he suggested.

"Somebody brought her beignets today," Gage noted, "so I don't think she'll really need breakfast from me tomorrow."

"You don't know that," Terrence argued. "She needs to eat. It's just a matter of whether she wants to be fed by your hand or not."

He winced. "I don't know. I'll see how I feel about it in the morning."

"Then go back to the hotel and take a break. Call me when you're feeling better," he said. "You've got me really worried."

"I'll be fine. "I'll head to the hotel now."

With that, he hung up on his brother and retraced his steps to the hotel. Honestly, he felt a little on the unpleasantly woozy side. Getting up to his room took more out of him than he had expected. By the time he made it inside the room, the door shut and locked, all he felt was relief.

He walked a few steps to the bed, then collapsed and was out within seconds.

CHAPTER 3

SKYLAR DIDN'T KNOW what to think. Today had certainly been odd on the barometer of oddity in her normal day. And she didn't know what to think about Gage at all. She remembered the old guy, Jonesy, but, other than that, what was she supposed to tell Gage? She didn't know what Jonesy was up to, and she didn't know why he wanted that old tarot card set—one that she didn't have anyway, and, if she did have it, she sure as hell wouldn't have sold it.

Things like that weren't meant to go to the uninitiated. Tarot cards had power, even though everybody liked to joke about it. But that kind of power wasn't something you should play with or squander. It was serious stuff, and, although she felt like Jonesy wanted to be serious about it, a part of him had a completely different reason for collecting tarot cards. She didn't know what that was, but now, according to the uncle's note found in his jacket pocket, this deck had something to do with murders. She didn't know if she believed any of it, but it was intriguing.

Tarot cards were not supposed to be used to determine negatives in this world and definitely not to tell people they would die soon. But not everybody followed those rules, and not everybody had the same sense of what was right and what was wrong. That kind of skill in the wrong hands could cause havoc to all kinds of young—and old—unsuspecting minds. Something she didn't dare have happen.

When she finally closed her shop for the day and locked the front door and made her way up the stairs to her apartment, she felt an odd heaviness and a really weird foreboding. She looked around and then mentally called to the ghosts down in her shop. *Anything weird in the ethers right now?*

And just as she hit the landing on the stairs outside her apartment door, she heard them calling out to her, "Be careful, be careful."

She took the hallway to its own balcony, next to the separate balcony to her apartment, and studied her surroundings. There didn't appear to be anything wrong, and she was desperate to go inside and to just relax. The day had been strange enough without having any kind of danger facing her now. She stepped forward and let herself into her apartment and, after a quick check around that confirmed her place was empty and was safe, she collapsed onto her bed, exhausted, needing a nap before her nightly cemetery visit.

Moments later, she became aware of somebody else lying on his bed, but something was very unnatural about it. It was a vision of Gage, the man she'd met today, the man who had already unsettled her life more than he should have. She saw him on his bed, his lips bloodless and something very strange hovering all around him. She swore, bounded to her feet, and, grabbing her amulets, she stuffed them in her pockets and raced down the street. Only one hotel had that type of design on the ceilings. When she got to the front desk, she asked what room Gage was in.

With a smirk, the front guy told her.

She slipped him a twenty dollar bill and raced up to

Gage's hotel room. She had no key to let herself in, but, using a trick she'd learned a long time ago, she held her hand over the lock, and, with a little help from Thomas, who was nearly always at her side, the door opened, and she slipped inside, racing to him. There was Gage, lying on the bed, his body cold, his face completely bleached of blood, and his lips almost blue. She reached out a hand and placed it over his heart, then stretched out her other hand to Thomas, making an energy chain all the way to those back in her shop, and she poured their collected energy into Gage's body. She felt it doing something, but it wasn't enough; the energy wasn't strong enough.

She cried out, "Gage, talk to me, get back here, where you belong," she roared. "Enough is enough. You can't do this."

And she kept pumping energy into him—blind, dark, light—any energy she could grasp from the surroundings went into this poor man, who had no idea what the hell was going on in his world.

When Thomas cried out, "It worked. It worked," she looked down to see Gage awake and staring at her in shock.

She sat back ever-so-slightly, slowly withdrawing her hand, so there wasn't an abrupt separation of her energy from Gage's. She stared down at him. "Well, that was interesting."

He rolled his head to the side. "You're in my hotel room."

"Yeah," she confirmed, as she shifted to the side. "Don't take it the wrong way." And then she smiled at him. "Glad to have you back in the land of the living."

"What happened?" he murmured, sitting up slowly and shaking his head.

She watched Gage's huge body shift into its spirit body, almost as if putting on a human suit, and she smiled. "Well, you were one step away from being dead."

GAGE STARED AT Skylar, feeling his body slowly warming up, but there was nothing for the shock in his mind at her words. He shuffled up onto his elbows and stared up at her. "Are you serious?"

She got up and walked around the small room, almost pacing now that whatever this catastrophe was had been averted. "Yes. What I don't know is why."

He looked around his hotel room. "I felt really drained, and I came in, and I just kind of collapsed."

"Well, you collapsed all right, but you collapsed too far, too deep."

"What does that even mean?" he asked, pushing himself into a sitting position.

"It means that you almost died, that you were basically in a coma. If you'd been in the hospital, I'm not sure they could have brought you back."

"Only you did, even though I wasn't in the hospital."

"Sometimes it's better not to be in the hospital," she noted. "Not everybody understands how energy works."

"But you do."

"I've had a lifetime of it," she stated, her gaze going dark, "but don't get me wrong. An awful lot out there I still don't know."

"How did you know to come to my hotel room?" he asked. "And how did you even get in here?"

She stared at him for a long moment and then in a flat tone replied, "You can get some of those questions answered but not all of them, so pick the ones you want that are really important. I don't have time or energy to sit here and argue or deal with your questions. I'm heading back home again. So whatever *single* question you might have, you better spit it out now."

Startled at her refusal to really give much of an explanation, he grappled with the priorities at hand and finally came up with his question. "How did you know I was in trouble?"

"I saw it in a vision, so I came running."

"And that spawns a million more questions."

She shrugged. "Too bad."

He took a long slow deep breath, uncertain how to get her to cooperate.

She looked at him and shook her head. "Don't even start thinking about it."

"Thinking about what?"

"How to get me to give you more answers."

He threw up his hands. "Is it really so hard to understand that I might want to know how I came close to dying?"

"I don't have an answer for that," she stated. "If that was one of your questions, it would be a complete waste."

He tried to breathe carefully again.

She looked at him and nodded in approval. "Control is really important."

"Could you please tell me what happened?"

"I can't because I don't know what happened," she said, with a toss of her arms. "And I'm heading home now."

"Are you always this difficult?"

"Yeah," she muttered, "I am. Particularly when people want stuff from me that I can't give them."

"You mean, like answers?"

"Like answers," she admitted, nodding. "Is it really so

hard to believe that I can't give you an answer? Maybe you need to go see a doctor and see if you've got some kind of a heart problem."

"Did it feel like a heart problem to you?"

"No," she snapped, "but then again I'm not a doctor."

"And you also said the doctors won't really be much help in my case."

"But I could be wrong," she added, shooting him a cheery smile, as she walked to the hotel room door.

Desperate to stop her, he asked, "Can I at least buy you dinner as a thank-you?"

She immediately frowned, and her mouth opened to toss back an angry no immediately.

He interrupted. "I'm really appreciative, sincerely, and just think, without you, I might not have been here to eat dinner at all."

She didn't like hearing that. She crossed her arms over her chest and glared at him.

He wasn't sure what it was about him that set off her prickliness, but definitely something was going on here that he was desperate to get answers for. "Is there any chance somebody did this to me?" he murmured.

At that, her smile fell away, and she stepped closer. "Is there any reason for somebody to have done this to you?"

"I don't know," he said, "but you're right about the business deal."

She nodded. "I know I am."

He winced. "Are you always this sure about yourself?"

"I don't tell people what I don't actually know," she stated, studying him carefully. "And when I know something, I know it."

"Have you ever been wrong?"

"Wrong? Not necessarily. Have I ever interpreted things imprecisely? Yes," she admitted. "Nothing is exact in this world."

"I get that," he murmured. "And I really appreciate you taking the time to help me out."

"I couldn't just stand by and let you die," she snapped briskly.

"And, for that, I owe you again."

She shook her head. "I don't like people owing me any-thing. There's no debt owed to me."

"Well, I'm glad to hear that too," he added. "I just wish I knew a little more about how this could have happened, so I could avoid it next time."

"Well, I certainly hope you find out," she noted, "be-cause I don't want to be running here to save your sorry ass all the time either. The front desk guy already has the wrong idea."

A note of humor filled her voice, meaning that she wasn't taking his words the wrong way. And he appreciated the jest, since it did lend a moment of levity to the situation. "You obviously have a very strong skill that I don't know anything about."

She nodded. "It's also not one that I advertise."

"You could probably make millions if you did," he stat-ed curiously.

"There's really no joy in going public."

He made a mental note to check deeper into her back-ground. He knew some of her story—thanks to Jonesy and his addiction to collecting bones and tarot cards—in that Skylar had had a problem with her growing reputation in another town and had quietly packed up in the night and left. Jonesy had tracked her down here. "Do you know why

Jonesy went to you for those tarot cards?"

"No," she replied immediately.

He hesitated, but he didn't sense that she was lying. Yet he couldn't understand how it would be possible that she wouldn't have understood why Jonesy had come to her, given her skill level. "He must have heard about your abilities."

"Nobody here has really heard about my abilities," she stated, with a shadowed gaze. "I don't advertise anything that I can do."

"All the more reason for me to be extremely grateful that you took a moment to step out of your comfort zone to help me."

"Whatever." She turned back to the door.

"Wait," he cried out.

She froze at the door, then pivoted and looked at him, her glare unmistakable. For some reason it struck him on the funny side.

"I'm really not trying to hold you captive, and I really am grateful. Please just let me take you out for dinner." He hesitated. "I'm feeling a little odd, and I guess just a little uncertain about being alone right now."

He could see her starting to relent, her shoulders easing back, as if all he were looking for was maybe a babysitter and not answers. His curiosity was well and truly piqued at somebody who could be so prickly and yet who could deal with the public so well. However, as soon as anything happened along the line of her abilities, she became incredibly defensive and immediately started putting up walls.

She finally spoke. "Fine. But only if you're capable of walking because I'm definitely not carrying you back up here."

He burst out laughing at that. "Nope, not unless I get another exhausted session, and I'm hoping not to experience that again."

"Did you feel anything?" she asked curiously.

"Not until I woke up. It's just like I'd been asleep, only to find your hand on my chest. Not that it was a terrible feeling, by the way," he teased, trying for more levity. "I mean, a beautiful woman in my bedroom is not necessarily to be taken as a bad sign."

"And yet you're still very cold," she stated, ignoring his remarks, yet witnessing his shaky hands that he rubbed together continuously.

He looked down at his hands and nodded. "That's another one of the reasons I'm hoping to go out for food and to walk around a bit—to get my circulation going. I feel odd." And the truth was, he did feel a strange hollowness inside.

She studied his energy—at least he presumed that's what she was doing—because she was walking around the room, staring at him.

"Can you see anything? What did you see when you arrived?"

"Same as now. Just a very pale, pale energy," she noted, "but that's the thing about these abilities. They aren't always there when you need them."

"Can you tell me exactly what your abilities are?"

She shook her head. "No, I sure can't because they keep changing. Just when I think I know what I'm doing, something else happens. And they're just different enough all the time that I can't ever count on them."

"I'm sorry. That's got to be frustrating."

"You don't know what half of it." She snorted. "Come

on then. Let's go get some food. I don't know about you, but I'm starving."

"And none of what you just did to help me out wore you down, *huh*?"

She shot him another look.

He shrugged. "I'm just worried that maybe you'll collapse or something."

"I doubt it," she replied, her tone turning distant almost. "At least that's never happened yet."

"Well, it's never happened to me either." He reached up, scrubbed at his face, checked that he had his keys with him and said, "Okay, let's go."

As they headed downstairs and outside, he asked, "Do you have a place to recommend?"

"Sure. A couple really good places are nearby."

"Good, you lead the way."

"They're expensive," she stated, as she pointed down the street.

"That's fine. I can afford it." And he walked beside her, enjoying getting out with her.

"Not if you crash that deal."

"I don't even want to think about that," he admitted. "After what you warned me about earlier, my stomach has already been churning steadily."

She nodded. "You should be worried."

"You can't tell me who the traitor is though?"

"Nope, I don't see any of those details. And I'm not looking either."

"Meaning that you could, but you just choose not to?" He hesitated.

She shook her head, looking around to see if anybody was close enough to overhear them. "No, it's like you have a great big black door, which means I can't go in there."

"Could that potentially be something I'm putting up?" he murmured, trying to find his way through how this all worked.

"Maybe," she agreed, "but it's just as likely that somebody close to you has put up that door instead. Particularly if they had any idea that I'd be looking." They had reached the street corner, and she waited on the traffic light to turn to Walk.

He frowned and nodded. "So mysterious."

"I don't like the idea of being mysterious either," she replied in a blunt tone.

He laughed. "I don't even know how to take you. You don't fit the norm of anything. I find that I'm on shifting grounds just trying to understand who you are."

"Why would you even bother?" she asked. "You're leaving here in a couple days and won't have anything more to do with me after that, so why waste the time and energy?"

He didn't even know what to say to that. "Haven't you ever met somebody who fascinated you so much that you had to learn more?"

"Yes, and I think I've cured myself of that by now though."

On that note, he had nothing to add. After all, what was there to say?

She motioned up ahead. "Let's go up this way."

"Fine, sounds good to me."

She led him in the direction of a restaurant with a large outdoor pub area, then looked at him and said, "They have the best po'boys here."

"I'm game," he replied immediately, and just then his stomach started to growl.

She smiled. "Now that's a good sign."

"What? That my stomach is crying out like it's afraid my throat's been cut?"

"Exactly." She smiled. "As long as your body is requiring food, the energy influx didn't cause any major problems."

And that just brought up so many more questions, all that he wanted answers for. But, from the expression on her face, no answers were coming his way, at least not right now. He might only have planned to be here for a couple days, but, if he didn't get the answers he needed, he could already see extending his trip for a whole lot longer.

He was fascinated, and she had information he needed, and, if there was anything he could do to help her share that information with him, he had to do it.

He needed to find the truth.

CHAPTER 4

A S SKYLAR LED the way into one of her favorite restaurants, she chose a table on the patio—and off to the side ever-so-slightly so they weren't in the way of the crowds. She still didn't know what to think about Gage. The fact that he had something weird going on that she had just barely managed to save him from set her on edge even more.

He didn't know this, but by saving him as she had, she had also taken on some of his energy and had gifted him with some of hers. The result of that was a bond, a bond that could go either way. It could strengthen, or it could weaken, but it would be there for decades, unless she could remove her energy from his system somehow.

As she studied his energy, she realized that hers was intricately woven throughout, and, as a matter of fact, she could see that Thomas had a fair amount of his energy in there as well. She sighed, her fingers thrumming on the table, as she studied the area around her.

"Now what?"

Her gaze darted around, at him, and away. Then she shrugged. "I don't know. I really don't know what to say about what happened to you."

"Is there a weird energy here in New Orleans?"

"There sure is," she admitted, smiling, "and many things are acceptable here and even sought out that aren't found in the rest of the world."

"Like the voodoo?"

She nodded.

"Is that why you're here?"

"Hiding in plain sight works pretty well," she noted.

"And people really don't know what you can do, do they?"

"Nope." She shook her head. "It might increase business but would also make my personal life hell."

"And you've been there before."

"I sure have," she confirmed.

Just then a waitress walked over toward them. She smiled brightly at Gage, hoping for a bigger tip perhaps, but, as far as Skylar was concerned, it was the age-old game, and she wanted no part of it. It was one of the reasons she tended to do takeout more than eating out, but she would do her best to be friendly and to hope that Gage left a generous tip for the sake of the waitress. Skylar didn't even want to look at the menu. She ordered her favorite—fried oyster po'boy— and the woman wrote it down.

Immediately Gage turned to the waitress and nodded. "If she's having it, I'll have the same." And then he added two cold beers to the order. The waitress sent one more beaming smile just to him and sashayed off.

Skylar ignored the flirting and asked him, "Are both of those beers for you?"

"Won't you have one with me?"

She frowned. "I don't normally drink." But she was just unsettled enough that it might not be a bad idea.

"Well, you can try it, and, if you don't like it," he said, "I'll finish it for you. How is that?"

"Are you sure you should be drinking?"

"No, I'm not sure at all," he admitted, his voice low. "Maybe you should tell me that."

"Nope, I ain't telling you nothing."

He nodded. "In that case," he muttered, "I'm fine. I'll have a drink. Besides, I could really use one."

"I get it. Some of this stuff is a bit of a shock."

"A *bit* of a shock?" he asked. "That may be the under-statement of the year."

She shrugged. "I forget about that—because it's some-thing I do and have done for years—so it's normal for me."

"Well, it's not normal for me," he stated flatly, "not at all. My accident was nine months ago."

Her gaze shot to him. "Right, so you said you had an accident, and this all started happening afterward."

"Whatever *this* is, yes," he agreed. "I just don't know what it is."

"You started to see apparitions?" she questioned in a low voice.

"Yes, some I could see clearly, and some I couldn't."

"Some are like that," she noted in understanding. "Sometimes they're easy to see, and sometimes they're not."

"Is that their choice, or is it just our abilities?"

And since it was a reasonable question, she answered this one. "Usually it's their abilities. Not all ghosts have the same ability to appear as if they're standing right in front of us."

"But some can?"

"Lots of them can," she noted.

"And what about what I was feeling and seeing in your store? I got the sense a lot of apparitions were around there."

"They prefer to call themselves *ghosts*—or actually *friends* in my case."

"So, they really are there?" he asked, his eyebrows shooting up.

She nodded. "Interesting that you could see them."

"Well, I couldn't, not really," he muttered, throwing up his hands. "I mean, I saw something but not clearly."

"So, you didn't see Thomas with his black suit and top hat?"

He looked at her and then slowly shook his head. "I could tell something was there but not clearly."

She nodded. "He's often the one who people will see. He's fairly advanced, as far as ghosts go."

"Is it something they can become more advanced at?" he asked, leaning in and oh so curious.

"Well, we'd like to think not," she explained. "I keep telling my group that they should be heading toward the light and leaving, but they won't. They're bound and determined to stick around."

"Why is that?"

"I don't know," she admitted. "I keep asking them that, but they just tell me that they aren't ready to go to the light yet."

"Have you lost any?"

"When you say *lost*, what do you mean?" she asked, with a note of humor. "If you mean, have any gone to the light? Then, yes, absolutely. Thomas is just having too much fun, so he doesn't want to go anywhere and refuses to leave me alone. I think he sees himself as somewhat of a guardian angel, watching over me."

"That's an interesting analogy," he murmured.

"Well, it's his version of it," she noted. "And he's fairly adamant about it all. In fact, he can follow me outside of the shop, which is not something the others have done."

"And do they do anything to help you?"

She slowly turned to look at him, checking to make sure that they were alone and that nobody was within hearing distance. "Thomas actually helped you earlier. It was hard for me to find enough energy right there to bring you back, so I enlisted his help."

Gage sat back, as if stunned at the idea of enlisting the help of a ghost.

"I mean, they are there all the time, and they talk to me, so why shouldn't I reach out and ask them for help when I need it?" she asked in a nonchalant way.

"Oh, *absolutely*." But his sarcasm got her back up, and she glared at him.

"They are family to me."

He raised both hands in frustration. "Sorry. I'm not trying to be difficult, but you caught me off guard."

"I don't think people do that very often," she noted.

"No," he admitted, "but, since the accident, it's happening more and more. I have to admit I was wondering if I was losing my edge."

"I don't think so. I think it's become more attuned."

"And yet you're worrying me, with all this talk about a business deal that could go wrong."

"It could definitely go wrong if you don't find out who is the traitor," she stated. "You wouldn't have been able to find the energy shift before your accident, but maybe now you can."

"How does that even make sense? I suddenly see apparitions, and now I'm supposed to understand if my business partners are lying to me?"

She smiled. "It's all about energy. The energy of somebody who is dead and gone looks different than the energy of someone you know very well is alive and healthy. But also the energy of somebody who is telling the truth and the energy of somebody who is lying look very different. The better you become at understanding energy, the better you'll become at understanding who around you can be trusted and who cannot."

"And you can make those kinds of decisions yourself?"

"Sometimes, though sometimes I get it wrong," she stated.

"But you're not going to give me any more details on that, are you?"

"No, why should I?" she asked, her tone turning flat. "I don't trust you."

He winced. "And that's from my energy or whatever? I would have thought I was quite trustworthy."

"Maybe to yourself," she murmured. "But there are people around you I don't want knowing anything about me."

"Well, that makes more sense," he replied, with a note of humor. "My brother struggles with what I've told him, and I know he finds it really difficult to accept."

"You're better off not telling people," she said abruptly.

"Then how are you supposed to have anybody to talk to so you can find out whether you're going insane or not?"

"Assume that you aren't going insane because everybody else will assume that you are," she stated.

"Yeah, I've been there, done that." He chuckled. "I was trying to avoid anything like that again."

"And that's good because you don't really want to end up down that crazy path again."

"But how does one avoid it?" he murmured.

"You learn to trust in yourself." She stood and checked around to see if the waitress was coming their way.

"Are you always this impatient?"

He seemed surprised to see her standing and pushing to see just how much longer they would have to wait. She sat down with a *thud*. "Honestly, something feels off, like wrong. I feel like we need to get going and fast."

"We can't just sit here and eat?"

She frowned. "I'm not sure that I can, no." As she started to look around again, the waitress returned with the beers.

Skylar immediately turned to her and asked, "Can you make those po'boys to-go, please?"

The waitress nodded and said, "Just give me a minute." And she took off.

Skylar snagged one of the beers and took a big long slurp. It helped to steady her, but, at the same time, it also enhanced her edgy feeling, noting something was seriously wrong. She watched as Gage did the same thing, and then he stood and stated, "I gather we're leaving."

"We are." She stopped and said, "Well, at least I am."

"That means we are," he stated. "Obviously, after what I've been through so far, I'm not taking any chances. If you say there's danger, then I'm not sticking around."

"Good." She sighed. "I'm just not sure that it's safe for you to even go back to your hotel room right now."

At that, he stopped and stared.

"Think about it. That's where you were when it happened."

"So, I change rooms or hotels or cities or what?" With her shrug, he added, "I'm in Jonesy's room on purpose, thinking I could find a clue or talk to a ghost or whatever."

"*Uh-oh.*" Surely she was wrong. *Could those tarot cards really cause the murders that they then knew about? This didn't bode well for Jonesy or Gage.* She'd have to do some research on this. Right now all she had were rumors and innuendoes.

"What?" he asked.

"I don't know for sure. For now, a bench is not too far from here, and it's a nice little picnic spot. We'll sit there and have our drinks and dinner."

"Fine." He still looked a little dazed at her vague warnings.

"Look. Sometimes I have to move fast in my world," she explained, "and there really are no answers sometimes. That's just the way it is."

"Got it," he said, shaking his head.

Just then the waitress returned and handed him a bill, which he promptly paid. Skylar snatched the bag and led the way out of the restaurant courtyard. He quickly followed suit.

She didn't even bother to check if he followed her or not. Either he would catch up or he wouldn't. She had the food, and, right about now, all she cared about was getting some sustenance. She had drained herself way too much, trying to save him. Normally she wouldn't begrudge that energy to anyone, but something so weird was going on with Gage, and she couldn't really understand it. It wasn't so much his own energy that worried her but those malevolent energies surrounding him.

So, as soon as she could get done with all this, and him, the better off she would be.

Leading the way to the bench that she had in mind, she moved quickly, keeping from the crowds as much as she could. When she was finally there, she stopped and sent out a silent warning beacon to see if anything nearby would trigger something unpleasant. She didn't always know what that could mean or how best to deal with it.

Ever at her side, Thomas shared, "Looks good," and

such cheerfulness was in his voice that she wanted to glare at him too. "Besides," the ghost added, "we're awful happy that you're actually having dinner with somebody."

"And that means nothing to me," she muttered, shaking her head at the thought of her shopful of ghosts, feeling gleeful because she was having dinner with this man she barely knew.

Gage, however, heard her grumbling. "Sorry. What was that?"

"This place will be fine," she muttered, with a wave of her hand at the surrounding area.

He nodded. "Okay, … if you're telling me that it's really better than the restaurant."

"Yes, it is," she murmured.

He sat down, and she handed him the bag. "Now, can you take a moment and explain to me why it's better?"

"No, I can't," she stated, "because honestly, I don't know."

"So, what then? You just honor your instincts without knowing why?"

"When it comes to this woo-woo stuff," she noted quietly, "that's often the only warning you get."

"But what could happen?" he asked, studying her intently.

"Remember that coma you found yourself in just a while ago?"

He reflexively choked. "Are you saying that could happen again?"

"Well, it happened once, so it can definitely happen again. I'm not sure what's going on here, but now, with your uncle missing, and something that theoretically could be attached to me somehow, plus the fact that you're here, and we had that little scenario in your hotel room—also attached to me—I'm definitely getting weird vibes around us."

"So, can you tell me—" Then he stopped, shook his head. "I can't even believe I'm asking this, but is it possible to tell who might be doing this, if in fact, someone is behind it?"

She looked at him with a sardonic glance. "Do you mean *someone* doing it versus *something* doing it?"

He shrugged and had the good grace to look embarrassed.

"I have met a couple not-very-friendly ghosts," she shared, "and I have heard horror stories of vindictive evil ghosts. Not all spirits turn into these wonderful, lovely people," she murmured. "A lot of them are looking for ways to get back to the world that they left. They haven't accepted the fact that they have actually died and thus have no intention of going on to the light, into the next stage of their life, only focused intently on trying to get back."

"Is that even possible?" he asked, curious.

"In theory it shouldn't be because everything we're taught in our normal world says that, when you die, either you go to heaven or hell."

"Do you believe that?"

"Oh no. I gave up on those overly simplistic fairy tales a long time ago."

She looked down at her sandwich and noted that her huge appetite had almost soured on her. She quickly took a bite, knowing that she would need the energy. Just because she had to help this guy out of one bad session today didn't mean she could skip going to the graveyard again tonight. She went practically every night for one purpose or another, it seemed, whether she wanted to or not. But Gage didn't know about that, and the less he knew, the better.

Skylar had nearly finished her sandwich, managing to scarf down most of it in what seemed like just a few bites. Gage sat beside her, watching her. She sighed. "Hey, nobody said I had good manners."

He laughed. "It didn't even seem as if you thought about it. It appeared as though you ate because you needed the sustenance, and that was all there was to it."

"This meal, yes." She nodded. "Unlike earlier, when I could take the time to just relax and enjoy."

"But you can't now," he stated, with a nod. "Got it."

That had him continuously looking around, trying to find whatever it was that had set her on edge. Good luck to him because she didn't even know what the hell it was herself. She just knew that something followed them from the ethers. The same damn thing that she had seen hovering over him in the hotel room. But she wasn't at all sure he was ready to hear about the evil murdering spirit of the tarot cards just yet. Indeed, she wasn't sure that she wanted to investigate it any further either. Better the evil spirit went straight back to where it came from and left her and Gage in peace and quiet.

But somehow she didn't think it would be that easy.

"YOU ARE THE most fascinating person I have ever met," Gage blurted out, as he studied his sandwich.

"That's not a good thing," she replied.

He looked up at her, startled.

"You have a vast experience of people in your world," she noted, "and a lot of varied relationships under your belt. I don't like the idea of being the odd or curious one who you can't figure out."

"I didn't mean it that way," he protested.

"Good thing," she stated. When she made this weird swipe of her hand, he almost felt it, like a slice in his belly. He stiffened and straightened.

She looked at him in surprise. "What?"

"When you made that hand movement, I could almost feel it viscerally."

She stared at him for a long moment. "Really?"

He nodded.

"Interesting," she murmured, as she turned to look around again.

That's all she did, constantly checking behind and around, as if she were looking for somebody either following them or who otherwise posed some kind of danger. She definitely wasn't resting or enjoying the space she was in. "Would you rather go home?" Gage asked her.

"No, I would not."

He had to be content with that because she sure wasn't forthcoming with any explanation. "Anything you're willing to tell me about this, I'm really desperate to hear." Then he took another bite of his sandwich.

"Better you just go back to whatever town you came from and forget about all this."

"You know I can't do that," he said, "because I have to find Jonesy and this strange new ability of mine is definitely something in my life that I have no control over. People are already starting to think something's wrong with me."

"Get used to it. There will always be those who think something's wrong with you from here on out," she declared. "I'm not sure if you were planning on getting out of the business world anytime soon, but you might want to consider it."

"Because?"

"Because somebody is likely to make a vote of no-confidence against you for any boards that you hold positions on."

He frowned and thought about it and nodded. "The trouble is, the more I've been asking questions, you're right. The more people have looked at me strangely."

"Of course they have, because nobody wants to know about this stuff. Everybody wants to stay in their nice quiet little beds and sleep their nice happy dreams, without confronting that their whole world isn't what they thought it would be when they come close to dying."

"As somebody who came damn close to dying," he added, "I can agree with that."

"You came damn close to dying twice," she said, "because, don't kid yourself, you were near dead earlier tonight. I almost couldn't save you."

He felt the shock bleaching the color from his face. "That's a little harsh to try to understand." He paused for a long moment. "All I did was walk up the stairs to my hotel room and collapse on the bed."

"And we have to figure out why," she stated, "because that's not normal."

"Well, I'm glad to hear you say that," he replied, "and that you won't completely desert me on this."

She winced, and he realized it had been a slip of her tongue. "I would appreciate any help you can give me," he noted, "and I'm definitely getting the heebie-jeebies sitting here now." He straightened and looked around, crumpling up the last food wrapper in his hand.

"Good, because we're about to get company."

"What kind of company?"

"At the moment"—she tilted her head—"it'll be ethereal."

"So, a ghost?" Gage asked.

"Yeah, let's see if you can actually see this one."

He shook his head. "You know I'm okay if I don't."

"Which is probably why you aren't seeing them. If you've seen one or two," she explained, "and you're not seeing any others, chances are you're putting up walls to tell them to stay away."

"Does that work?"

"Sometimes," she confirmed, "and then eventually you realize it takes more energy to put up the walls than it takes to just ignore the ghosts."

That startled a laugh out of Gage. "Well, maybe you should tell me what I'm looking for."

"Nope." She shook her head. "You tell me what you're looking at."

He twisted to look at her, but she was serious. He sighed, settled back down, and looked around the area where they sat. "It's a nice little garden area," he mentioned.

She nodded. "It is. And generally it's ghostly quiet."

"So why is it not now?"

"Because something has disturbed them," she stated sadly.

"And what could possibly disturb a ghost?"

"All kinds of things," she murmured, "but often it's when somebody they care for is about to be hurt."

At that he winced. "Seriously?"

"Very seriously. And, in this case, too many ghosts are gathered here, so they're disturbed about something else."

"Well, I'm glad to hear that," he muttered.

"Doesn't help much though," she countered, "since we still don't have any answers."

"Can't we get any?"

"Maybe. This is the French Quarter. This is where voodoo and hoodoo and all the good stuff exists," she replied on a laugh. "Ghosts are always in this city, and they're always upset over something. It can be as simple as a building coming down that they didn't want destroyed because they have a connection to it," she shared, "or the fact that somebody on the ethers has a gripe against one of them, and he's coming to try and destroy the life of someone he doesn't want to continue to live."

"Does he get to make that choice?"

"No, of course not," she declared, turning to look at him. "Yet that doesn't mean they stop trying. And I have heard about cases of possession, where a strong spirit will actually overtake a weaker physical body and try to live the life through them."

"Wow," he said, "that is just terrifying."

"You should be terrified," she agreed. "You should have just enough knowledge now to realize how twisted and warped the energy world out there is."

"Sure," he admitted, "but I wasn't thinking it was twisted and warped *after* death."

"It's no different," she noted. "Seriously the people over there are just as twisted as they are here."

"Are you talking about those who actually made it to heaven?" Then he stopped and asked, "Wait. Is there even a heaven?"

"There is," she confirmed. "There is a light for those of them who get to go there. I'm not sure what happens to those who don't—or if there even are those who don't. All I know is, when I see the light, I try to convince the ghosts to go toward it. They don't always cooperate." And then she muttered under her breath, "Most of the time they never cooperate."

"Why do you think that is?"

"I think a lot of the time it's because they think it'll be boring, or they're scared of change, or they're having way too much fun over here to want to go over there."

At that, an apparition appeared in front of them, so close that Gage jumped.

"Don't worry about him," Skylar told him in a calm, almost bored tone. "That's Thomas."

Gage took several slow deep breaths, remembering that she had mentioned how Thomas was from Abraham Lincoln's era. Gage tried hard to see what he was supposed to see.

"You're trying too hard," she murmured. "Just accept that he's there and don't worry about what he looks like."

"All I see," Gage noted, "is this ghostly white."

She muttered out loud, "Thomas, can you crank it up a bit?"

Instantly the apparition in front of Gage started to shine brighter and brighter.

"Now don't look directly on," she explained. "Look slightly to the side."

When Gage twisted his head to one side, he could almost see somebody walking nearby. "Seriously?"

"Yeah, if you try to focus too much fully on, when you're not used to it, it's really hard to pull all of it together to show an image. But peripheral vision is quite a bit stronger, especially when it comes to this stuff. So tell me what you see."

"Well …" Gage stopped. "It'll sound stupid."

"Of course it does. It always sounds stupid," she shared.

He laughed. "Well, I see an older man in a black suit and a top hat."

"Right. So, as I told you, that's Thomas."

He nodded slowly. "He's holding a young child by the hand."

"Yeah, that's Ada, his granddaughter," she murmured. "She died with him."

"So why has she not crossed over?"

"Because her grandfather won't cross over," she answered. "So the two of them are stuck here, but they have each other."

"And over there they won't?" Gage shook his head. "You know what? This is just a little bit beyond belief."

"Yeah, it is," she agreed, "but that's just the facts of life."

"Not for anybody else," he murmured.

"Nope, not for anybody else. Anybody else wouldn't give a crap about this stuff because they wouldn't believe you and would want to lock you up for even mentioning it."

"Do you ever get worried about that?"

"All the time, but I tend to keep my mouth shut and to keep out of all this."

"And what do the bones have to do with anything?"

"That is none of your business," she snapped, and her answer was so fast and so sharp that he knew it was a huge deal.

"And what if I want to make it my business?"

"Then you'll probably regret it," she declared. "Some things in life you should never play with. And talking bones is one of them."

"And how do you know a talking bone versus a

nontalking bone?" he asked in exasperation. Getting that look from her again, he continued. "I get it. You don't have all the answers, but I surely don't have them. You're really good at this stuff, and you can do things that I probably can't even begin to imagine. But all you do is keep telling me not to do something, when I don't even know what it is that you're talking about. How can I avoid doing something if I don't even know what it is that I'm supposed to stop doing?"

She burst out laughing, and he was stunned at just how beautiful her face shone, when she was filled with a delighted joy. When she had finally calmed down a bit, wiping tears from her eyes, he quipped, "I'm glad I could entertain you."

"I am too," she admitted immediately. "I hadn't realized how much I needed that." Nonplussed, he just stared at her. She reached over, patted his hand gently, and added, "You have been very good entertainment today."

And that was so not what he wanted to hear.

At the look on his face, she smiled and suddenly added, "I understand. You want to be anywhere but here, and you don't want to have any of these kinds of conversations that make you feel like you're an idiot. You're not an idiot, and I'm just trying to warn you that some things are not as fun and as pleasant as we think they'll be."

"No worries there because I don't think any of this is fun or pleasant," he stated in a harsh tone. "I was just looking to find a way to save my sanity, while I tried to find my uncle."

"Well, you may have to do one or the other," she noted, "but, in this case, I'm not sure that both are doable."

He stared at her. "Do you mind elaborating?"

"It has to do with the tarot card set your uncle was after," she replied. "It is fairly well-known in the collector circles as having predicted several murders—and, having predicted them, people then believe firmly that the tarot deck itself has powers. And anything with power is what people naturally want, whether they are gifted or not. And generally they want power so they can abuse it."

He nodded. "This makes a lot of sense so far."

"Good. I hate to think I'd lost you at this point. The other issue that comes up is that particular tarot card set hasn't been seen in at least a century, as far as I know." She gave him a one-arm shrug. "And I have no idea what the connection is to the bones."

"Jonesy thought the bones were of the people being murdered."

"And why would he care?"

At that, Gage took a deep breath. "From his notes, I gathered he thought it was an ancestor of his, and he felt compelled to return the bones to the proper grave."

"And what grave is it from?" Then her facial expression changed. "Ah, right. Got it. I know what I needed to know."

He nodded slowly. "And how do you know that?"

She gave him a grim smile. "Well, let's just say I'm intimately knowledgeable with this cemetery."

CHAPTER 5

OF COURSE IT would be that cemetery. The very one and the same where she spent hours every night. Well, what was she supposed to do if his uncle had come to her with the bones? And that bone was still in her shop, so it was something she needed to return to the cemetery tonight. She'd already managed to pick up twinges of the dark energy on the bone, when she'd picked it up, even with gloves on. She couldn't imagine trying to touch it without some protection.

Sometimes people didn't realize just how lucky they were to not be affected by this stuff. His uncle hadn't worn gloves when he was in her shop, or Skylar would have noticed. It was often a sign of somebody who did energy work, and having a bone in his hand would have been even more obvious.

As she sat here, pondering her next move, Gage added, "Not only do I need your help, but my uncle does too."

She glared at him. "And I really don't need any emotional blackmail right now."

"What do you need?" he asked instantly.

She sighed. "Well, some sleep would help."

"Why can't you sleep?"

"I can. I just don't get enough of it," she replied.

"You work in the evenings too?" he asked in surprise.

Her lips turned up in a quirky smile. "You could say

that."

He frowned.

She hopped up off the bench. "Look. I need to go back to my place. I didn't get a chance to finish up at my store or anything else either, so I have a lot of work there to do. Thomas is still disturbed by something here, so I want to get him home and get him settled."

"Is that something you typically do?"

"Only with him. He sees himself more as my protector, but, because he doesn't have a physical body to actually protect me with, he's always on the alert, looking out for trouble and danger. The problem with that is, he becomes very restless, and his restlessness transmits to me."

"All in all, that sounds perfectly normal," Gage admitted in a dry tone, "that is, if Thomas were in human form."

"Right," she agreed, "but he isn't. So this is just what we have to deal with." She nodded at Gage. "Thank you for dinner. Now I'll head back to my place ... alone," she stated firmly.

"And what do you suggest I do?"

"I suggest you go back to your hotel room and rest," she replied.

"And if I have another attack?"

"Well, maybe don't lock your door, so I don't have quite so much trouble getting in."

"How did you get in anyway?"

She smiled. "Thomas, actually. He used to be a safecracker in his day." At the shocked look on Gage's face, she burst out laughing. "That's how he died. He was murdered by his partner, when they were out robbing a bank. And, when the partner realized little Ada had seen him kill Thomas, he murdered her as well."

"Good Lord," Gage murmured.

"Yeah, those who hang around tend to be colorful characters. Those who led a more peaceful life are more likely the ones who went across to where they belonged, without any kind of issue. Only, when all these things start to come up, and you look closely at their lives, then you realize some weren't necessarily the nicest people."

"Is he trying to atone for it?"

"Thomas, you mean? I don't know about that. He's hooked on to me, and he's certainly working at trying to make my life either better or more difficult—depending on your point of view, I suppose." She smirked. "But I've become quite comfortable with him now."

"And the others?"

"There are a lot of others," she agreed, with a nod. "It would be so much easier if I didn't have quite so many."

"But how do they find you?"

"In many ways." She shrugged. "I would be very interested in knowing how your uncle found me."

Gage nodded, validating the questions, then shrugged, since he didn't know the answer.

At that, she said goodbye, with a quick finger wave, and raced off. She knew she had to get back to close up the shop and to take care of any number of other headaches that would have come up by now. She had left the ghosts in charge, which meant that the door would be jammed, so nobody was allowed inside. At least she hoped that was what had happened. Otherwise, people could have gone inside and cleaned out her store.

As she walked up to her shop's entrance, she heard Dodi on the inside, calling out, "She's here. She's here."

When Skylar walked inside, the doorknob turning easily

under her hand, she asked, "Is everything okay?"

Immediately came a chorus in the affirmative. Dodi, the same pioneer woman she'd been talking to earlier, stepped forward. "We took good care of it for you."

"Good," Skylar said. "Now if only you guys could learn to work the equipment, so you can make sales for me at the same time, I'd be all set."

Dodi replied, "A group was trying to get in the door earlier, and they were quite disappointed they couldn't get in. We did discuss whether we should let them in or not."

"I'm glad you didn't," Skylar stated. "That wouldn't have been good."

"Why not?" Dodi asked.

"Because they might have tried to steal something."

"Well, we would have stopped them."

"Exactly," Skylar noted, with a half laugh. "And then you would have chased them away, and this place would have become known as haunted."

"But that could bring you a lot of good business," Dodi replied.

"It could. It could also chase me right out into the public eye, if the store became known as *too ghostly*," she murmured.

The other woman frowned, as if not having considered that. "We wouldn't want to cause you any trouble."

"I'm glad to hear that," she told Dodi. "Now, let me lock up, and then I'll go up and have a shower and get ready to go out again."

"I do wish you wouldn't go out all the time," Dodi said.

"Wouldn't that be nice?" Skylar replied. "I don't have much choice. We have to do some things regardless."

"I know. I know," Dodi agreed, "but you do realize

some of those people out there—"

"You and I both know that they're dangerous," Skylar noted, "but you also know an awful lot of lost souls are out there, who need my help."

"And you're the only one who does," she snapped. "That's why we worry about you so."

"I have Thomas. He goes with me," Skylar reminded Dodi.

"What about that nice man who was here today?"

"Nope," Skylar argued, "not going there."

With that, she quickly locked up and raced upstairs. She changed into her other working clothes, which was black, top to bottom, and picked up her tools. She wasn't ever sure what she would need whenever she was out there. Lastly she grabbed the bone that she felt Jonesy had left behind. Now she slipped out the back and headed toward the cemetery that needed her attention tonight. It was usually locked up at night, after being open for tours during the day, but she had managed to get a key made and could get in and out as she needed to.

Of course, if she ever got caught, it would be troublesome. But, so far, her ghost leads were quite capable of keeping her away from that kind of trouble. And it was trouble. The law didn't look kindly on people going through graveyards after-hours. Some of these graveyards weren't locked up, so it didn't matter, or their locks were so insufficient that she could easily bypass them.

However, with all the trouble they'd been having since Hurricane Katrina, with more people coming and stealing bones from the cemeteries, a lot more care was being taken. Skylar was all for it, except that, in her case, it cost her a little more time and trouble than it was worth. She couldn't talk about this to anybody on those commissions, responsible for looking after the graves, so she had to keep doing it all privately.

First she would take care of her bone left in her shop. *Anybody claim this bone?* she asked. All that came back was a vague humming. Sensing energy calling to energy, she followed the hum, as it got louder and louder. When she reached an unmarked grave, she sighed. "You were either poor or unidentified. I hope this helps you get home. Follow the light." And she buried the bone in the grave.

As she walked into the central area of graveyard, she called out gently to the ether, *Who needs help? I'm here.*

Immediately a voice clamored off to her side.

She walked to the left and studied the ground. And, sure enough, peeking out from one of the corners, was a bone. She reached down and, with a deep breath, wrapped her hand around the bone. Almost instantly, it started talking. His name was James, and he had been just nineteen when he had been run over. She didn't really want all the details, but she did want to know where he belonged and why he was out here.

This one was a typical flood story. Most of the cemeteries in this area had been subjected to multiple floods and unfortunately a lot of looting over the years. But getting a last name for James was a whole different story.

As she wandered through the graves, trying to find where he belonged, he kept trying to give her directions that he felt were useful but weren't, having absolutely no bearing on the physical plane. So all she could go by was energy.

So she walked with her hand out, touching each and every one of the headstones to try and find the one that felt right; she felt an odd sense coming up behind her. She immediately ducked behind the headstone, the bone still in her hand, and waited. When nothing else moved, she stopped and peered around the corner, not sure exactly what she was sensing but knowing that something wasn't quite right. She looked down at the bone and whispered, "Hey, I might have to put you down and come back."

Instantly James argued for her not to, but she wasn't sure that she had a choice tonight—since the last thing she could afford to do was to get caught. She waited in the darkness for whatever it was to pass. But when it didn't and just stood in front of her, off to the side, she took another chance and peered around the corner. And, sure enough, almost immediately, recognition slammed into her.

She stood up slowly. "Gage, what are you doing here?"

He winced and came toward her. "Hey."

"You were following me? Why?"

He shook his head. "I don't know," he stated honestly. "I don't know. But I needed to."

"Great," she moaned. "More amateurs out here is all I need."

He asked, "What are you doing?"

"You don't want to know," she replied.

"Actually I do," he argued. "I really want to know."

"Well, that's too bad. You'll have to wait until I have a chance to figure this out."

He looked at the bone in her hand. "Do you come here to steal bones?"

"Good God, no," she snapped. "But, since we have so many grave robbers since Katrina, with so many bones flooded out from these graves, I come here and try to put them back together again. Some people are not capable of leaving if they aren't complete."

"But wouldn't they have left a long time ago?"

"Some of them would have, and some would not. Some of them take too long to make a decision, and some of them only get woken up when they get spread apart," she explained. This time though there was much less disbelief on his face, as if he'd heard just enough for some of it to settle in. She nodded in approval. "I'm glad to see it's not shocking you."

"I just couldn't comprehend what you could possibly want the bones for."

"Unfortunately a booming business is here," she noted, her voice soft. "And it's for the spell-casters mostly. ... Stolen bones taken from the graves are always wanted. Of course, for the people left behind, that's the last thing they want."

He stared at the bone in her hand. "Is that one of them?"

"Yes. James here was run over about, what? Eighty-five years ago?" she asked the bone.

The answer came through her head. *Ninety-two.*

She nodded. "I was off a bit. Ninety-two."

"And what are you doing now?"

"I'm trying to find where he belongs," she replied, "but he can only give me a bit of information about it."

"Do you have his last name?"

"Wainwright," she said.

"Is there a map of this place?"

"No, not that I've found. Not that's accurate anyway. I found some Wainwrights over there, but I checked all the closest graves."

"Who thought rising waters would disturb all their bones? You would think he wouldn't have floated too far over," Gage murmured.

"You'd think so, but it doesn't always work out quite

that way," she explained. "And it's quite possible that the rest of his skeleton was already scavenged and taken."

"For what?"

"Tourists a lot of the time. Nothing I can do then," she said. "It's not as if we have a market for buying replacement bones for these guys. If I find any of his body parts in town, I will always recognize the signature, now that I've met him. But, until then, I won't know that."

"So you do what?"

"Right now? Try to find where his resting place is, so I can put him back. And then, if he's complete, try and get him to walk into the light, so, if this should happen again, he won't care."

"Ah." Gage nodded. "So there is an end to it somewhere."

"Yes," she murmured, "at least most of the time."

"I don't think I want to hear about that other ending."

"No, you don't," she added cheerfully. "But it doesn't change the fact that there are no certainties in this."

"Sounds like you've had a hard set of life lessons."

"Well, they certainly weren't the easiest."

"You know what? I'd love to hear your story."

"No, you wouldn't," she stated instantly. "And, even if you were ready, it doesn't matter because I'm not telling you."

"Stubborn to the end," he said on a laugh.

"Let's not waste time," she whispered. "I spend way too much time out here as it is, and I need to get some sleep."

"Do you do this every night?"

"Almost," she agreed. "Unfortunately an influx of souls cry out to be pulled together again. So it's something that I'm trying hard to do. Otherwise I lay awake at night because of their cries."

"That has to be tough."

"It is. It's one thing to do something when you can actually help. It's another thing to be involved in something where you can't help them."

"Right, it makes perfect sense," Gage added. "Well, let's keep looking then."

The two of them searched the headstones; he used his phone as a flashlight and read off names as he went.

"Hey, check over here," she said. "James is telling me to go in this direction."

With that, Gage quickly reversed direction, going ahead of her, and together the two of them moved until she said, "Stop."

He stopped, then bent down and checked one of the big engraved headstones. "Looks like this might be it."

"Good," she murmured.

"Now what the hell do you do?"

"I'm hoping there's a way to tuck the bone underneath. Otherwise"—she shrugged—"I have a small shovel with me, and I just bury it as close as I can." He looked at her, and she shook her head. "Some of these graveyards are underground, but most of them are all above. In this case it's an underground grave, which is why the flooding caused so much trouble. It's been going on for over a decade."

She pulled out her compact shovel and quickly dug a small space, big enough to bury the bone. Then she put the bone in and buried it, putting the soil back on top. As she stood here, she sent James a quick goodbye, asking him if he had enough bones yet.

The cry came back, "No, no, I don't."

"Okay, fine," she noted. "But do you see the light?"

"I can see it, but I don't see much of it."

"Can you walk toward it?"

"No, I can't. I can't," he cried out urgently. "I need my bones."

"In that case," she replied, with a heavy sigh, "you'll have to wait. I don't know where the rest of you is."

And, with that, she swept her energy clean of his. Then moving Gage back with her, she said, "Come on. We have to leave."

"You only do the one?"

"No," she stated, "but the energy is changing, and I don't know what's going on."

He looked at her in surprise, and she placed a finger over his lips and whispered low, "Stay quiet. Something's definitely afoot."

And, with that, she turned and raced toward the front gates. As she got there, she realized the gates were locked again. She turned to look at him, then, reaching up, she whispered into his ear, "Did you come this way?"

He nodded. "They weren't locked when I got here."

"That's fine, but now we'll have to get out."

He asked, "Can't you do whatever you did to get into my room?"

She looked at him, then rolled her eyes and said, "I'll have to. I just prefer not to do this kind of stuff with people around."

He reached out a hand and placed it gently on her shoulder. "I'm not the enemy here. I promise I won't do anything to jeopardize your position."

"What you don't understand," she explained, her voice a whisper, "is that you already have."

With that, she turned and focused on the lock, then

called out to Thomas to give her a hand. Within seconds, he had it open for her. She quickly slipped out and called Gage to come through behind her. As soon as they were free and clear, she turned to the gate and locked it.

As they stepped back, a voice behind them called out, "Who's there? Who's there?"

She froze.

INSTINCTIVELY GAGE STEPPED forward, facing the security guard. "Good evening, sir."

"Hey, what are you doing here?" the guard asked, his voice suspicious.

"We were just going to take an evening walk around the graveyard."

"Well, the gates are locked for the night."

"Yep, we see that," he noted. "We were wondering about doing one of the tours."

At that, the security guard seemed to relax ever-so-slightly. "That's the best way to do it," he agreed. "They're not all locked up tight during the day, but most of them are."

"That's a sad state of affairs," Gage replied. "I'm only in town for a few days, so I just thought I'd check things out to see what was what. It's a priority on my to-do list."

At that, the other guy snorted. "Most guys are down on Bourbon Street, enjoying the open-air booze."

"We're heading there next," Gage stated, injecting humor into his voice. "I just thought we'd take a little walk around first. Once we start in on the partying, walking to the hotel is about all we can handle."

The guard nodded, with a smirk. "Yeah, well, I'm off in

an hour, so I'll be down there myself."

"Is it just a touristy area, or is it for everybody?"

"Nah, some of my favorite places are down there. Tourists are just a necessary evil." And, with that, he waved his flashlight at them, then turned and walked off.

Skylar let out a slow exhale.

Gage turned and looked at her and asked, "Was that okay?"

She nodded quietly. "He didn't shine the flashlight on my face, so he didn't recognize me."

"Would he have?"

"I hope not."

Something was odd about her voice. He really wanted to turn on his own flashlight and check out her face because she had the ability to do things he had no idea about. "Would he have been able to recognize you? Maybe that's a better question," he muttered. She didn't answer, and he chose to take that as a no. "You really can do things with energy, can't you?"

"I can do all kinds of things," she whispered. "We all can. Not everybody is prepared to do what they can to learn, though."

"Sure," he agreed, "but a lot of people don't even know what the options are; and if it were to hide your identity in front of a security guard, that's not something we really want the public to know about, right?"

She laughed. "No, it sure isn't. None of the things I do are really of interest."

"You mean, like talking to bones."

"Hey, the bones talk to me," she argued in a harsh voice.

"And did you come by that skill naturally?"

She burst out laughing. "You could say that. My father

used to work in a funeral home. I went to work with him, and my mom worked the night shift."

"You slept in a funeral home?" he asked in horror.

"I don't know how much sleep I actually got. My father said I was always telling stories about dead people."

"And were you?"

"Well, I was telling *their* stories," she murmured, as they walked back toward the busier streets. "But I can't say that I was making them up. At least I didn't think so at the time."

"But he convinced you of that?"

"He did for a few years, until I went to the funeral of a friend of mine, who sat up in the casket and started talking to me. That freaked me out pretty good, but that was nothing compared to how me talking back to her freaked out everybody around me. I spent quite a bit of time talking to a therapist, who made the assessment that I was just over-wrought from the loss of a good friend."

"And what did you think?"

"I thought it was time to shut my mouth," she stated succinctly.

At that, he burst out laughing. "Isn't that the truth? I'm afraid I didn't learn that lesson very quickly."

"That's because, when you woke up from the coma, you were more interested in learning how to control it," she noted. "And learning how to control it meant asking questions, and, if you don't have the right people to ask the questions to, you end up asking the wrong people."

"Yeah, you could say that," he agreed. "I saw shrinks myself for quite a while."

"After the accident?"

He nodded. "Yes, and they told me it was basically a

result of the trauma from the accident, and I was just trying to find a way to deal with it."

"How were you changed?"

"Yeah, that's a good question," he noted. "I lost my best friend in the wreck. He was driving at the time. Thankfully I wasn't, but then maybe it wouldn't have happened if I were. No point in dwelling on that. I think the biggest change was the fact that I was dealing with some brain damage, though I think it's cleared up at this point. But I don't have the same drive that I used to. I'm looking for a complete lifestyle change now, something that's a whole lot easier on my body, which obviously suffered in ways that I hadn't even imagined," he admitted. "I'm healed physically. Emotionally I'm still grieving, and there's still that survivor guilt," he added calmly.

"At the same time, I would like to think that maybe this whole thing that started after this accident would be something that I can either live with or at least turn to doing something solid with. And I don't know what that would even look like right now. I didn't really plan on coming out here and putting bones back together," he noted, with half a jolt of laughter.

Her smile gleamed in the darkness. "No, I wouldn't recommend it."

"How is it that you feel like you can't *not* do it?"

"I don't know," she replied. "It's just, when you think about it, how do I *not* help these people?"

And yet," he murmured, "if you get caught …"

"Getting caught isn't so much the problem, it's trying to come up with an explanation that makes everybody happy," she murmured. "If you think about it, these are not very easy things to explain away."

"Not at all," he agreed, with shock in his voice. "I mean, just that security guy alone. If he had caught us on the other side of the gate, how would you explain having gotten in?"

"I don't know that I could have," she admitted, "except to display some ignorance and hope that he bought it."

"What? That the gate was left unlocked?"

"Exactly," she said, with a nod. "What else could I do?"

"I don't know," he replied. "That's your department."

"Hardly," she argued. "Nothing in this is my department really. Like you, I'm just finding my way. It's a learning process, and you do the best you can, but there are no guarantees that somebody won't look at you sideways and think that you belong in the looney bin. No way to know how any of this will pan out over time. I don't want to spend all my life doing this, but, when I have a shopful of spirits, what the hell else am I supposed to do?" she muttered. "They tend to be quite the nags."

At that, Gage burst out laughing. "You're serious, aren't you?"

"Very," she muttered. "You have no idea what it's like to have dead people wanting you to go help somebody else that they hear crying out."

"Oh my God." Gage stared at her. "Is that what they do?"

She nodded slowly. "They've certainly been known to. They also keep watch on my store for me, letting me know when things are off, telling me when customers are coming, and basically just keeping me company." She gave Gage half a smile.

"That sounds absolutely fascinating," he murmured.

"Although I've seen some—you know, like I told you—I haven't really had the same kind of an experience, and I certainly haven't been able to talk to any but the one."

"But really," Skylar noted, "what you're probably doing is looking for your friend."

CHAPTER 6

SKYLAR LOOKED OVER at Gage, wondering if he had acknowledged the death of his friend in his world. "Right?"

"It would be nice to know that he's okay," Gage replied quietly.

"What kind of an accident was it?"

"He missed a corner," Gage said, with a casual shrug.

"Deliberately?"

He sucked in his breath. "I hope not."

"Well, of course you hope not, but, at the same time, you're wondering."

"You really like to go right for the jugular, don't you?"

"Don't really have time for much else," she muttered, hating to hurt him but knowing that it was easiest to cut through all the smoke screens. "You might want to pussyfoot around, but I don't. I've got way too much on my plate."

"And I get that," he noted. "However, this is also rather new for me, so it does feel a little bit abrupt when you get right to the point like that."

"Get used to it," she stated. "Ghosts do not care about niceties. They do not care about where your feelings are."

He asked, "Really?"

"Often they're the same as they were on this side," she explained, "and sometimes you'll find that they'll be nice.

However, sometimes they'll cut to the chase and ask why you're doing something stupid." She laughed. "Believe me. I've had a few of them get to the point a whole lot faster than I would have liked."

"And again that just sounds fascinating to me."

"Fascinating, yes, but not necessarily the easiest to deal with."

"No, but, if you don't want to waste time, it's much better to figure out exactly where you're at, isn't it?"

"Yep," she agreed. "Now, let's get you back to your hotel, and I'm going home to my place."

"Do you ever worry about any dangers at the graveyard?"

She was silent for a long moment.

"You do, don't you?" he asked.

"Well, there are dangers, and there are other kinds of dangers," she stated, her voice fading ever-so-slightly. She tried not to involve people in the uglier side of this, but there was that uglier side. And, if he kept pushing, he would find it.

"And then what?"

She shook her head. "Look. I get that you really want to explore and want to get to know a lot of this new side of yourself, and I understand that drive. It's been a long time since I first came into any of this stuff," she noted. "It's not as if I've forgotten, but you need to understand that not all of it is pleasant, not all of it is upbeat and fun. People died, and they don't like it sometimes. Others are grateful because it released them from a very painful existence, and sometimes they're angry because they were murdered, or they were trying to do something terrible and were killed in the process. Not all ghosts are happy-go-lucky friendly apparitions."

"Right, it's like you said earlier," he replied. "They're not any different as ghosts than when they were alive, and some people are just not very pleasant."

"Exactly," she admitted. "And not only are they just not that pleasant but they have the distinction of being downright ugly sometimes."

He laughed at that. "We don't really think of it that way, do we?"

"No, we don't," she said, "and that's why I'm warning you."

"Yet that warning seems to be fairly strong."

She shrugged. "I've gotten the impression that you don't really take kindly to mild warnings."

At that, he burst out laughing. "Wow, I've really made quite the impact, haven't I?"

"You have," she agreed. "I'm just not sure it's the kind you really want to make."

"Am I that bad?"

"No, not that bad," she said, "but I don't want to say you're that good either."

He shook his head, as if unsure how to take her comments.

"Look. Just be careful with whatever you're doing."

"Something happened to me in that hotel room, and I don't even know what it was, not to mention how to fix it," he noted. "I get that you don't really want to help me, but you are kind of it for me. You're the only person I know who has any experience in this field."

She hesitated.

He frowned and asked, "Or are there others?"

"There are others, and some are willing to help, and others are not so willing. And some are so in demand that they don't have time."

"Right, because people are people."

She smiled. "Yes, that's a good way to look at it. People are people, and they aren't necessarily always very helpful."

"But *most* people," he added in a craftier voice, "are perfectly happy to help, if there's money involved."

"As long as they're not on the ghostly side—because what those people want isn't usually anything you can give them."

"What is it they want again?"

"They want resurrection. They want forgiveness, and, in some cases, they want to live again."

"Ouch, talk about tall orders."

"You mean *impossible* orders. The forgiveness they have to get themselves, and, when it comes to other people who are still alive, you could spend a lifetime hunting down the people who matter to them. Geography doesn't matter. In some cases, you'll get people from other countries. And then there is the time issue. Time has no meaning either."

"I thought people were connected to where they died."

"They're connected to places that matter to them," she clarified. "And that's not always where they were living. Think about somebody who was off on a trip around the world and died here—say, in New Orleans—but really they're from Scotland. They want to go home to Scotland."

"Why can't they just—" And Gage stopped.

She looked at him with a wry expression. "Just what?"

He threw up his hands. "I don't know. I was just thinking, why don't they go to Scotland then?"

"Sure, and sometimes they can. However, if they're tied to their physical body, they can't because, wherever their body is, they are."

"Does that happen a lot?"

"Yes, it happens a lot," she confirmed. "You can also get people who have come up with some kind of attachment to living people here, either because they find out that it's a living relative they didn't know about—or, say, a granddaughter lived here, and they don't want to leave them. That becomes their new lockdown attachment, and they aren't in a position to actually unlock and move on. Also a lot of people are afraid to cross over. They don't know what's waiting for them, particularly depending on what they were like in life."

"Oh, so we're back to that heaven or hell issue, aren't we?"

"And, for you, that might seem light and funny, but, for people who are stuck in-between, it can become a terrifying reality. Particularly if there's no light for them to follow."

"Everybody says there'll be a light, don't they?"

"They say that, and supposedly you can walk forward and connect to that light. But, if you don't see that light, then what?" she murmured, looking over at him.

"I don't know," he said. "You got me. If there's no light, then what?"

"Usually no light is because they aren't ready to leave, but what if there's no light, and they want to leave? Then you've got a problem, and you have to figure out why they can't see the light."

"And are there actually reasons? Is there a logical system in play that you have to work out for these people?" he asked curiously.

She shrugged. "A couple times I've had it happen, and it was because they were either hooked on to an earthly presence or to an earthly event and weren't ready to leave, or they were trying to stay somehow and were refusing to see where they needed to go. There can be all kinds of scenarios, as many as you could come up with for people who are alive can also be applied to people who are not."

"And who would have ever thought it?" he murmured.

"I know." She nodded in agreement. "Nothing's easy about any of this. Once you start talking to these ghosts, it may not be the one you want to talk with. Some ghosts demand attention more than others, and sometimes ghosts are sitting there, just waiting for somebody like you to talk to them, and they'll talk your ear off because they're lonely."

He groaned. "Now that would be my aunt Jess," he muttered.

"Again, people on that side are just the same as the people on this side, and individuals can have the same issues they've always had."

"I never thought of it that way."

"And they collect in groups," she added. "So, when you open the door to talk to a ghost, you have to be careful that you don't get drowned out by a bunch of other ghosts. Sometimes they're well-mannered and orderly, and they're happy to just, you know, stand there and talk to you, but then they usually want you to pass on a message to somebody. Otherwise what's the point of talking to you or to me personally? So often they just sit there and wait in the background, hoping that you'll trip over their loved one, so they can jump up and knock you on the head, letting you know it is important to them."

He started to laugh at that.

"Hey, I get it. It sounds funny to an outsider, but it's really not funny when it happens to you."

"Does that really happen?" he asked in shock.

"Yeah, it has certainly happened to me," she muttered, "and never at the most convenient of times either."

"You must have the most interesting stories to share," he murmured.

"Yeah, too bad I'm not really the social kind," she stated bluntly.

And again he grinned. "Maybe not the *social* kind, but I do think that what you do comes from the heart."

"It comes from the heart, but that doesn't mean it'll get me any brownie points," she murmured.

"And yet that isn't what you're after, is it?"

"No. It's a good thing though," she said. "Just being after brownie points won't do it for you."

He smiled. "Fascinating. It's all really fascinating."

And that's when she stopped. "Here's your hotel."

He looked up in surprise. "I didn't realize we were here already. You sure you don't want to have a drink down on Bourbon Street? It sounded like it might be fun."

"You go for it. I'm tired, and I need to head home and get some rest."

"And will your ghosts let you?"

"I hope so," she replied on a yawn. "It all depends on what's stirring on the ethers."

And, on that cryptic note, she turned and walked rapidly away.

GAGE WATCHED SKYLAR go, wishing that she were the kind who would open up and share, but she'd obviously been hurt by doing just that, because she was certainly against it. And he could understand if she'd tried it with bad results. People like him, struggling to find answers, looking for anything to somehow provide clarity, were desperate without someone like her to help. He also knew that when you were a specialist in any field, people were always out there trying to grab information from you to increase their own specialty.

He hoped she knew he wasn't trying to pull one over on her or to use this information for anything other than his own healing. But he wasn't exactly sure that was even something she would understand. It was a sad world when it came down to not wanting to help people because you'd been burned so badly that you couldn't trust anyone.

Yet was he any different? He'd had a couple deals go sour because of business partners screwing him over, and a couple other deals he had reluctantly made because he wasn't comfortable with the people involved, getting out as soon as he could. People would be people. It was disheartening to think the world had gone to hell in a handbasket.

He looked around his hotel lobby, before calling for an elevator, recalling the moment Skylar had asked if he was hoping to connect with his friend. It had been a direct hit that neither had discussed further. He wasn't sure he'd thought of it consciously in that context, but he knew she was right.

Alone in the elevator now, he whispered, "I don't know where you are, Linden, but anytime you want to talk to me, I'm here, and I'm listening."

Of course he had to learn exactly how to be here and to listen, but he could only hope that maybe one day his buddy would show up, and they could actually talk. Skylar had also hit the nail on the head asking if the accident had been intentional. Gage really hoped that his friend hadn't been trying to kill both of them and that maybe he had just been terribly upset and had missed the corner accidentally.

But … maybe Linden *had* done it on purpose. Gage just wanted clarity from his buddy, and, because Gage had survived, he also wanted to tell his friend that it was okay, that he forgave him. Right or wrong, that stage of Gage's life had come and gone, and Linden was no longer part of it. His friend had been in such a messed-up state prior to the accident. Linden had no desire to be a part of the sale of the business, so Gage figured he'd buy out Linden early, so he could avoid the headache of these negotiations. And, when Linden wanted out, Gage had let him go easily enough.

Yet Linden had been upset about that too. It showed his mental state, and it bothered Gage that he hadn't been aware of it in a close enough way to have done something to help his friend of all these years. Gage hadn't realized just how unstable Linden had been.

Until it was too late.

Shaking his head, Gage quickly walked up to his room and inside. He studied the bed. Sleep might be impossible tonight because of all that had gone on earlier. He still wasn't sure about that black presence he had felt over his chest and had seen behind her when he woke up. He really wanted to ask her about it but knew she wouldn't be happy about it. Which was a pain in the ass because she was literally the only one who could answer these questions. He looked down at his phone, wondering if he should call her.

He hemmed and hawed and then finally mustered the guts and said, "Screw it. I need to know."

And he dialed the phone number he had for her.

When she answered, her voice distant and not exactly friendly, he jumped right in. "I didn't have the guts to ask you this earlier, but I really need to know," he began. "In the hotel room, I sensed a huge dark presence atop me, before I went under. It was something new to me. Then I woke up again and saw it was behind you. Do you know what that was?"

There was shock in her voice when she replied, "No, I don't, but I sure as hell wish you would have said something about it earlier."

"Why?"

"Because that kind of shit," she snapped, "it's not good. And you need to nip it in the bud right off the bat, just as soon as you can."

"And do what?" he asked her in bewilderment.

"Disarm it, for one thing," she stated firmly, "or dissipate the energy. The fact of the matter is that something knocked you out, and it was likely that dark presence."

"But then wouldn't you have noticed it yourself?"

"No," she said, "I was totally preoccupied trying to gather enough energy to keep you alive."

He winced. "Right, and of course you don't have answers to everything anyway."

"No," she snapped, "I don't. But I do know that, right now, if you have done any kind of research, you know you need to keep a protection spell on you, particularly in that room. I'm hoping that the dark energy is not connected to something that might have gone on in that room beforehand. You might need to ask or do some subtle research for some time period in history, then try and get some sleep."

"I do know about protection spells," he noted, a little dazed that she would bring up something like that. "I just didn't think they were for real."

Her voice was harsh when she snapped, "Damn right, they're for real. So when you go to bed tonight, make sure you put one on." With that, she hung up.

He stared down at the phone, wondering if he should call her back to apologize for not being forthright from the start, but realized that she probably wouldn't answer a second time. She could only put up with so much from him, and she had been generous with her time so far and hadn't even lost it when he had followed her to the graveyard. But he'd probably exhausted her goodwill, … for tonight at least.

He smiled, as he thought about his brother's suggestion and realized that it did make sense to try again in the morning, with food. At least it seemed to work today, so he'd do it again tomorrow.

CHAPTER 7

SKYLAR SAT DOWN on her balcony, with a glass of white wine, relaxing in the warm, humid New Orleans air. She was dreaming if she thought she wouldn't see Gage again tomorrow. Elena, one of the ghosts that she let into her upstairs apartment, walked out and sat down beside her. Decades and decades and decades ago, Elena had been a beautiful light-skinned ex-slave and mistress of a plantation owner. She hadn't survived her first childbirth. Her voice was musical and soft, and she was more hooked on this location.

Having had such a short life, she was content to sit around and to have an extension of that life in this ghostly form. No matter how much Skylar tried to convince her to go to the light, which was there and available to her, she refused. Even when Skylar told her that maybe she would then come back and live this existence all over again.

"He's nice," Elena noted.

"He is, and he's also in a tough spot," she murmured, taking a sip from the wineglass, before leaning back and closing her eyes.

"No, I hear you. He is in a tough spot. I could see his energy, but I couldn't actually appear before him."

"That would shock him," she noted, with a laugh. "He hasn't been able to see anybody really clearly yet."

"But, as he works at it, he might though, right?"

"Maybe," she agreed, turning to look at this ghost that she would have called a friend, if they were both in physical form.

Elena looked at her, smiled, and stated, "You know we're friends now."

"We are, except that you're supposed to be off on your own journey," she murmured, "not sitting here, keeping me company."

"I thought it was the other way around," Elena teased, with a light tinkling laugh that filled the balcony. "I was here first."

Skylar grinned. "Point taken," she murmured. Then she added, "And who knows? I could have been here at the same time you were here. Maybe we were friends in physical form before."

"I wouldn't be at all surprised," Elena agreed thoughtfully. "You should check your Akashic records, which with your skills I'm assuming you can, and see where and when your other lifetimes appeared."

"We've talked about the existence of those records before but I've yet to try to access them," she stated, "but my hands are a little full at the moment."

Elena nodded complacently, as she rocked gently on the rocking chair. And, yes, the rocking chair did move and was just one more of the nuances of a ghostly life, where there was really no rhyme or reason or answers because Elena had no physical form and no weight to make the rocker move. Yet it did. And whether it was just a push of a rocker that she managed to make from a certain specific corner, it was the one trick that Elena could do.

Skylar had had physical company over early on, when

she had first moved to this area. But taking one look at the rocking chair seemingly moving itself, her guest had freaked out and had abruptly left, never to return.

Elena had laughed and laughed. "I guess they weren't cut out to be the kind of person you need in your life."

"Well, I could have used any kind of friend," Skylar murmured.

"Nope," Elena had argued. "That's not quite true. You need people like you."

"There aren't many people like me," she muttered.

"No, but you need that tribe."

"*Tribe*," she repeated softly.

That was one of the current catch words that always got her, because how did you know who your tribe was from the outside?

"You have to trust," Elena answered her thought.

"I'm not really good at trusting."

"Nope, you're not," she agreed, "but I love you anyway." She spoke in such a breezy tone that in no way could Skylar be mad at her. Besides, Skylar had discovered early on that it was completely a waste of energy to be mad at ghosts. They had their own way of doing things, their own way of looking at things, and you could try to argue with them until you were blue in the face, and it didn't make the tiniest bit of difference. They still thought they had the answers—or at least knew more than you did.

And sure, Elena had been around a long time. She had been part of the New Orleans scene for a very long time, but that didn't mean that she had actually been as active as she was now. Because, in reality, she couldn't have been very much of a part of it. Only as Skylar had come and had opened up more energy, as it became more available, did a lot of this actually open up for Elena, who was loving every bit of it. She didn't want Skylar to leave, but, at the same time, Skylar would do whatever she needed to do for her own security and peace of mind, and Elena knew that. Yet, at the same time, she didn't want to hear it.

Skylar smiled at that because, once again, it was all about doing what you needed to do and hoping that everybody around you would either understand or, if they didn't, that they would stay out of your life enough that you could do what you wanted to do regardless. And, in this case, it was more about Elena understanding that, when she left to go into the light—if and when she left—that increased energy that Skylar provided to Elena may fade with her crossing over. Skylar just didn't know. They had discussed it a couple times but with no answers. Elena wasn't prepared to argue about it. She was just enjoying life as it was for her right now.

"It really is nice to see everybody so happy out here."

"What about when you see the brawls?"

"That's just a part of it," Elena admitted, with an airy wave of her hand. "When you think about it, there were always brawls and fights, particularly with men … and always over the ladies." Elena smiled at that.

Skylar got the impression that Elena had seen more than a few such conflicts, perhaps over herself. "Well, you are beautiful in this form," Skylar noted, "so I imagine you must have been a stunner when you were in your full physical form."

"I was," she agreed, with a complete lack of guile. "And my master was very proud to have me on his arm."

"Did he treat you well?"

"Yes, absolutely," she replied, with a smile.

"Would it have lasted?"

"Not likely, not when I became old and gray with ten babies at my feet."

"So, he would have moved onto somebody younger, slimmer, less occupied, I presume."

Elena nodded. "The good thing," she explained, "was that I didn't have to live through that stage of being discarded."

"No, and I can't imagine that would have been very much fun for anybody."

"No," she replied, "and I am very happy now that men don't have quite the same options"—she paused—"or maybe women have more options now."

"Women have a lot more options," Skylar agreed, "and women of color have far more options."

She nodded. "We never thought we'd see that day come."

"Well, I'm sure a large part of the population would say there are still a lot of problems, and it's not come anywhere nearly as far as it could be, but at least it's progress."

"A hell of a lot of progress," she murmured. "But you're right. I don't think it's enough." She looked down at the street and pointed. "Look. An awful lot of partying down on that corner."

As Skylar looked over the rail, she saw a group of twenty or so. But the energy around them was gentle and fun-loving. "I think they're just having fun."

"And that," Elena agreed, "is really good to see."

"You didn't get to have a lot of fun, did you?" she asked Elena.

"We sang a lot," she replied, "and I was treated well enough, but my own people didn't particularly appreciate the favors that I was given."

"Of course not," Skylar noted. "Every society has its own microsocieties, and, within them, there will always be jealousy and anger."

"Yes," she murmured.

"But you died in childbirth, correct?"

"Yes, as did my baby daughter."

"I'm so sorry about that," she murmured.

"I'm not," she stated, with surprising force. "She would have been born into slavery—and likely would have been beautiful and become the property of a man."

"Born to a slave, she already was," Skylar noted quietly.

Elena looked at her, glared, and held up her hand. "I'm just saying that's what the life was like. I know I shouldn't get mad at you, but, if I could live now," she snapped, "I think I would be a force for men to contend with."

"I'm sure you would," Skylar declared, with brilliant laughter. "If nothing else you'd break hearts with every step you took."

"Because I'm beautiful, right?"

"Yes, absolutely because you're beautiful." Skylar chuckled.

"And yet you laugh," Elena noted, with a frown.

"Not at you," she explained, "just at the thought of how the men would be overwhelmed by your beauty, which is only the half of it," she murmured.

"It would be easier for them if they were," she stated. "Men are simple creatures."

At that, Skylar burst out laughing. "I won't argue with that."

"You really should be nicer to him, you know?" Elena noted.

"Why?" Skylar asked bluntly.

"He needs your help."

"He does need help, but that doesn't mean that I'm the right person to help him."

"You're just afraid of getting hurt again," Elena murmured.

"Maybe that's one of my lessons to learn though, right?"

It was really hard to turn off the ghosts when they got to know you because they really thought that, once they did, they then had the right to make judgments about your life and share how they thought you should lead it. Sometimes Skylar would tune them out; sometimes she would tell them to keep it to themselves, but Elena generally stayed within the boundaries. Yet tonight she seemed to really want to discuss Gage.

"I like him," she stated.

"He's male," Skylar said in a dry tone, "of course you do."

Elena burst out laughing. "I'm not so simple as that."

"Yes, you are." Skylar looked over at her ghostly friend.

Elena shrugged. "Maybe so, but still he is very good-looking."

"I hadn't noticed." Then Skylar rolled her eyes at Elena's laughter because, of course, it was really hard to hide any of those kinds of reactions. "Okay, fine," Skylar agreed. "I'll give you that. He is good-looking. Big deal. That's on the outside, and it doesn't mean it's all good on the inside."

"He's good-looking on the inside too," Elena stated, with a nod.

"Maybe, but then I've been wrong about that before," she muttered.

"That's why you're scared to move in that direction

again."

"Maybe I'm just not ready. I don't like the way this all went down today, and I don't like anything to do with his uncle." She looked over at Elena. "Now, if only you could tell me if Jonesy were alive."

"Can't tell you," she said. "I don't know anything about other ghosts."

"And yet you know about the ones downstairs."

"I know about the ones downstairs, but it's not like I converse with them much. And they don't even converse with each other very often," she noted. "A couple seem to be able to, but most of the others don't. Yet I think they create bonds," she stated thoughtfully, "but I'm not sure how that works."

"That's because the only bond you've formed is with me," Skylar explained. "And you really should be going into the light."

"But I'm not going to," she argued, "because this is way too much fun."

Skylar groaned at that. "What will it take for you to go in the light? Maybe you can try another lifetime here."

"What if it's worse than the last one?" she asked. "With my luck I'd come back as a man. An especially simple man."

Skylar couldn't do anything but laugh. "Well, I would hope," she added, "that you would have a little more tolerance for those simple males, if you did come back as one."

"Well, according to you, we're coming back for each lifetime to learn something," she said, "and that's not really something I want to learn." And, with that, she disappeared.

Skylar sat here, pondering her world that had more ghosts than actual humans, considering the conversations and friendships that she had with both humans and ghosts and realizing that most people would consider her three bricks short of a load. As long as nobody really understood what was going on, and she could keep that secret safe, then it was fine. But the minute she started making the mistake of talking to these ghosts around other people, it would be a whole different story.

For that reason alone, she tended to keep people away because it was too easy for her to forget about these ghosts being ghosts and not humans. Since she talked to them on a regular basis, it was hard to remember to hide their presence, and, once that secret was out, well, she didn't want to think about what her life would be like. And that just brought Gage up again because he already knew way too much, and that was disturbing in itself.

She shouldn't have told him so much, particularly after he had followed her to the graveyard. That was a step too far in her book, and yet somehow she didn't feel threatened by it, and that bothered her. How is it that she was giving this guy a level of leniency, especially when she wouldn't have given anybody else the same? It didn't make any sense, except that the ghosts and her own abilities had confirmed she had nothing to fear from Gage.

And now that she had actually worked to save his life, it was even more apparent. She understood his energy more than he probably did, just from the experience of trying to save him. Not that it was a nice feeling by any means. Still, she could only deal with so much at one time, and he was not it. Plus, as long as Jonesy appeared to be missing, it would only bring more and more police and investigators around.

She feared he was dead.

Taking a deep breath and calming her thoughts for a moment, she said, "Jonesy, if you're here, I'd like to talk to you."

A weird muffled sound came on the ethers, and she tilted her head to the side. "That doesn't sound like Jonesy." She spoke softly because she wasn't sure exactly what she had heard, and it was more like she was speaking to herself.

When another voice spoke up, it said, *I'm not Jonesy, but I'd like to speak with you.*

Startled, she bolted to her feet and looked around, but no human form was here. Yet that ghostly voice had been strong, too strong for her not to first think it may have been human. "Why?" she asked.

He took something from me.

She looked up to see an apparition, standing in front of her. "What can you do with it in your form?"

None of your business, he stated in a brisk tone. *But I need it. And, if you know where it is, I need to know what you know.*

"I don't know where he is," she said blankly. "People have been asking me off and on all day. I don't even know him."

You didn't answer my question. The apparition wobbled in place for a long moment, and she saw the darkness of anger, first just at the edges, then slowly taking over. There was a bland haze on the outer layer, and she immediately covered herself in a protective energy.

He laughed. *You might do that now,* he noted, *but you won't always be able to hide from me.*

"I'm talking to you now," she stated in a calming voice. "I can see that this really bothers you, but have you considered that maybe you need to let it go?"

I can't let it go, he argued. *He had something of mine.*

"What did he have? And, if I can find him and get it back, what is it that you want me to do with it?" she asked, trying for a reasonable tone of voice.

Jonesy had the tarot cards but no longer, he stated, *and I need them.*

"What good will they do?"

They will help me live again.

"No, they won't," she argued. "That's not possible." She spoke with a surety that she didn't feel because something was always happening out there in the ethers, something odd and different enough to make her realize that she could never count on anything. But this guy seemed so sure that he could live again that she didn't even want to go there or to consider it as a possibility.

Yes, it is possible.

"And how do you figure?"

Jonesy already had my bones, he murmured. *And my life was taken from me.*

"Many lives have been taken from many people," she noted. "It's a sad fact of the state of humanity, but that's no guarantee that you can live again." She hadn't ever heard from anybody that it was even a possibility. "When your life is gone, you need to go to the light, and then you need to come back again as a different person with a different life lesson."

He snorted. *I like the one I've got just fine.*

"Maybe so," she admitted, "but apparently it was taken from you, and, therefore, it's not the life that you have any longer."

More anger built in her unwanted ghost, and she stood fast, not letting him see any sign of fear at all. Ghosts like this lived on fear; they thrived on it. The worst thing she could do was actually let him see that she felt anything; otherwise he could use it against her.

Finally he eased back and spoke. *You're strong.*

"Have you talked to very many of the living?" she asked, with a note of humor.

A couple, he noted. *They didn't last long.*

At that, a whisper of a warning trickled down her spine. "Didn't *last?*"

Nope, they didn't last at all. I'll have to see how you do.

"*Last* during what?"

Possession, he stated, with a cheerful voice. *I've become very good at it. The trouble is, my subjects don't handle it very well.*

Skylar now felt that Jonesy was dead. By this ghost possessing him. And all about getting the cards. And, if Jonesy were dead, she then wondered if this angry spirit were the black entity who had sought to possess Gage earlier today, which had almost killed him too. Of course she had nothing to prove either theory, just her gut. Regardless, this spirit was to be avoided at all cost.

Therefore, I'm always looking for somebody new, somebody stronger I can experiment on with my abilities. ... And it looks like I found one.

And, with that, he disappeared.

Of course he could try. That didn't mean she'd give him—or any other ghost—the opportunity.

THE NEXT MORNING Gage woke up and walked to one of the recommended breakfast spots. He had slept surprisingly well but was antsy to get out of his hotel room. He didn't know why, but he definitely felt that sense of getting away from there free and clear, and he was okay to follow that dictate because he didn't really want to be sitting inside anyway.

It was a beautiful day out here, and he would only be here for however long it took to find Jonesy, so Gage wanted to explore and to learn. Besides, he was also going on one of those graveyard tours today, without his private nighttime tour guide. He wanted to see just what people were actually saying about these graves and about the ghosts. Even if he saw some on the tour, Gage didn't expect that he could say anything to any of them. But he'd never know until he actually got there.

He looked around at the restaurants nearby, chose one, picked up several beignets, and then decided that something more was needed. So he picked up several egg sandwiches too. As he walked toward Skylar's store, Gage checked the atmosphere around it. He couldn't tell a whole lot, but it seemed like everything was fine. He saw no dark sense of foreboding, saw no stormy weather, like they always talk about in the movies. It just looked like a normal day.

As he walked into the store, he thought he heard a youngster inside, and he remembered what Skylar had said about the ghost kids often letting her know when people came in, so he called out, "Thanks for giving her a heads-up."

After a moment of silence, Skylar's head popped around the corner, and she glared at him.

He smiled suddenly. "I brought breakfast."

She frowned and sighed.

"Yep, it's a good day, isn't it?" he asked, chuckling.

She shook her head. "How come you won't be chased away by my temper?" she asked.

"I'm not sure, but, no, I won't be," he replied. "Nice try though."

"Not likely if it didn't work." She motioned to the space to the left of him. "Do you see anything?"

He looked around and down, then shrugged. "Nope. Am I supposed to?"

"Well, the little boy you said thank-you to is standing there, grinning up at you."

He turned and looked for a minute. "I can see … something, like an ethereal kind of a cloud maybe."

She nodded. "This little guy's name is Jackie. So go ahead and say hello, if you like."

He knelt and said, "Hi, Jackie," as he held out his hand. Instantly an icy wave crossed his palm, and he immediately retracted it. "Jesus."

"When you held out your hand, Jackie put his in it. His little hands are very cold," she noted.

He stared at her in wonder, then again at the space, but the ghostly apparition was gone.

"He's gone off, grinning from ear to ear," she noted, with a smile. "Looks like you made his day."

"Good God, it'll take a while to get used to this."

"A long while," she added cheerfully. She took the bag from him, now looking inside.

"You don't ever tell me what you like or don't like," he stated. "Except you don't seem to like being in crowds, so I'm guessing you don't like walking through the graveyards in the daylight."

"I like all those things," she replied. "All at the right time. And, so far, we haven't had the right time."

He nodded. "I get it."

She offered him one of the egg sandwiches, and he nodded with relief because he was pretty damn hungry, and, after that touch from the little ghost, Gage was also on the nervous side. "Should I do anything for these ghosts? Are there any around me?"

"Lots of them," she stated, "but don't worry about it. They'll always be there, just watching you. Particularly now that you tried to interact with one of them."

"And what now? So the others will try to interact with me too?" he asked, frowning.

"Maybe. You can never tell what ghosts will do." But then she tilted her head, as if listening to something, and thereafter she shrugged. "Posey here wants to know why you're back."

"Posey?"

"An older woman, who passed peaceably in her rocking chair."

"So why is she still here?" he asked. "Aren't they supposed to just naturally go off to the light and have a new life?"

"Well, whatever afterlife that they're supposed to have, she decided she didn't like it. She still had family living here at the time, so she figured she might as well stick around too. But it does drive her nuts that they don't come and visit." Skylar smiled. "And you can't really explain to her that they've all since died now and are gone, and their ghosts didn't hang around, like she did."

"*Are* they all dead and gone?"

"I did check once, and she has quite a few cousins and grandchildren spread out across the country, but I don't think anybody lives in New Orleans anymore."

"And you've told her that?"

"Many times," Skylar confirmed, with a wave of her

hand. "Now she has locked on to me, so I just became the next family member she didn't want to leave."

"It's really fascinating, you know?"

"It is. Yet it can also be crazy and disturbing."

"Have you ever had scary ghosts lock on to you?" At that, her smile fell away, and he leaned forward. "Tell me."

"I don't really want to," she murmured, "but considering what happened last night, I guess I'd better."

His eyebrows shot up. "You had a visit from an unfriendly ghost last night?"

She nodded. "He's looking for Jonesy because Jonesy had something of his, and he mentioned the tarot cards."

At that, Gage's heart sank. "Did you ask him if Jonesy was dead?"

She shook her head, not wanting to share this news until she had proof in the physical world. "Ghosts don't know if somebody is dead or not."

"How is that not a thing?" he asked.

"Do you know if somebody's dead?" she asked him.

He looked at her, considering the question. "Well," he began, then stopped. "I guess not, since an awful lot of people are in this world, aren't there?"

"There are, and, if it's not somebody in your state, in your world, in your actual circle of friends and family, how would you know if somebody was alive or dead?"

"I didn't really think of it that way," he muttered, "but, yeah, that makes sense."

"Listen. This malevolent ghost is looking for a body to possess, a strong psychic body, because he wore out the last one—or two. I know that sounds horrible," she noted, looking at Gage, "but you have to understand that it's more important than ever that you use protection circles around you at all times."

"So, it's really that serious?" He knew he sounded dazed, but what else was he supposed to do when having an actual conversation on ghostly possession. "Is it even possible that a ghost could possess me, a living body?"

"I have to wonder if that isn't why you passed out yesterday," she noted, frowning. "And, if so, his possession attempt almost killed you. That would also explain how he found me."

"Because you're the one who came to help me?"

She nodded. "And, because I did help, it also shows I have some strength in this field, which he is now attracted to."

"Does he have the ability to actually overtake someone?"

"I won't say no because we've all heard of possession horror stories over the years. Have I come across it myself? No. Do I want to? Hell no," she stated in a strong voice. "But that doesn't mean that we always get what we want."

"And yet you're still fairly ballsy about it."

She looked at him in surprise. "Not really, but I won't go borrowing trouble before it gets here either." She didn't even know what to say because it sounded so far-fetched. She shook her head. "And again you're at a crossroads here. I don't care if you believe me or not," she snapped, "but don't waste my time. So, if you don't believe me, the door is behind you."

He immediately shook his head. "Don't get so riled. It's just a foreign concept to me."

"It's a foreign concept to a lot of the world. The fact of the matter is, he was angry, and I mean *very* angry about something, and it had to do with the tarot cards. He did say that your uncle had bones that were his and something about somebody taking his life."

"Wow," Gage murmured, trying to sift through it all. "He isn't implying that my uncle killed him, I presume?"

"No, he looked like he was from a different era," she noted quietly. "I couldn't tell you when or where."

"And time really doesn't matter, unless you're trying to track down a murderer," he muttered.

"Maybe, in that case, yes, but, at the same time, maybe not. Remember. Back then, there were no records of importance in so many of these cases."

"Right, so people could get away with murder, and, other than the deceased's immediate circle, nobody really cared."

"There is also the possibility," she murmured, "that somebody may have killed him while he was in the process of doing something illegal."

"Just because he was doing something illegal doesn't mean that the death was justified."

"The person who killed someone might very well think it was justified. I mean, if you are protecting your own life or that of your family, then you would definitely consider it justified. But the criminal himself, the one who came there to do the job and got killed in the process, doesn't necessarily agree."

"Wow," Gage repeated, shaking his head. "So people are stuck and still believing their own lies, even on the other side."

"Remember," she murmured. "Everybody should be looking at their own world and dealing with their own issues because everybody else has their own take on it."

"It's all so very strange to consider."

"Strange, but it happens all the time."

He nodded. "So, back to last night. Did you have any

problem getting rid of the possessing ghost? Has he been back today?"

"Not so far," she said, looking at him. "I don't know if he's planning on staying away or if he'll show up again at some point."

"Yes, you do," Gage countered instantly. "You wouldn't have even mentioned it if you didn't think he'd be back."

"I know he's still hanging around," she admitted, seemingly unoffended, adding a shrug. "I can only wait and see if he'll become a problem."

"I'm sorry," Gage replied. "I never intended to bring anything negative to you."

"Well, I can't see that you had anything to do with it," she clarified, "so I can hardly blame you for that."

"A lot of people would," he noted.

"But I'm not a lot of people," she murmured. "You need to remember that."

"Oh, don't worry," he said. "That is not something I'm likely to ever forget. You are fascinating, irritating, frustrating, and incredible, all at the same time, and you know so much that it's amazing. I can't help but find myself captivated."

"I know a lot," she muttered, equally ignoring both the critiques and the compliments, "but that doesn't mean I know everything, and it doesn't mean I know the right things at the right moment."

He tilted his head at that. "What do you mean by that?"

She fell silent.

CHAPTER 8

SKYLAR WASN'T EXACTLY sure how much she wanted to tell him.

"Look," she began. "Every situation is different. We don't have any research or anything that gives us a manual on how to deal with ghosts. There's no guidebook on how to make your life peaceful and quiet with them," she stated. "Each one is different, and every ghost comes with an agenda of their own. Most of the time they're harmless. Frequently they are lonely, looking to go home or for loved ones. Some spirits out there are malevolent and dark, who rejected what they were supposed to do in favor of their own agenda. So, it's important that you realize that this guy, even though he might have an agenda, that doesn't necessarily mean he has the ability to make it happen. However, if he does, he will need to be watched and carefully guided into doing the right thing, instead of doing what he thinks he wants to do."

"Which is?"

"He's looking to live again," she stated, "and, so far, he has managed to find people he can inhabit in a way that gives him a semblance of the life that he craves. And he seems to believe that the tarot cards will help, along with getting his bones back."

"Is that even a doable thing?"

"Maybe. … It's something I haven't come up against, so

I don't have answers for you on that."

Gage asked, "So the bone left in your shop? Could that be one of Jonesy's bones that he had for this angry ghost?"

Skylar shook her head, glad he hadn't asked where that bone was now. But he might still. If he did, she could just tell him that she buried it. "I don't know who the bone belongs to. Like I said, not many records on deaths from long ago."

"Right. And, of course, it's not as if you can walk to the library and find reference materials on the subject."

She nodded, with a smile. "Now you're starting to understand."

"What about other people in this field?"

She shrugged. "There are a couple of fairly famous ones, no shortage of charlatans, and probably a lot of people with lower-level information. But from my experience? I don't know *very* many at all."

"But you do know some?" he pounced.

She slowly nodded. "I do."

"You could ask them for help."

"Why would I do that?" she asked, with a raised eyebrow. "It's not as if I need any help yet."

Gage frowned. "Do you have to wait until you're really in trouble before you ask for help?"

She considered that for a second. "That seems to be what I would do, so yes. I guess that is what makes sense to me."

"It doesn't make sense to me," Gage argued. "Why wouldn't you ask for help ahead of time?"

"Because that would mean raising my hand in alert to this scenario, which would be a mistake. I don't really want other people to know about it or to even know where I am, for that matter," she murmured. "And, once you point that energy in a certain direction, it has its own kind of life force. I really don't want to stir up that energy."

"Okay," he replied slowly. "Have you at least tapped these people, so, if you do run into trouble, they'll be there for you?"

"Nope."

He frowned.

She just smiled, then picked up her egg sandwich and started to eat.

It would be hard for him. The business CEO side of his personality was definitely coming out. The problem solver was saying, do this or do that, advice that she generally ignored, which obviously frustrated Gage to no end. But this wasn't a business, and he didn't understand this world. She did and would follow her own instincts and experience, even if it bruised his ego a bit. This was serious, something he couldn't play around with.

Frustrated, he looked at her, while she enjoyed her sandwich.

She pointed at his and asked, "Aren't you going to eat?"

He nodded, snatched it from the wrapper, and munched away.

She smiled. "It's very good by the way. Thank you."

He nodded. "It's really bothersome that you won't do anything to help yourself."

"Well, I haven't needed to, so why complicate things?"

"But what if you do now?"

"In which case, it will all come back to this Jonesy problem, something that you brought my way," she stated, with a harder edge to her tone.

He nodded. "It was unintentional. I assure you."

"Maybe so, but doesn't change anything in the end, does

it?" she muttered.

"No. It doesn't." He stared down at his sandwich.

"Keep eating. It's really good."

His lips curled.

"It really is, and you shouldn't waste food."

He laughed. "It's not like I'm trying to waste food. I'm just not getting the answers I want."

"No? Well, if you have anybody you can talk to, then do so. That might help you."

"I think my brother has been doing a lot of research into that," he murmured. "Maybe I should see if he found anything."

"Do that, and then you can leave me to operate my business day as I need to," she murmured.

And just then, the front door opened, and several tourists walked in.

She looked at the beignets and asked Gage, "Are these all for me?"

"Will you eat them all?" he asked.

She smiled, with a nod. "Absolutely."

"Good, then they're for you. I'll come back later, and we'll discuss lunch and dinner." And, with that, he was gone.

She didn't even have time to stare at his back in outrage because the tourists were already right in front of her, asking for items they had been searching for. Gratefully she allowed them to take her attention away from that irritating man and on to the business at hand.

AS SOON AS Gage got back to the privacy of his hotel room, he called his brother. "Who was that person you called when I had the accident?" he asked.

At first came silence at the other end. "I talked to a lot of people, bro. Which one are you talking about, the psychic?"

"You talked to a psychic?"

"Yeah."

"I mean, that healer person, the one who did so much good."

"Are you sure she did any good?"

"Well, I'm walking around when I shouldn't be, aren't I?"

"Well, that's true," Terrence admitted. "That was Dr. Maddy. She's pretty famous, which is one of the reasons I went to her. And she's local. To me. And to you at the time, what with your accident being in Oregon."

"And did it make a difference?"

"You tell me. You're the one who just said you're walking around because of her."

"You think there is any chance that she would talk to me?"

"I would think so. She certainly did some work on you, or at least she told me that she would look into it. When you showed so much progress, I contacted her and asked her if there was an invoice or something to pay, and she laughed at me and asked what she had done. It was kind of nebulous. So, I made a donation to her big project instead of paying an actual invoice and called it good. I wasn't even sure that she had done anything, but you were incredibly improved, so I wouldn't take a chance."

"Do you have her contact information?" Gage asked abruptly.

"Yes, I just don't know what you'll do with it."

"Well, obviously I'll contact her," he muttered.

"Is there a reason?"

"There's always a reason. I'm just not sure that I want to tell you right now."

He sighed. "You know that you didn't start talking about all this weird psychic stuff until after she had done whatever she did. I wondered at the time if she had done something to bring it into being."

"Because she's a psychic and a healer as well?"

"And I don't even know what that means," Terrence cried out in frustration. "I was desperate to get you out of that coma and back to a normal functioning human being again," he muttered, "so I didn't look into her methodologies too closely, when you were showing such tremendous progress."

"Well, I am happy to be alive and mobile, but I do have many questions."

"She apparently runs her special hospital unit here in Portland, and I think she oversees several huge departments in multiple hospitals around the world, all with some kind of psychic healing processes."

"Fascinating," Gage murmured. He also frowned and noted, "You still haven't given me her contact information."

"Just go easy with her, will you? She's different."

"Well, my world is full of different people right now, so thanks."

"Meaning?"

"Oh, I'd barely even arrived when I met a woman who is definitely what you would call different."

"The one that Jonesy went to see?"

"Yeah, her."

"*Hmm*," Terrence muttered. "I did a little bit of investigation into her too, but there wasn't a whole lot to find."

"That's always suspicious, isn't it?"

"Well, that's been our take on it, right? We don't generally do any business with shadow people."

"*Shadow people.*" Gage smiled at that phrase because it was one that they had used time and time again to discuss people who absolutely had no history, so little history, or such a perfectly clean history that it made them suspicious as hell. "I get it," he said to his brother, "but this one is different."

At that, his brother snorted. "Aren't they all? At least until they get what they want from you."

"Maybe so, but I do need to talk to this Dr. Maddy."

"Have at it then," he replied in disgust. "Just don't go any more into that crazy line, will you? At least not until we get this deal sealed and you out of there. Your heart is no longer in big business."

"Well, it isn't in big business, but it'll finance whatever comes after this," he corrected, sensing an old fatigue inside him. "I just don't want it to be that same kind of cutthroat business that I was doing."

"And yet you were so good at it," his brother stated, his smile coming through the phone.

"Yes and no," he replied. "I just don't want anything to do with that kind of hardcore life again."

"Meaning?"

"Meaning, I want ethics to be dominant. I want honor to be a strong component." He paused. "I came close to dying, and, when I took a deeper look at my life, even though we ran a solid company, we certainly could have adopted a much more philanthropic approach."

"You mean, give away money?"

Such horror was in his brother's tone that Gage burst out laughing. "Let's just say that I've been doing a lot of soul-searching since I woke up."

"Yeah, that's what I'm afraid of," he said in disgust. "The shareholders won't be happy."

"Well, if this deal to sell the company outright doesn't go through, I can step out of the public eye, and you can be the CEO."

"Do you mean that?"

"Hell yes, I mean that. I'm serious. I want to get out of this kind of business."

"Interesting," Terrence murmured. "Well, we'll see what happens with the outright sell. We're a long way from that yet. Any progress on the deal?"

"They've got the paperwork in front of them," Gage noted. "I'm waiting for them to come back with changes."

"Why are there always changes?" he asked.

"That's one of the things about business that I would be okay to walk away from."

"What's that, the stress?"

"Yeah."

"You used to thrive on it, bro."

"I used to, yes," he agreed, "but not anymore."

"And that's just sad because you were damn good at that."

"Easy on the past tense," he murmured. "I still know how to make money and lots of it."

"Yet you're not looking at making it the same way anymore," Terrence whined.

"Look. I just want to find an easier and gentler way on my soul."

"Soul?"

The shock filling Terrence's tone made Gage wince. "Don't worry about it."

"Bro, you're making me nothing but worried every time you bring up that kind of shit. It gives me the heebie-jeebies, and it makes me realize just how delicate your profile is in the business world."

"And again that's why we're taking me out of the company," he muttered.

"Oh, I remember. I get it. No stress and give away the money. Jesus."

He did his best to try to reassure his brother. "Don't worry about it. I'm fine. I'm just looking at the world a little differently these days."

With a doubtful note in his tone as he said goodbye, his brother hung up.

Not wasting a moment, Gage quickly made a call to the number his brother had given him.

When he got the receptionist, he explained who he was and asked if it were possible to speak with Dr. Maddy.

"Not in the next couple hours," the woman replied cheerfully. "She's working with patients all day."

"Okay, could you leave her a message, please?"

With that done, he hung up and again left his hotel room. He was outside on the street, staring around, not even sure what he was doing. He shook his head. After following Skylar to the graveyard last night, he had been spooked. Talk about a step too far. If his brother had any idea what Skylar had been doing out there last night, Terrence would have Gage committed. He was certain of it. Gage knew in his heart of hearts that his brother would only tolerate so much, and then it would be a case of *Dude, you're done.*

Gage didn't want to get to the point where his brother felt he had to do something legal about this. But who was out there to even talk to about it? He walked inside his hotel again and asked at the reception desk about the graveyard tours.

The woman immediately brightened. "That's one of our most popular tourist activities." She handed him the brochure and added, "I think they run about four to five a day. So, if you contact these guys, they'll let you know when the next one starts."

He smiled and thanked her, then took the brochure outside, sat down on one of the many benches, and called. Sure enough, a tour would start in about forty-five minutes. Arranging to meet at the starting point, he quickly put away his phone, thinking he'd walk a bit, while he waited. As he stood, his phone rang.

Frowning, he looked at the screen but didn't recognize the number. He hesitated but decided to answer it. When he did, he heard a woman's voice, so musical and gentle.

"Hello, Gage. How are you feeling?"

He froze for a moment. "Do I know you?" he asked quietly. Something was almost memorable about her, definitely memorable that he recognized her voice, but he couldn't quite grasp who this was.

Her laughter trailed through the phone. "Absolutely, but maybe not on a conscious level."

He froze because that was like talking to Skylar all over again. "Would you mind explaining that statement?" he asked quietly.

"Your brother contacted me when you were in a coma, after your accident."

"Is this Dr. Maddy?"

"Yes," she replied, her smile easily coming through the phone.

"Thank you for returning my call so quickly," he stated,

feeling quite stunned. "I understood from your staff that you couldn't get back to me until much later in the day."

"Things are going well this morning, so I had a bit of time open up."

"Thank you," he said.

"Are you having trouble still?"

"I don't …" He stopped. "It depends on what you mean by *trouble*. I'm seeing things, feeling things, hearing things. Things that I've never dealt with before."

After a moment of silence on the other end, she asked, "What kinds of things?"

Such understanding and acceptance filled her voice that it was almost like he could have told her anything, no matter how outrageous, and she would have been perfectly okay with it.

At his hesitation, she added, "Gage, let me assure you that nothing you can say will surprise me."

"I just, … I don't know what kind of healing you may have done," he explained cautiously, "but I woke up with the ability to kind of, well, see spirits."

"Oh, good," she replied, with a laugh.

"Good?"

"Yeah, not everybody sees it as a blessing," she noted, with a smile in her voice, "but it truly is."

"Says you." Gage tried for a laugh. "I'm really not sure what I'm seeing or feeling, and it has come to my attention that somebody not very pleasant could be in my space."

"Now that's an entirely different story," she noted briskly. "Who told you that?" When he mentioned Skylar, Dr. Maddy interrupted him. "Is she in New Orleans?"

"Yes, that's where I am right now. My uncle came to her shop and has been missing ever since."

"Well, I doubt Skylar had anything to do with it," she replied instantly.

"I would hope not," he stated cautiously. "And talking to her, she doesn't seem like the type, but she's hesitating, and, well, I don't know how to say this but, she's ... different."

At that, Dr. Maddy laughed. "Yes, she definitely is different. But she's a good kind of different. She's real, although she can be stubborn and cranky and argumentative." Dr. Maddy chuckled.

"So, you do know her then," he said, with relief. "And you understand this stuff too?"

"Yes, I definitely know Skylar, although she probably wouldn't be happy if I acknowledged that relationship."

"I don't get that," he admitted. "If there aren't very many of you who work in this field, why wouldn't you want to stick together?"

"Well, there's sticking together, and then there's sticking together," she murmured. "You also don't understand everything or the fact that there is no distance in our world."

He thought about that. "No distance in time or physical space, is there?"

"No," she agreed. "Seeing people who have gone is just a natural extension, even in my case, and it's not my forte. I'm a healer, but, because I cross time and distance, I do see the dead on a regular basis."

"And there's no doubt that you brought me back from whatever nightmare I was caught up in."

"You were definitely dying, and I would say that a part of your soul was still clinging to the hope that you could be pulled out of it, but it was touch-and-go there for quite a while."

"Well, I thank you for that," he stated, "although my brother would not necessarily be grateful anymore because, now that he's heard about this other ability I have, he thinks I'm no longer capable of running our company."

She replied, "And that is a common problem with people who have no experience or exposure to this kind of world. There are masses of us out there, but we do tend to keep quiet."

"Except for all of those who definitely don't keep quiet."

At that, she burst out laughing again. "So what's the deal with this malevolent energy?"

As she asked about it, he almost felt something weird behind his head. He shifted and shook his head a little bit.

"That's me," she confirmed. "I'm just checking your energy to see how the healing is doing."

"Are you saying I'm still healing?" he asked.

"Oh yes, healing is an ongoing process as we age. So, the more you heal as you age, the healthier you are," she murmured. "And, in your case, you'll have a little bit further to go than a lot of people do."

"I was really badly hurt, wasn't I?"

"You were definitely dead there for a short while," she admitted, "but you have a very strong will. Honestly, I'm not sure that something else wasn't keeping you alive."

"Interesting," he muttered. "All of this is. It's just so fascinating, but it's also very new and different."

"Of course," she agreed. "So are you feeling a little overwhelmed?"

"Yes. I know it sounds strange, but is there any like …" Then he stopped.

She filled in, "Like someone to talk to, courses to learn from and to understand this? There's not really anything that we do too much in the public eye. We definitely have a way to provide training sessions for people who are struggling with this, but it's not something you can just walk into off the street."

"No, I can imagine," he stated, "and the people you get that way would probably not offer the level of detail of what I need to know."

"And that's quite possible too. Honestly, Skylar would be your best source of information, if she is willing."

The fact that Dr. Maddy had even added that comment about Skylar just immediately brought the problem to light because the fact was, Skylar was not very willing. "She hasn't been very cooperative," he noted instantly.

"And yet she's the one who mentioned this malevolent energy?"

"Yeah, she also thinks it's hanging around her, how it wants to live again. But that seemed a little on the far-fetched side, so I'm really hoping that you could disperse that nasty little fear from my heart."

"In that case, I would be doing you a disservice," Dr. Maddy replied, sounding very serious, "because definitely malevolent spirits are out there."

"Damn. I was really hoping you would tell me that it was all a load of malarkey."

"No, I would never tell you that because it's not true, and it wouldn't be safe for you to even begin to believe that."

"So, what does one do?" he asked in shock. "I mean, how does one actually function in this world, if malevolent spirits are out there, ready to possess us and take advantage of us?"

"One of the things you need to do," she stated, "is learn to protect yourself."

"I've studied a little bit about that," he replied.

"Yes? And yet your energy right now is way too open and far too easily impacted by everything I say."

"What do you mean?"

"We have to watch and see just how much people listen and believe what we tell them. We can't take a chance of influencing other people. And that works inversely too. Don't let others influence you either. So it's important that you come from a distance in your new world. Being defined and safe within your own space."

"And that's different than the distancing I thought I was doing?"

"You just need to not be so—how shall I say it? Not so dependent on what other people say. You need to have a belief within yourself that everything will work out fine and that the information I'm giving you is coming from a point of information only."

He kind of understood what she was saying, but, at the same time, he didn't totally understand and surely had no clue how to go about doing this distancing. She laughed. "It's all right," he stated, yet questioning his own words.

"I just don't want you to automatically believe in everything anybody says, without using your own cognitive reasoning. And that includes me."

"Ah"—he shook his head—"and no, I won't just obediently believe whatever you tell me. I'm already starting to question why I'm even here."

"Good, that's a healthier way to look at it."

"And what about the malevolent energy?" he asked.

"Well, I'd really hate to see anybody ruin my work," she noted. "I worked long and hard on you for that, too damn long and hard. So add a layer of protection to your energy."

And she walked him through the process.

He frowned. "I don't suppose you would care to tell me exactly what you did to heal me, would you?"

"I helped mend bone and muscles," she replied, "but that was only on one level. The energetic damage was pretty extensive as well. That usually comes from some kind of trauma at the time of the accident."

"Well, I was in a major accident."

"No, from before the accident."

He frowned.

"Were you fighting with somebody? Arguing?"

"Ouch," he automatically said. "Yes, I was, with the driver of the car. I kept telling him to calm down, and we would sort it out, but he wasn't having any of it."

"No, and I definitely got that. Also I found some energy that was a little bit unhelpful, as if he were still hanging around you."

"You mean, the same guy? Linden was driving. We were best friends," he shared quietly. A moment later he felt a humming around him. "Are you checking my energy again?"

"I'm checking something," she noted, "and I find that this energy is the same energy that was there during your accident. So, I can only presume that it's your best friend, still here, even after his death."

"Really?" Gage felt his heart lighten a bit. "I have been caught up in trying to talk to him."

"Now there's not necessarily any ability in place for these people to talk to you," she explained. "And remember. Just because you want to talk to him doesn't mean he wants to talk to you—or that he even has the ability. And I also get the impression that he is still very angry."

Gage frowned. "We never got the chance to settle up the

argument," he replied, "but I would hate to think that he took that kind of anger with him."

"It does happen, and, human nature being what it is, it happens a lot," she stated. "So, you just have to understand that it'll quite likely be an ongoing issue for him."

"Well, that sounds really crappy. All I want for him is to head off to the light and to be this happy soul on the other side, doing whatever comes next in his journey."

"Those are all the right words," she agreed, "but whatever happened between the two of you isn't something he is capable of letting go of at this point."

"So, what are you saying then, that he's hurting?" That idea really upset Gage and was painful to even think about.

"You may need to just work on your survivor's guilt and let Linden go because his anger is his problem to deal with," she said abruptly. "And I do sense another energy around you, by the way."

"Great," he groaned, "apparently I'm wide open."

"Ah," Dr. Maddy added. "I see Skylar's healing energy in here. Were you visited by a dark entity recently?"

And Gage explained the whole scary process to her.

"Good thing Skylar was there for you. Now you have a piece of her energy too. Like you have some of mine."

"How does that happen exactly?" Gage asked.

"That is possibly because of all the work we did," she added. "We had to leave some of your energy open in order to keep checking in to make sure you were doing okay."

"Did you remember to close these holes afterward?" he asked, only half joking.

"There will always be a certain connection between us now," she explained, "because that level of healing happens in a way that results in our energy always being there. That's just how energy works. It's not like we have a relationship or any kind of back-and-forth, but my energy was recorded and a few more as well," she admitted. "I can see that Stefan's is in there too."

"Stefan?"

"An extremely talented psychic," she murmured, "and a gifted healer who steps in to give me a hand when needed."

"And that was needed in my case, I assume?"

"Absolutely," she declared. "Bringing you back from the brink of death was not for the fainthearted either. I'm just wondering if we brought something else back unintentionally. I need to look into this. I'll get back to you." With that, she hung up.

He stared down at his phone in horror.

"What the hell does that mean?" he whispered to himself. "What could they have brought back?"

CHAPTER 9

S KYLAR'S MORNING WAS incredibly busy. It was a good thing Gage had left her all the beignets because, by eleven o'clock, she was reaching for yet another one, just to keep going. Gage hadn't shown up again, and maybe that was a good thing too. The customers were moving swiftly through the shop, picking up trinkets and dropping cash. She was good with that. She made a point of trying to keep the energy gentle and open but never did anything to influence people into wanting to spend money or not.

There were ethical standards involved in this, and she also knew there could be very negative consequences to a lapse in integrity. She was always careful to stay well on the right side of it all. By the time the last of the crowd stepped through the door with waves of goodbye, she sagged into her chair by the counter and looked around. Just something about having people in the store left things in a disarray, with bits of their energy everywhere.

She went to the front door, propped it wide open, and walked through, doing a massive sweep of energy, sending out the multiple old bits and pieces of religious trauma, fights, and discussions. When people fought in the store, it was the worst, but sometimes they came with a spouse they weren't even talking to or were in the midst of an argument prior to coming in. Either way, it was just bad news all around because they left those energies related to their argument lingering in her space.

Having the front door wide open allowed her to at least move it outside again. She walked through and opened up the back door as well, then ran a mini burst of her energy all the way through to clean it out from one end to the other. By the time she went to the rear door and locked it up again, as she turned and headed back to the front door, she saw Gage stepping through again.

He looked a little rattled and yet somehow stronger. She eyed him carefully, as he held up another bag of takeout. She smiled. "What are you going to do, just feed me continually?"

"Will that work?" he asked.

"I don't know," she murmured, then studied him. "You look different."

"Yeah, I connected with somebody who had done a lot of healing for me, when I was recovering from my accident," he shared. "She also kind of scared me."

"Did you actually speak to Dr. Maddy?"

"How did you know?"

"Well, 'she' and 'healing' were pretty good clues."

He frowned and then slowly nodded.

She whistled. "Wow, somebody must have money."

"Why is that?"

"I've never tried to engage her services myself, but that woman is in high demand."

"She helped bring me back from the dead as well—in her words," he noted. "My brother told me how he couldn't get an invoice from her, so he made a donation to whatever project she was working on."

At that, Skylar laughed. "Yep, she'd do anything to keep

her projects going."

"I'm not sure that's a bad thing."

"Probably not," she agreed, "but if you had Dr. Maddy working on you, that would explain a lot."

"Like what?"

"Well, one of your walls is quite blue, as if there's still a healing vibration going on."

"She did say something about me still needing to heal, which I didn't quite get. She also said something that kind of terrified me."

At that, Skylar's eyebrows shot up.

"Not that it would take all that much now," he muttered.

She laughed again. "You've come a long way since you've been here."

"I know." He shrugged. "Maybe that was the impetus to come in here, you know? In your store. So I could learn some of this stuff."

"So, what did Dr. Maddy say?"

"Something about she brought me back from the dead, but now she's wondering if something came back with me. She seemed a little unsettled by the possibility. Does that make sense?"

At that, Skylar's heart froze, and she sucked back her breath. Was this tied to the tarot cards? "Will she check into it?"

He nodded slowly. "You actually found some value in that comment, didn't you?"

"Well, there's always value in what others have to offer," she admitted in a hopeless effort to sideline the question. But he wouldn't be sidelined, and she really couldn't blame him because this was serious business.

"I need the truth from somebody," he snapped, the brutal honesty of the statement seeming to surprise even him.

She nodded. "Dr. Maddy will be your best bet in terms of getting the help you need—and the fact that you even got a call back speaks volumes."

"She mentioned something about being connected now. Do you know what she meant?"

"That's another truth," she stated, "and that would explain why she got back to you. There'll always be that connection between you now. I'm almost jealous." He stared at her, but she just shrugged. "Dr. Maddy is really brilliant at what she does. She runs multiple centers now, and she offers training for people who are very gifted, but she's incredibly talented in her own right."

"I'm glad to hear that," he admitted. "And I'm glad to know that I got the best person for the job, assuming that she did what she said she did."

"Absolutely. The only other person I know who could do that would be Stefan and maybe some of his cronies. I know he's been collecting a group of like-minded and gifted individuals as well."

"SHE DID MENTION Stefan," he muttered, thunderstruck. "Is he another gifted person?"

"You have no idea. Stefan can do things most people couldn't even dream up for their most horrific nightmares," she added. "Yet he is one of the nicest people you could ever meet."

"This whole other world is fascinating." Gage stared at her, realizing she was the most fascinating of all. At least to him.

"Careful," she warned. "Once you get too far down this pathway, there's really no going back."

"I think I'm already there." He knew she would be furious if she figured out what he was thinking.

She nodded. "Just remember. Not everybody in your circle of friends will take it kindly, and you'll quickly find yourself out in the cold."

"Again, already there," he admitted, staring around her shop. "My brother is very unimpressed that I'm continuing to pursue these lines of inquiry."

"Did you ever think about having a serious discussion with him? You know, the kind that involves both talking and listening?"

"No." Gage chuckled nervously. "I mean, he's really not interested in me doing any of this. And that kind of conversation isn't something my family has much experience with."

"Well, the fact is, you will take a serious hit to your reputation," she stated. "So, if your world or your business is built on your reputation, this is not the pathway for you."

"That's another reason I'm trying to get out of what I'm doing."

"You're blessed to have this second chance at life," she said.

He nodded. "I will owe my brother forever."

"Well, if he's a good brother, he won't want you to owe him."

"I'm thankful he's there to take over the reins if the company doesn't sell, or, if the sale goes through, that he's there during the interim period, to help with the transition by the buyer. Yet he already wants me to step out of the company because he's afraid that I'll be a danger to the company now. Is that possible?"

"Yes." She nodded. "If you continue to pursue this new life, your name will get linked with all kinds of weird and wonderful scenarios that will make the business world extremely uncomfortable."

He nodded. "That's what he's afraid of."

"And it's justified," she agreed. "So, ultimately it's up to you and how you choose to live your life. Most people who go through something like your accident and then subsequent healing go through a life-changing reassessment of how they want to live. I can't say that what you're doing is anything different than what I would expect."

"That's what I tried to explain to my brother, but he just wasn't hearing it."

"So, you need to finish this deal and be done with it."

He smiled. "Isn't it nice to think of everything in such simple terms?"

"Life isn't simple at all," she argued. "I find it to be messy, dirty, and dark. Sometimes it can be fascinating and fun and enlivening, but it is never, ever simple."

He burst out laughing. "You're certainly not simple."

"I'm a hell of a lot simpler than Dr. Maddy."

"I don't know," he countered. "Talking to her wasn't anything like trying to talk to you."

She shrugged. "Why should it be?" she murmured. "I'm staying in the shadows, while Dr. Maddy is well and truly out in the public forum. She has done incredibly well for herself—and not just for herself," she admitted. "Everything she does is for others. That selflessness is really what has made her so incredibly popular."

"And she doesn't have that same stigma?"

"SHE DID WHEN she first started out, but her results are—" She stopped and considered her words. "It's people like her who validate us. I'll put it that way. Everything she does seems like it's been touched with gold. She's had losses of course. She's had people choose to cross over, even though she'd done everything she could to keep them on this side. But, as she will tell you, once people make that choice, it is truly out of her hands. She can't do anything about it then. But trying to explain it to the families is a whole different story because then they feel this horrible guilt that, if they could have been there or could have done something way different, something better, it might have made that other person want to stay.

"We don't always understand the journey of our soul, what it is that our souls are here to do, and what lessons we may have come for. Maybe it was a quick hop, and they wanted to get out in, say, eight years, and so they took this lifetime so they were done, gone, and dead within so many short years. But we don't know any of that from the outset. It all makes people very leery, and, since Dr. Maddy can save so many, they all want to know why she can't save their loved ones too."

"I never thought of a soul not wanting to be saved."

"Your friend didn't want to be saved," she stated bluntly.

Gage sucked in his breath and stared.

"I told you that before—and about the fight that you had with him. I'm pretty sure he thought you should go with him."

"And that may be true, and he was really angry. But I would hate to think that anger would have translated into a desire to kill me."

She snorted. "You do realize that love and hate are two

sides of the same coin?"

He tilted his head. "I hope you don't mean love in the way that it sounded like you meant it."

"I definitely do," she stated. "Did you not know?"

"Know what?" He stared at her, and she watched, as the color shifted and slowly drained away from his face. "You really didn't know he loved you, did you?"

He slowly shook his head. "No idea, not in that way," he added carefully.

"Well, for a lot of people, there is no *that way*," she noted. "Love is love, and, whether or not it results in a physical relationship, doesn't really matter."

He took a long slow breath, his gaze both horrified and fascinated, as he stared at her. "You're just guessing about that, right?"

"Meaning, am I actually talking to him and getting confirmation about how he felt about you? No, I'm not talking to him directly," she confirmed, "but there is guilt all over your energy."

He shook his head. "No, that's because I lived, because I survived, and he didn't."

"Yes, and because, deep inside, you knew that he wanted more from you than you could give. Isn't that what the argument was about?"

He frowned. "You know what? I don't even remember most of what we were arguing about. It seems stupid now. I think it was about an old relationship and business."

"Exactly." She nodded. "An old relationship and business. He was a business partner too, wasn't he?"

"Yes." Gage frowned. "He definitely was."

"And is his estate cleaned up?" she asked curiously.

He looked at her and shook his head. "No, not really,

it's all tied up with lawyers."

"Why?"

"Something to do with my business and the fact that he basically left me everything, even though he had a wife, although they were separated, they were working it out."

Skylar smiled, as she nodded. "And yet a separated wife hasn't got the same punch as a *longtime best friend*, does it?" When he remained silent, she added, "And because she thinks you might have had something to do with his death, is that it?"

"I imagine she does," he guessed, "but then she's always been after his money, so I don't think any of the reasons why I might be fighting against her lawsuit, or the will for that matter, would make any difference to her. … She got a hell of a life insurance settlement, millions in fact."

"The more people have, the more they want," Skylar noted automatically. "Particularly if she's always been jealous because she couldn't compete with you for Linden's affections."

"What? No, it was never like that."

"Not for you perhaps, but it could have been for him. And that would certainly explain her ill will toward you and the feeling that you owe her."

He winced. "Is everybody so greedy?" he asked, as he stared at Skylar in instant dismay. "Is there really no such thing as honor and virtue left in this world?" He felt sick and terribly confused.

She looked at him and pinned him in place. "You tell me. Did you have any?"

"Yes. I did. I do. I will." He stared at her and frowned. "It's like there's this old world and the new world."

"Well, there definitely is this old world within the new

world. There's before your accident and after the accident. You've changed. You don't have any choice, and you'll be much more aware of all that now because of Maddy."

He stared. "What does Maddy have to do with this?"

"Because you're now connected, and Maddy can only function at the level that she functions at if she comes from a completely pure space of love. And now that you have that Dr. Maddy energy inside you, the corporate business world really won't suit you."

She watched as Gage slowly sagged into the single chair she kept in her store.

"Good God," he murmured. "So that's why I feel like we need to be more philanthropic and should be giving away more money and helping those who need it?" he asked. "My brother is beside himself because I keep talking about sharing more."

"Of course he is. He doesn't have the same new mind-set that you have, and, for that, you should be grateful for Maddy because, although she is part of the reason why you're here with us still, it wouldn't be happening unless you really wanted it to. Of course now you care, whereas before you cared, but it was much more distant."

He nodded. "I had no idea my life would take this kind of a flip."

"And your brother didn't either. He was only focused on keeping you alive, but that focus on keeping you alive will now be about trying to keep you from giving away all your money."

"He already is," he noted thoughtfully. "Who knew?"

"Well, at least now that you understand that aspect, when you get these urges," she explained, "you'll know to make sure that you're dealing in reality. Dr. Maddy is very realistic, and she has a lot of businesses that she runs, only because it's a fact of life that she has to have money to keep these centers open. She has to have the law on her side to keep lawsuits at bay. She has to keep the bureaucracy moving in her favor. Otherwise these centers shut down."

He nodded slowly. "You don't think about somebody with a gift like that dealing with those kinds of headaches, do you?"

"No, and she does have a solid team around her, but that's not the same thing as what you'll deal with, as you slowly acclimate to this new way of thinking."

"And is it my way of thinking?" he asked. "Or am I taking on her beliefs and ideas instead of my own?"

"I think this is probably always who you were," Skylar stated. "But I'm sure you probably worked at it and easily managed to keep it deep inside your psyche, so it wasn't as prevalent. Were you always fighting your brother to give away money?"

"Yes, I was actually"—staring at her in surprise—"so I guess really all Maddy did was amplify it."

"All she did was release it," Skylar corrected quietly. "It's not about amplification. You are who you are, but now you have a little bit of Maddy with you, and that won't stay suppressed. So that little sprinkling of her energy just amplified those parts and pieces of you that already wanted to be more altruistic anyway."

He sighed. "My brother won't like this."

"It doesn't matter what your brother likes," she stated. "Let him do his thing, and you do your thing, and make sure you have enough money to do what you want to do with your life, free of the constraints that you had before, which no longer fit. Those people from your old world and those pressures they add to your days will be on your shoulders for a little while, before you figure out how to get free of them all. But, at that point in time, when you actually realize what that freedom will be like, when you step into your true self," she noted, "you'll never go back." His fascinated stare locked on her features as she threw up her hands. "Look. I'm just passing you information. Do with it what you will."

"I will," he agreed, "but that information is absolutely fascinating. I feel like I haven't even lived before."

"Well, you have, but now you've got a whole new world ahead of you," she added, with the gentlest of tones. "Who you become will be something that'll be interesting to watch."

He slanted her a gaze. "Does that mean you're okay to stay in touch?"

She shrugged. "I don't really have a choice now."

And then he got it. "Because of the other day, when you had to heal me, right?"

She nodded. "Correct."

"Wow. All of a sudden I've collected this whole pile of people around me, without even meaning to."

"And whether we particularly wanted it ourselves," she noted, with a wry tone.

"I guess that's another aspect that I didn't consider either," he murmured. "I do thank you for my life though."

"And Dr. Maddy and apparently Stefan too," she added, shaking her head. "When a lineup like that comes to you, it's like a golden team. So you need to make sure you do everything you can to not squander that gift."

"I hear you. But what about this entity that she mentioned may have come back with me?"

"If that actually happened, then you need to trust that

she'll find a solution for it," Skylar stated.

Just then the door opened again, and she looked up to see the store filled with tourists. By the time she dealt with them, and the store had emptied out again, Gage was sitting beside the cash register, ringing up orders for her.

She looked at him, smiled. "You're handier than I thought."

In a humble voice with a twinkle in his eyes, he replied, "I aim to serve."

She rolled her eyes at that. "*Uh-huh.*"

He pointed out the gyros sandwiches that he had slipped out at one point and picked up for them for lunch.

She smiled, snatched one up, and started eating. "At least you bring food," she admitted, "and you do work when you're here."

He laughed. "I also went on a graveyard tour this morning."

"Oh, how was that?"

"Interesting," he replied, "but kind of flat."

"Yeah, well, you won't always get the private tour that you got last night," she noted wryly.

"Do you go out every night?"

"Not every night," she replied, "just whenever the call gets to be too strong to ignore."

"Does Dr. Maddy and Stefan know what you do?"

She nodded. "Most of us who work in the ethers know about the others. We all stir energy, and energy that obviously gets stirred can impact them too. So, it's important for them to keep track of what I'm doing, just as I understand that all this healing is happening over in her corner of the world," she explained. "And should I ever need to be healed, that's where I would be calling for help."

"So, you really do have help, if you need it."

"Yet I haven't needed it to date," she reminded him.

"I get that, and I do feel better to think that they would be there for you, should you ever need such a thing."

"You have no idea," she muttered.

He tilted his head, ready to ask more questions, but more tourists walked in. By the time they left, he was trying to bring up the subject again, but she wouldn't bite. "What are you doing after work?" he asked.

"Hopefully going upstairs to crash." She yawned. "I didn't get a whole lot of sleep last night."

"No, I didn't either," he shared. "I did try a couple drinks though."

"Well, you might find booze affects your energy thereafter now too."

"Yeah, I wondered," he admitted. "I don't drink much anyway, something else my brother never really approved of."

She looked at him in surprise. "He actually wants you to drink?"

"It's part of big business schmoozing," he noted. "And being somebody who's starting to pull back from that, it was just one more thing that bothered him."

"Your brother needs to learn to let go."

"No, I think, in this case, he probably just needs to learn to take over," he said, with a smile.

"Are you okay with that?"

"I think so. I mean, I no longer want to do it, so I need somebody to do it instead, and he is the one who has been there and who understands the business more than most. So he would be a great CEO. However, I prefer to sell the company. So my brother could be the transition agent, although the company offering to buy ours will probably never offer him a permanent job, instead wanting all their own people in those positions instead."

"Good, it sounds like a perfect solution then." She stopped, then frowned and asked, "Does he have anything to do with this Jonesy business?"

"I have no idea. Well, he's the one who tracked Jonesy to your shop," he noted, "and that information came from a private investigator he had hired. And from Jonesy himself it seems, per the note in his jacket pocket, which the cops found."

"Right, let's never forget that Jonesy is a character in his own right."

"And what the hell is with these stupid tarot cards?" he asked. "A lot of elements are here that are just getting very confusing."

"That's how it works," she stated. "Lots of confusion and finally, if you're lucky, some answers emerge."

"And if there are no answers?"

"Then you live with the fact that you won't get any answers, and that's just the way life is," she replied, "particularly in this field. Some people want to know why their loved one died, but there is no answer sometimes. Others insist on justice because somebody has been killed, yet there is no answer. There are just a lot of questions."

"That's the worst part, if you ask me," he murmured.

She nodded. "It can be."

"Have you ever tried to help anybody find answers?"

"Yes. Sometimes it works. Sometimes it doesn't." And, with that, she turned, then looked at him and said, "It's time for you to disappear again."

"Meaning, you're no longer hungry?"

"Meaning, you're a distraction, and I need to get to work."

"Nobody's in here."

"No, but now I have to clean the place out," she noted, "and your energy is part of what I need to clean out."

His jaw dropped, but she shrugged. "People come in here because the energy is fresh and clean, and they always see new things because it's not covered in the bits and pieces of everybody else's energies," she explained. "So, I clean the energy out of here on a regular basis. I've already done that once today, but it's full again," she stated crossly.

"I never heard of dusting energy before." He chuckled at his own attempt at humor.

"That's because you haven't been around long enough in this new world." She smiled. "Go find some touristy thing to do in the meantime."

"Yes, ma'am." He hopped to his feet and headed toward the door. Before he stepped outside, he turned and asked, "Are you okay to go out for dinner tonight?"

She looked at him. "Do you really not have any plans outside of sitting here and bugging me the whole time that you're in New Orleans?"

"Well, at the moment, I'm thinking about relocating because this certainly seems to be more my kind of place."

She stared at him, horrified, yet intrigued at the same time.

"And some of the people are definitely more my kind of people." Then, with a wicked grin, he turned and left.

She wasn't even sure what to say to that, but Thomas wouldn't stay quiet about it for a single moment.

"Would you look at that, girly?" he chortled. "Seems you've hooked yourself a live one."

"Doesn't mean I'll keep him though," she argued. "I might just decide to throw him back."

He laughed and laughed. "Oh no you don't. This one's a keeper. He's got your number. He knows how you function, and you're all over him."

"I most certainly am not," she stated crossly.

"You are too," Thomas countered. "There's got to be some advantages to being here without a body. We see energy, as you well know."

She groaned. "You don't have to tell him that you can read my energy," she muttered. "And isn't it time for you to go off for a spell and do something else?"

"Nope, I'm going to sit by and watch how this plays out."

"Damn it," she muttered. "I really don't want an audience while I try to figure out this relationship."

"Well, don't take so long to figure it out then," Thomas replied. "I don't know what's to figure anyway. You like him. He likes you. *Boom*. It's done."

"Hardly," she said. "I like a lot of people in this world."

"Really?" he asked. "How come I never met any?"

She glared at him, but he was too busy having fun with his own joke. At that, Elena called down from upstairs, asking if Skylar would be long.

She groaned. "Not too long," she called up, "but I have to close up the shop yet."

Then she spent the next hour and a half cleansing the energy and closing up the shop. By the time she said good night to everybody downstairs and headed upstairs, Elena was sitting outside on the rocking chair, moving gently in the evening air.

"Are you going out with him tonight?"

"I don't know," Skylar replied, an edge to her voice. Everybody was asking her questions that she just didn't have answers for.

Elena immediately held up a hand. "Not trying to push."

"Yeah, I can tell. Come on. Sure you are," she stated. "Just like Thomas, you want to see me happy with a partner."

"Of course I do. Is that so wrong?" she asked, as she gently smoothed her nonexistent skin. "Youth only lasts for so long, you know."

"Well, we rarely have death in childbirth anymore," she noted, "so it can last a whole lot longer than you're thinking."

At that, Elena smiled. "You're getting edgy again, which means I'm getting close to pissing you off, and you know what? I think I'm okay with that."

The longer the ghosts hung around, the more they had started to talk like Skylar, as if the ghosts were learning all the idiosyncrasies of modern day English. It was both fascinating and irritating because now Elena could swear with the best of them.

"I don't know what to do," Skylar groaned. "Gage mentioned going out tonight."

"Perfect," Elena said. "You need to."

"Why is that?"

"Because he really appeals to you, and you need time with him to see if something's there."

"That's a more realistic answer than Thomas came up with."

"Well, Thomas is male," Elena said. "He's probably all worried about the physical aspect and getting down to business."

"Maybe I don't feel like getting down to business."

"Of course not, you want to be wooed with romance first."

Skylar didn't want to bring that up, considering Elena's past, but Elena was already nodding her head.

"Yes, even though you're not asking, I was treated very well. He was very anxious to receive my affections."

"Well, I'm sure the trinkets he kept bringing you helped," Skylar teased.

"Very much so," Elena replied, with a light twinkling laugh. "It's nice to know a man understands how to get to a woman's heart."

"There are definitely other ways to get to a woman's heart," she stated.

"But none quite as effective as jewelry."

"I don't know," Skylar replied. "In my case it seems to be food."

Elena stopped for a moment, then burst out into beautiful laughter. "Oh my, that is so true," she said. "He keeps feeding you, doesn't he?"

"Yes," she muttered. "And, dammit, it's working."

Still chuckling, Elena nodded. "Everybody is different. Every relationship will have its own bond," she noted, within a surety that drove Skylar nuts.

"That's hardly a fair way to look at it though," she countered.

"How else would you like to look at it?" Elena murmured. "If you think about it, he already has your number. He's just waiting to see what it'll take to coax you out a little further from that fortress you keep yourself guarded in."

"Hey, I like to have walls up," she stated.

"Absolutely. I have walls up too," Elena noted. "But that doesn't mean you have to keep them up all the time."

"Maybe not," she murmured. "But, for a while, I will."

"That's fine. He has already gotten under them a couple times anyway. I have faith in this one. He seems like he knows what he's about."

"He's just a big businessman."

"Business is good," she noted, with a trill. "They make money."

And, of course, in Elena's world, it had been quite simple. As long as she was well kept in the manner that she wanted to be, Elena was quite fine with whatever happened. She hadn't lived long enough to see the darker side of these relationships. And it seemed like her education hadn't matured over time either. Skylar wondered at that. "You do know that our relationships aren't like yours, right?"

"I know," she agreed. "I'm not a fool. I do understand that things were much less than they could have been."

"That's one way of putting it," Skylar muttered. "And even today things are much less than they could be."

"Well, I think that, as long as you are content and happy," Elena stated, "nobody gets to judge you."

Skylar smiled. "You're really taking this nonjudgment stuff, women's independence, and *doing what you want* thing to heart, aren't you?"

"Why wouldn't I?" she asked. "It's a magical world out there for you women today."

"In some ways, yes," Skylar agreed. "In other ways, not so much."

"So, you have to strengthen the ways that are good and deal with the ways that aren't," Elena noted, shaking her head. "This guy is for you. You need to spend time with him and see just what there is between you."

"Hey, I'm not even talking about some permanent thing right now. We were just talking about a dinner date."

"A date is a good start, but you'll never be a person who takes a long time to get to know them."

"I was hoping to." Skylar glared at Elena.

"Nope, not happening."

"Why not?" she muttered, almost petulantly, knowing all the while that there was no way to get answers from these ghosts if they didn't want to give them.

Elena went on. "Because you'll find that connection, and that connection is real. You'll know it. You'll feel it, and it will be a done deal, just like that."

"And what if I haven't already felt it with this guy?"

At that, Elena looked over at her and started to chuckle. "You *have* felt it," she exclaimed. "That's one of the reasons you keep the walls up, so you don't have to actually let him in. He's knocking on that door, whether you like it or not, and it's up to you to open up and to say yes or no. He won't hang around forever, so do you really want to be alone for the rest of your life?"

"That's not fair," Skylar said. "Just because this guy is here doesn't mean he's the only guy on the planet."

"You're not getting any younger," Elena stated, with a condescending note.

She groaned. "Thank you, Elena. Thanks for that." Skylar hopped to her feet. "On that note, I'll go have a shower."

"Yeah, you should do that, since he's already on his way."

"What do you mean, he's on his way?" She turned to look at Elena.

She shrugged. "I suspect he'll be here within about twenty minutes."

"*Great.*" Skylar picked up the pace and raced through a shower.

Thankfully it was about twenty-five minutes before Gage rang the bell to her shop. She let him in, locked up again, and brought him upstairs to her balcony, where Skylar sat down on the rocker beside Elena and looked over at Gage.

"I wasn't sure if you were interested in going out to eat," he stated, his thumbs hooked into the belt loops of his jeans, as he studied her. "I was thinking maybe dinner out on the river."

"That would be lovely," she replied, with a smile.

He looked at the second rocking chair, and his eyes widened.

Skylar noted it was rocking. "Meet Elena." She gave a casual nod of her head.

"Hi, Elena," Gage said carefully. A gentle rose smell wafted through the air. He sniffed it. "Is that her?"

Skylar nodded. "It's her favorite scent."

"Wow. You really do have them everywhere, don't you?"

"I sure do, whether I like it or not."

"And the rocker rocks all the time?"

"No, only when she's here, or when she's being difficult," Skylar noted, sending a look at the ghost in the rocking chair. "She has very definite ideas of what I should be doing."

"And what is it that she thinks you should do?"

"Honestly, she thinks I should go out with you."

"Oh, I like her," he said instantly.

At that, the rocking chair almost jerked, as if the woman seated there was laughing hard.

He stared, fascinated. "I really wish I could see her."

"And she is memorable," Skylar stated, "because she's so beautiful. An absolutely stunning woman who died in childbirth a very long time ago."

"Everyone has a story, don't they?" he asked softly.

She looked up, smiled, and said, "Very much so."

"Why does she hang around you?"

"I'm not exactly sure why she hangs around me, but she does." She turned to look at Elena and asked, "Why do you hang around me?"

Elena laughed. *I'll hang around you until you find somebody to look after you,* she shared. *And, until that point in time, I guess you're stuck with me.*

At that, she turned and looked at Gage. "She says that she hangs around with me because she doesn't think I can look after myself. So she's waiting for somebody to step in to do the job for me."

"And then she can leave you alone?"

She turned to look at Elena, who just shook her head. "Well, she's shaking her head, so I'll say no."

"Wow, so it won't even matter what happens?"

"They get curious," she noted. "Even though I've tried hard to get her to go home, she won't."

"Any particular reason in Elena's case?"

"Not so much," she stated. "She died very young and feels like she has missed out on a lot and isn't too interested in heading back in that direction, without getting the full experience here. I keep telling her that, if she would go back toward the light, she could recycle into a whole new experience and come alive again, but she's not too interested in that because, since there's no proof of it, she doesn't believe me."

"Wow." Gage shook his head. "I never before thought

about trying to get souls to cross over or to get them to try to experience coming back, because you always tend to think that's what they would already want to do."

"Not all of them." She frowned. "There is no shortage of those who seem to just want to hang around me."

"You in particular?"

"Yes," she stated, "and mostly because they can talk to me. I give them ..." She stopped and frowned again. "It's not really a reason to be here because that would be even worse for me. But it's almost like, because they have that connection, they don't want to lose it. They don't have any guarantee of a connection on the other side, so they don't want to make that step to cross over and then to find out they made the wrong choice. And, of course, they can't come back," she noted with a smile, "or at least not in the same way."

"And is that really what happens? They come alive with a whole different life?"

She smiled. "I guess for some of those questions you'll have to wait and experience it for yourself."

He rolled his eyes. "Then let's go get dinner. I'm actually really hungry. Like really, really hungry," he said. "I don't think you shared lunch with me at all," he accused.

"Oh, that can't possibly be true," she teased, "but I was certainly working on getting enough for myself. Where do you want to go?" she asked, hopping to her feet and heading for the stairs.

"I don't know. I was hoping that a local might be able to show me."

"I've only been here a couple years, but I do have a few favorite haunts," she said.

"Well, Skylar," he replied, with a bright smile, "show me

something in New Orleans that I haven't seen yet."

"There are a lot of choices," she added, with a hint of warning.

"And that's okay too. I'm game to try a couple things."

She looked over at him, seeing his energy a little bit on the rattled side. "Has something else happened?"

"No, not really. Just a sense that everything is changing. And I'm changing with it."

"Does that mean you're eager for change or are you feeling hesitant?"

He shook his head. "Honestly, I think I'll say, *Both*."

"And that's not a bad thing either." She looped her arm through his, just as they hit the block on the street level. "Come on then. It's time for a night out on the town."

THE NEXT MORNING Gage woke up, still feeling slightly buzzed from the previous night. He didn't think it was alcohol-related as much as it was energy-related, resulting in a glow. A part of him had hoped maybe that Skylar would end up in his bed overnight, but that hadn't happened.

At the same time, he'd had a blast. They had danced, drank, and danced some more. It had been an awesome evening, one that had allowed him to totally forget all the troubles weighing on his heart. It had allowed him to really step back from all that and to step forward as his true self. He didn't know whether she would like that or not, but it was who he was, and, if he hoped to have anything with her, he needed her to see him, even though he was very different than he had been before the accident.

Before then, he'd been a man of decision, a high-powered CEO, driven by ambition to do the best at all times. And yet that lifestyle hadn't served him all that well. He hadn't had a permanent or even long-term relationship and was on the outs with several board members. Stress had been clawing away at his insides, and it had been hard to see his future as anything other than a heart attack waiting. The accident, in a way, had been almost inevitable, except that his best friend had died, which had hurt beyond measure. The suggestion that it might have been deliberate or possibly intended to take out Gage as well had just added to the hurt. There are just some things that you never know.

Gage still desperately wished he could talk to his friend and could make sure Linden was okay. Gage desperately hoped that the accident hadn't been a suicide attempt—or an attempt to kill them both at the same time—but Linden's actions at the time held so much determination that either his intent was to take them both out or he just didn't give a damn if Gage had died too.

His friend had been so angry at the time that Linden's knee-jerk reaction almost made sense. Gage understood temper. He'd had a bad temper himself prior to the accident, but he didn't remember losing his temper at all since then.

However, now with the additional thought that maybe Linden had been in love with Gage, Linden's rage took on another level. Here Gage had sought to better his life, to sell his company, when Linden probably saw it as Gage never wanting to see his best friend again—a breakup of personal and professional magnitudes that, unfortunately, Gage only comprehended now.

Linden must have felt rejected by Gage on so many levels: in love, in friendship, in business. Gage sighed, shaking his head, feeling such remorse that he had failed to see his best friend, to really see him, and to actively listen to him throughout all those years. *I must do better in this reiteration, for me, for Skylar, for those in my new world.*

As he lay in bed, he checked his watch and noted that Skylar's store would be closed on a Sunday, or at least it should be. He frowned at that; this was a pretty heavy high-tourist area, so maybe her shop wasn't closed. He quickly sent Skylar a text, asking about it. She texted back almost immediately, saying she kept it open every day during the summer season.

Then you never get a holiday.

Sometimes I have a friend or two come in and look after things for me, so I can leave for a few hours in the afternoon. Why? Did you have plans?

He smiled. **Not yet, unless you have a suggestion.**

No, no suggestion, she texted, **but it's possible if you want to do something.**

I do.

Fine, she typed. **I'll see if I can get Regina in to cover for me.**

He waited for a bit, wondering what that would mean, and then she texted back.

Fine, free from one to five this afternoon, and then I'll come in and close.

Perfect. Any suggestions?

There was no answer at first, and then she wrote, **I kind of want to go to a different cemetery.**

He winced at that. **I guess I've inhibited your ability to continue your graveyard work, huh?**

A happy face emoji showed up.

He smiled. **Can I come with you then?**

Sure. Be here at noon then. A thumbs-up symbol came back to him.

He checked his watch, already nine o'clock, so he really

hadn't left himself all that much time. He got up, had a shower, and, by the time he was dressed and ready to head out, his phone rang. Thankfully it wasn't her canceling. Instead it was his brother. "Hey, what's up?"

"Just checking in on you," Terrence replied. "How are you doing?"

"Much better. Feeling a whole lot less stressed about things."

"That's a good sign. What about Jonesy?"

At that, Gage winced. "Nothing, no progress in any corner."

"Damn," Terrence said softly.

"We'll have to accept the fact that we may not get the answers we want as fast as we want them," Gage noted, with a yawn.

"You don't sound like you're very awake."

"Went out on the town last night." He stifled another long yawn.

"Well, at least you're enjoying yourself," his brother noted grudgingly.

"Yeah, I didn't really expect to, when I came down here," he muttered, "but, when you realize there's not a whole lot you can do about something, it tends to shift gears for you."

"As long as you're not wasting time. Are you coming back if you can't find Jonesy or any other leads? Because you certainly have a lot of work to do here."

"Oh, and I thought you were handling everything."

"I am. I absolutely am, but normally you're a very hands-on guy."

"Like I said, I needed to take some time, to back up a few steps, and to ease up on things."

"I know you keep talking about it," his brother grumbled, "but you must understand that, if this deal doesn't go through, we're all screwed. So I can't have you stepping off the accelerator now."

"No, I'm aware of that," Gage replied. "I'm very invested in this deal too. We just have to keep everything quiet about my current focus on Jonesy. This family matter is as important as business deals to me, although many in the business world would disagree."

"At least he wasn't involved in the deal or the company," Terrence muttered. "Then we would have even more delays."

"No word on the contract yet from our interested buyers?"

"No, nothing yet. They're still going over the terms."

"Well, we know it can take a while."

"I know. I was hoping to have it locked up by now though."

"I hear you," Gage stated, "but we haven't changed anything from the approved draft document, so it shouldn't take too long."

"No, no, we haven't."

An odd note in his brother's voice attracted Gage's attention immediately, and he knew his brother was lying. "Or did you?" Gage asked, his tone sharp.

"What do you mean?"

"Did you change anything before the final contract was sent out?"

"Well, I couldn't have changed anything without you," he replied in exasperation.

"That's not necessarily true," Gage stated slowly. "So, tell me. Honestly. Did you make any changes to it before it went out?" After a moment of silence came, Gage knew it.

"Jesus, you did."

"Just a small change," Terrence admitted, "and I told you about it."

"We didn't discuss any changes to that contract," he argued, almost yelling now. "We had the lawyers go back-and-forth on it for days. So what did you change?"

His brother hesitated.

"You need to tell me," Gage demanded, his voice allowing no argument. "What the hell is going on here? Why would you make a change at the last minute?"

"It's not like you were paying attention to things," he whined. "And it was just something simple."

"Then tell me what it was."

"I'll send you a copy of it," he snapped. "You probably won't even notice."

"Then you need to tell me, and you need to tell me right freaking now. I am beyond frustrated with you at present."

"So what then? You'll return and take over?" he asked. "I thought you were talking about me taking over."

"And remember what you just said about me needing to stay at the helm in case you screwed this up?"

"I didn't. It was just dates."

"And why did you change the dates?" he asked loudly.

"Just the closing time frame," he replied.

"That could be why they're taking longer to look things over because we're pushing for a faster time period."

"Well, I also changed the time they had to consider it," he finally added.

"You what? Why the hell would you do that?"

"I don't know," Terrence said in frustration, "because I wanted this over with. I didn't want to give them too much time."

"But you have to give them enough time. Jesus Christ, Terrence," Gage yelled. "Otherwise it looks suspicious as hell. They need time for their lawyers to go over it all, and, if you try to push it through too quickly, they'll wonder what you're trying to hide. We'll be lucky if this doesn't blow the whole thing right out of the water."

"I wasn't trying to hide anything. I just wanted it done." And, without saying anything else, his brother hung up.

Gage stared in frustration at the phone in his hand. "Why would you even do shit like that?" he grumbled, wondering what was really going on. It's one of the reasons Gage was selling his business, refusing to hold any position thereafter, even limiting his transition time involved. He didn't want to worry about all these things. It would be up to other people, other board members, to determine who should stay in power or not. But a stunt like this made Gage wonder if his brother had what it took to be successful on his own.

The last thing Gage needed was his brother making things too awkward or making changes that weren't discussed, which made everyone involved very nervous. His brother should know that. So why the hell would he have done it? *Everybody* wanted this deal over and done with. *Everybody* wanted it signed.

No. Technically the last thing Gage needed was to accuse his brother of intentionally tanking this deal.

And the fact that it now came down to something this dicey made his heart pound in fury. He took several calming breaths, trying to release the stress knotting up his gut and twisting the back of his neck. He would end up with a migraine if he kept this up and briefly wondered how he had handled all this crap before the accident.

It had seemed like it had been small peanuts to him back then, but it really hadn't been. It's just that he'd handled it all differently, but now it seemed like everything caused him major trauma. Which was too damn bad because it was starting to get to him in a big way.

Shaking it off, he raced downstairs to the hotel lobby and burst out onto the street. If only he could find something that would make a difference in his world, like locating Jonesy. … That would help.

As he walked down the street, somebody from the hotel called out, running behind him. Gage stopped when he heard his name, then turned and spoke. "Sorry. I didn't realize you were looking for me."

"I was waiting for you to come down," the manager explained, catching his breath, "but you charged right out, and I didn't get a chance to talk to you."

"What's up?" Gage asked.

"There was a message for you this morning," he replied, as he handed over an envelope. "This was dropped off." At that, he looked back at the hotel. "I must return now. I left the desk unattended." Then the man turned and bolted toward the hotel.

Gage stared at the envelope, wondering why the hell somebody would leave something like this instead of coming up to his room. And was no answer from him expected? *Odd.* Holding the envelope, he walked down to the small restaurant that had some of the best beignets he'd ever tried, and there he chose a table outside and ordered a fresh coffee, then waited for the waitress to leave.

As soon as he was alone, he opened up the envelope and studied the message.

Jonesy is gone. If you want to know where his body is,

meet me at noon.

His heart sank.

The message also included the name of a cemetery.

"Jesus," he muttered to himself. "How the hell did that work?" He immediately took a picture of it and texted it to the detective Gage had contacted when he'd first arrived in town.

The cop phoned him. "When did you get that?"

"I just left the hotel, and the guy from the front desk ran down the street to hand it to me," he explained. "Apparently whoever it was came in this morning but didn't want to go up to my room and just left it for me at the front desk."

"Very suspicious."

"You think?" Gage quipped. "I don't know what the hell this means at all."

"No, neither do I, and I don't understand the cloak-and-dagger nature of it," he replied quietly. "I presume you want to meet him."

"Absolutely I do," Gage stated. "Finding Jonesy is the reason I came to New Orleans."

"Right, we definitely need to meet your mystery person there."

"I'm also bringing Skylar from Skylar's Heaven," Gage added.

"Why?" the cop asked in alarm. "The less people you bring, the better."

"Maybe so, but it's a cemetery that she knows very well."

"How is it that she knows it?" he asked suspiciously.

No way would the detective understand, so Gage avoided answering that question directly. "Don't worry about it. The bottom line is that I'm bringing her along."

"Whatever. I'll meet you there at noon." With that, the detective hung up.

Gage then texted the same photo of the message to Skylar. He was just sipping his coffee and waiting on his beignets when she phoned him.

"When did you get that?" she asked, but no accusation was in her tone, more curiosity.

He explained the scenario, like he had to the detective.

"Interesting," she noted. "I guess it's possible that people saw you out partying last night and didn't want to wake you this morning."

He smiled at that because it was the nicer answer. "Yes, that's definitely possible."

"Still, I'd already arranged to be gone," she added, "so, if you want, I can come with you." Yet she sounded hesitant.

"No, I would definitely like for you to come," he stated.

"Are you sure?"

"Yes," he murmured. "I don't know what you might see or understand about what's going on, but just the fact that I've been asked to meet at a cemetery makes me more than a little suspicious and apprehensive."

"You're thinking that Jonesy's been buried there?"

"I have no idea," he admitted. "I wouldn't know how anybody could tell."

"It would be a fresh grave," she replied almost instantly.

"Right, like that'll help much though. It's a graveyard, so there'll be a lot of fresh graves."

She chuckled. "So I can see why you're thinking maybe I should go with you, in case there are any ghosts to talk to, is that it?"

"Maybe, but there could also be a lot of people around, so I don't know how much actual talking you could really do.”

"Oh, you'd be surprised," she murmured.

"I don't know," he told her. "Where you are concerned, I'm not sure anything will surprise me at this point."

"Well, it was a fun evening last night," she said. "Maybe you got to see a little more of me than you expected."

"I loved every moment of it," he shared warmly. "You were natural, friendly, and open."

"I had a blast."

"Good, so maybe we can do it again sometime."

"Sounds good," she agreed, "but let's deal with some of these crazy issues first."

"I'm all for that." He sighed. "None of this makes any sense."

"Well, let's hope, after today, it does," she suggested. "Are you coming here just before noon then?"

"How far away is the cemetery?"

"Walking distance," she noted.

"Okay, I'll be at your store at one-quarter to noon." With that, he hung up and realized that he didn't have all that much time left. As he studied his phone, his beignets arrived. The fresh smell wafted up to his nose. "My God, these are absolutely divine," he murmured.

The waitress laughed, then smiled brightly. "It's not the first time I've heard that or a similar comment."

He grinned. "These are definitely from the gods."

She nodded. "I don't know about the gods' involvement, but they're definitely a popular item," she confirmed.

"And with good reason," he murmured, as she left him to his breakfast.

He picked out the first one and took a bite of the fresh soft sugary dough and moaned. It was absolutely divine. By the time he finished two cups of coffee and all but one of the beignets, he wrapped that last one up in his napkin and slowly worked his way to Skylar's place.

When he got there, he was still a little early but not by much. He walked into the store to find her busy with customers. He put the beignet on the counter in front of the register, then wandered around the store, waiting until she was done. By the time she'd finished with her last customer and had locked the front door, putting up the Be Right Back sign, it was almost time to go.

She looked at him and blew a few tendrils of hair from her face. "It's been crazy busy this morning," she murmured. She looked at the beignet and sent a big fat smile in his direction. "This looks lovely."

"I didn't know how many you got these days."

"I'm fairly blessed. A friend of mine is working his way toward making the best beignet in town," she noted, "and, of course, he's up for some pretty stiff competition."

"I see." Gage nodded, with a sly smile. "So he brings you samples?"

"All the time." She picked up the beignet, took a bite, and swallowed. "But this I need right now, before we head out. Otherwise I might collapse on the way."

"Did you eat breakfast?"

"Nope, didn't have time."

"Right, we were out late last night."

"We were, indeed. And I woke up late, so I just ran downstairs in time to get the store open."

"Only you didn't have to commute anywhere."

She laughed at that. "Nope, I've been in a job where I did have to commute a long way, and it really ate into my day."

"It sure does, doesn't it?"

"What about you, did you commute?"

"I did for a while, and then I bought a condo closer to work," he explained. "I don't know what I'll do with the place now."

"You won't go back there?"

"I'm not sure I fit in there anymore." He shrugged. "I already felt a bit that way immediately after the accident, but everything is surely different now."

"It is. It really is."

"It feels odd, like my old life doesn't even fit anymore. It's not just that I'm different but that nothing in that world really fits me anymore. It's the weirdest sensation."

"I get it," she agreed. "And when you do find the right place, it will fit perfectly and will feel right."

"So, is that why New Orleans feels right then?" he asked, staring at her.

"I don't know. You tell me. Maybe because you're getting answers."

He nodded. "I wondered if that was something I was looking at. It's a little confusing at times."

"It's very confusing at times," she confirmed, with a smile, "but that doesn't mean it's not worth sorting out."

"No, I will, and I'm not limited to the time frame that I'm here either," he noted. "So I'll stay as long as I need you to help me figure this out."

"Good for you. I gather you're independently wealthy."

"Wealthy, yes, … and, if this deal goes through, I pretty well won't have to work anymore," he shared, with a shrug.

"Is that what you want?"

"No, it's not that I don't want to work anymore. Not at all. I want the deal to go through because that culminates the business I built, and I'm ready to walk away from it," he explained. "I just don't want to give it away."

"Of course not," she murmured.

Just then her doorbell rang. She looked up and smiled. "And now we can go."

And, with that, she slipped her arm through his, and, after saying *thank you* to her friend, they walked out.

"We need to go straight to the cemetery for this meeting."

She nodded. "Let's go."

By the time they walked through the cemetery gates, the detective stood there, waiting for them. He impatiently shifted from foot to foot. "You're late," he snapped.

Skylar immediately apologized. "It was my fault. The store was busy."

He just glared at her. Then he turned to Gage and asked, "Did you get any more instructions as to where you're supposed to meet him?"

"No." With a nudge from Skylar, Gage pulled out the note and handed it to her.

She frowned as she read it, then turned to look around. "I presume Jonesy's body is here."

The detective glared at her.

She shrugged. "Why else would he choose a cemetery?"

At that, another voice broke through their conversation. "She's right, you know? Why else would anybody choose this location?"

She turned to look at the man and frowned. "Do I know you?"

His gaze was focused as he studied her, and then he slowly shook his head. "I don't know, do you?"

She didn't like hearing that which was obvious. She

turned to look at the cop, who was studying the newcomer.

"Are you the one who sent the note?" the detective asked the stranger.

"I am," he stated. "I wasn't expecting a whole party of you to come though."

At that, Gage just shrugged. "No reason not to."

"I guess. It's a little bit gruesome though."

"What is?"

"Your uncle's body." Then the stranger led the way through the cemetery to one of the crypts at a back corner. It seemed broken on one side. But then so many of the crypts were broken. He pointed. "I think that's him in there."

Startled, Gage gave the stranger a harsh look and then bolted forward, pulling out his phone and clicking on the Flashlight app, as he shoved his phone behind the rubble and deeper into the crypt. He had just enough light to, indeed, see a body. He turned to look at the detective. "Can we access this to get a clearer picture?"

Immediately the cop stepped forward, pulled back a few rocks, taking a look inside, taking a photo of the man's face. "This is a fresh body, so I need to get forensics down here." He handed his phone to Gage to view the snapshot, then turned to look at the stranger. "Did you have anything to do with his death?"

"Me?" the guy asked, then he laughed. "No, I didn't."

Gage nodded, his expression grim, returning the detective's phone to him. "It is my uncle." Then he turned to the stranger. "Did you see anything? How did you find him?" Gage asked.

"I was studying a couple of these crypts here, looking at their history," he explained, "when I noted something was wrong with this one, like it had been recently vandalized. So

I pulled back a few of the loose rocks, which are easy enough to maneuver, and saw a fresh body in it. And I recognized him."

"How did you recognize the body?" the cop asked, all business. He was already pulling out his phone and sending messages off.

"Because he had been asking around town about a set of tarot cards. Then it didn't take long after that to hear the rumors that you were here now, looking for your uncle."

"That's quite true," Gage noted. "It sucks that this is the way I found him."

"Sorry about that," the man said, "but at least you'll get some closure. Too many people go missing and nobody ever knows what happened to them."

The detective demanded this guy's ID and continued to grill the witness, and apparently the man had been in New Orleans for about a week, doing research for a book. He had seen Jonesy asking around the French Quarter about a rare set of tarot cards, which had piqued his interest.

Gage turned to Skylar and whispered, "Do you sense anything off or strange about this guy?"

She turned a bland stare Gage's way, and Gage realized that his voice was a little louder than intentional. He glanced back at the other two, but they were fully involved in a heated discussion. When Gage turned back to her, an odd look was on her face, as she studied the two men.

"What's the matter?" In the distance he heard sirens, and the sound was getting closer.

She groaned. "It'll get crazy here." Stepping back, she said, "I should never have come along."

"Why?" he asked, stepping back with her.

"Because of the publicity."

"Well, it's got nothing to do with you. This is all about me."

"It won't work out that way," she argued. "As soon as my name gets linked with this, it'll be a hot mess."

"Let's go then," he suggested. "We'll head down to the restaurant, and I'll buy you lunch."

"You just ate," she noted.

"I'm a growing boy," he teased.

She smiled but shook her head. "No. If I try to run away now, it'll get even worse. I'll just wander around the graveyard," she added.

He nodded. "That could work, too."

CHAPTER 10

EVEN THOUGH SKYLAR had stayed out of the crime scene, Gage knew where she was, yet she remained far enough out of all the congestion as to go unnoticed. As soon as Gage walked toward her, she started to move away, so people wouldn't think they were together.

When he caught up with her, she asked him, "Are you done here?"

"Yes, I'll be contacted later, as they get an update."

"Good enough," she agreed.

"Did you see anything about Jonesy?"

"No, nothing."

"What about the journalist?" he asked, his tone very suspicious.

"Well, nothing about it is normal," she noted, "but I certainly don't have any reason to suspect him."

"I do," Gage argued. "He led us right to the body, for Christ's sake."

"And I'm sure you told the cop that."

"Of course I did. It's a very odd situation."

"Yes, it is, but, at the same time, it could be that he's completely innocent in all this."

"He could be," Gage admitted, "but why not call the cops? Why come to me directly?"

She pondered that. "You're right, which makes me wonder if the journalist removed the bricks to see if Jonesy had the tarot deck with him. More concerned about his story than helping anyone."

"And you're thinking this guy might have found it?"

"I don't know. Maybe he's really looking for the tarot deck and was checking to see if your uncle had it. There's a story there but if he knew about the history of the cards, he'd understand their value."

"Jesus." Gage was moving but now his footsteps slowed. "You know what? Something is nagging me about that guy."

"What about him?"

"He seemed familiar somehow."

"Well, maybe you've seen him around town," she offered. "If you think about it, he's been here for a week, and you've been here most of that time."

"Yet he said himself that he was here when my uncle was here as well," Gage noted. "So I'm not sure the guy's *week* actually holds up. You know I might have seen him at Mom's one time? But I can't be sure."

"And maybe it was ten days, but that's for the cops to determine," she stated. "However, if you figure out where you saw him, that's a different story."

He groaned. "That'll be the thing that bugs me next."

"Prioritize," she said quietly. "And, right now, there's a break in your uncle's case."

"And confirmation in a way I didn't want. It does, however, bring closure."

"No, of course this isn't how you wished this to end," she murmured, "and I'm so sorry."

"Thanks." Gage nodded, considering this and more. "It is difficult to process Jonesy's death, but something's just different about this guy's energy."

At that, she stopped, looked at him, and asked, "Seriously?"

He nodded. "I know I'm not the right person to make that comment, being the newbie."

"You're absolutely correct to make that comment," she noted, with a shrug. "I do better with dead people." He looked at her in surprise, and she laughed. "All of us don't have every skill," she explained. "I can manipulate all kinds of things, but I don't always see everybody's energy. And, if they're blocked or in any way cloaking their energy, I don't do very well with it. Now tell me," she added, "what did you mean about his energy?"

"He seems like way too easy of a fall guy for this."

"Meaning?"

"He has to know that the cops would immediately suspect him of killing Jonesy just by finding the body. So why would our supposed witness even put himself in that position? It's not like most people would encourage the cops to charge them with a felony. Hell, most people would worry about their petty crimes coming up, with a standard background check."

"That's true," she agreed, pondering that bit of logic. "So, my earlier theory, about whether our witness checked Jonesy's body for the tarot cards—and found them—was just one side of the coin. What if the witness checked and *didn't* find the deck on Jonesy, so now he hopes he can let the cops lead him to the deck? By locating the body, our witness has opened up an official investigation that might shake something loose."

"And that," Gage admitted, "makes a hell of a lot more sense."

"What we have to do now," she suggested, "is wait to see

if they found any forensic evidence."

"Well, Jonesy's *dead* now," he noted, turning to look at her. "You did say that you do better with the dead."

"Yes, I do better with the dead," she agreed, "but that doesn't mean the dead do better with me. Remember. The ghost's abilities come into play here. Not just mine."

"Oh, right." Gage groaned. "So, in other words, we still don't have any answers."

"No, we don't, and that's how this game goes."

"It's hardly a game though," he murmured.

"Well, it is a game of sorts," she countered. "Don't kid yourself. It all comes down to business, one way or another."

"Can you imagine if big business could ever monetize this?" he asked, shaking his head.

"That's the CEO in you talking," she noted, with a smile.

"Maybe so," he agreed, "yes, that's quite true. Yet just think about it."

"I don't want to," she declared. "Do you know how many people come to New Orleans because of the dead as it is? That part is already monetized. Imagine if they could actually see what I see. Or talk to my ghosts," she murmured. "It would be a nightmare forever after."

"I wonder if your ghosts would like it."

"Maybe, and at what point in time are we taking advantage of them too?"

He winced.

"See? All kinds of things come into play. New Orleans is special, and my ghostly friends are mostly quiet and peaceful. I wouldn't want to do that to Thomas or Elena or the kids or any of them," she stated. "These ghosts have already dealt with humanity, some of it at its worst."

"Let's not bring them into that now. Besides, they couldn't appear to everybody, could they?"

"No, not at all. Otherwise believe me, that thought in your head about monetizing their ability and their presence would have been taken advantage of a long time ago."

"You're quite right there," he agreed, "and it's not as if it's an original idea. It is in the sense that I'm sure other people have thought of it. Yet nobody has the ability to make them show up for the public. Thank God. Can you imagine?"

"I don't want to," she stated. "I like the peace and quiet as it is right now."

"And yet they don't leave you alone, do they?"

"Nope," she replied, with a grin, "but it's a whole lot better than dealing with humanity, and the living people wouldn't leave me alone either."

At that, he smiled and agreed.

GAGE WONDERED ABOUT it again later that afternoon, while Skylar closed up the store, and he sat on a bench at one of the nearby parks, just staring at the water. People walked up and down a large pathway at his back, but Gage was content to just sit. Then his phone rang.

When the detective identified himself, he said, "Your uncle appears to have had a heart attack."

Gage straightened up. "Seriously?"

"Yes, that's the cause of death."

"That was fast."

"I put a rush on it," he replied, the fatigue in his voice evident. "So, we don't know that any foul play was involved."

"Except for the part about him being bricked into the mausoleum."

"I wondered about that," the detective agreed. "Whether that was somebody trying to hide the body from the public or to just dispose of the body or perhaps to do it a service. You know what? In this day and age, I have no idea anymore," he admitted. "I've heard it all from so many people that it could be any of the above."

"Was there any forensic evidence found?"

"That's all with the forensics team right now. After they are through with any of it, it'll probably be turned over to his next of kin," he noted. "However, since Jonesy died of a heart attack, and it wasn't foul play, criminal charges are not likely to be pursued."

Gage frowned at that. "What if he was scared to death?"

The detective laughed. "You mean because he was prowling around the graveyard? That could be, I suppose, but I don't know that we'll nail anybody on a murder charge if that's the case," he shared. "I suspect this will close as death by natural causes."

"Somebody may have tried to close up the crypt or maybe just piled a few more bricks around him, thinking that Jonesy had a death wish and wanted to die in the mausoleum himself."

"For all I know," the detective added, "your uncle was hiding in there because he wasn't supposed to be in the graveyard at all."

Gage winced, knowing it wouldn't be the first time somebody had gotten locked in to a cemetery. "I suppose that's quite possible. Maybe Jonesy was just trying to find a place to hole up in, and then the shock of it all and the fear of getting caught brought on the heart attack," he guessed, with a nod.

"That would be my take on it."

"Well, at least he wasn't murdered," Gage murmured, more for the detective's sake.

"Exactly. That cleans up my case nicely." And, with that, the detective stated, "I'll follow up, if we have any other questions or if we find out anything else."

With that, Gage hung up, and then quickly called his brother. When he got voice mail, he tried again a few minutes later, and this time left a message, asking his brother to call him. Gage walked over to a vendor and picked up a coffee, then headed back to his same place on the same bench. It was a gorgeous day, and the crowds were pretty intense too. He could see the appeal of the graveyards, so quiet and peaceful, and, if his uncle had any reason to be in a graveyard, Gage could only think it had something to do with Jonesy's bone collection. Still, Gage had no idea why Jonesy was in the graveyard, much less why his uncle collected dead people's bones. He just didn't know.

Just then, his phone buzzed with an email. He checked it out and frowned, when it supposedly was from his uncle. Actually it was from Jonesy's lawyer, who happened to be Gage's as well.

When you get this, call me.

Gage quickly called, and Charlie answered, his voice tired.

"What's up?" Gage asked.

"I have an envelope here, which Jonesy set up to be handed over to you when he died."

"So, I gather you heard the news."

"Yes, I did. Can you confirm it?"

"Yes, absolutely. I identified his body. He's been dead a

couple days, but we don't know how long exactly. Looks like he may have gone into hiding inside a crypt in the graveyard and had a heart attack. No apparent sign of foul play."

"I understand some of the bricks were replaced."

"The detective thinks Jonesy may have crawled in to get out of view of the cops who patrol the area at night, when the cemeteries are all locked up," Gage murmured. "And so Jonesy may have put the bricks in place himself."

"You know what? I can almost see that too. What the hell was he doing in the graveyard in the first place though? Particularly after-hours when it's all locked up?" Charlie asked.

"Considering I was in a similar situation only a few nights ago, … it does kind of make sense."

"Right. Crazy tourist things? So, we don't suspect the guy who found him?"

"I don't think so," Gage replied slowly, "but I'm not sure I'm ready to write it all off as much as everybody else is."

"Do you believe the police about no foul play?"

"Yes and no," he murmured. "I can certainly see that, given how absolutely obsessed Jonesy was to find the tarot cards, plus his bone-collecting proclivities, if somebody had agreed to meet him there about that deck, he would have gone."

Maybe," Charlie noted, "but why would somebody meet him there?"

"I don't know," Gage murmured. "And I don't even know how important those cards are."

"Well, you go through the email that I just sent you and let me know if it's something you want me to get involved in."

"Will do." And just when he was about to hang up, he added, "Hey, Charlie, about the deal pending right now?"

"Yeah, what about it?"

"Did you know my brother made last-minute changes to the dates?"

After a moment of quiet his lawyer exploded. "He what? After all the changes that we went back-and-forth on? How did he do that without everybody's permission?"

"I don't even want to know," Gage murmured, "but he did. Supposedly he shortened the dates, so the buyers had less time to think it over *and* less time to close the deal."

"But the buyers had asked for those specific dates, and we had all agreed," Charlie yelled into the phone. "Why in the hell would Terrence do that?"

"I'm not sure," Gage admitted. "I don't know if it was just a case of flexing his muscles or whether he really thought that this would be an advantageous move."

"Jesus," Charlie mumbled. "You'll be damn lucky if the whole thing doesn't get tossed because of his shenanigans."

"I know. I was wondering that myself."

"And this is a deal you really want, isn't it?"

"Absolutely it is," he confirmed. "Either way, I'm stepping out of the business though. But, since it is my business, I want to sell it and move on."

"Well, let's hope this deal still works out." Charlie hesitated. "Look. I know he's your brother," he began, "but that's kind of a dick move. Is there any reason he wouldn't want you to sell?"

"Well, he has invested a lot of money," Gage noted. "Therefore, he stands to make a very healthy profit. So, no, I see no logical reason for him to tank this."

"But he doesn't get the same crazy amount of money like

you, right?"

"Well, it is my company," Gage said, "so he shouldn't make the same amount of money as me."

"What about your buddy, Linden?"

"*Yeah.*" Gage shook his head at the memories and some of the new revelations. "I don't know where everything stands with the wife now."

"She has withdrawn all her protests. At this point in time she has run out of legal litigation options, so it only makes sense."

"Well, in that case," Gage added, "my buddy had the same number of shares as my brother. So technically I get Linden's shares as well now, as per our preexisting business contract among any business partners, resulting in an even bigger payout for me."

"And would *not* selling the company be a bigger payout for your brother—over the long-term?"

"Oh, yeah, maybe. I guess. Depends on the success of the business going forward, which, as you know, I can't predict or promise such things—especially if I no longer have an active hand in it."

"Well, that's something you might want to take a look at."

Gage nodded. "Okay. Listen. He sent me a copy of the changed contract to look over, since I confronted him over it earlier today. I'll send it to you."

"Yeah, you do that," Charlie agreed. "I still can't believe he did that."

"I know. Me too. I'm a little worried that I'll discover that's not all he's done."

"How much do you trust him?"

"Until this?" he asked. "I had no reason not to."

"Well, that's as good a reason as any," Charlie noted, "but I'm not happy. He shouldn't have touched the damn contract."

"Nobody is happy with this deal now. That shouldn't have been something he even had access to change."

"Yeah, I'll have to look into that," Charlie added, "because you're right. Terrence shouldn't have been able to change anything. Now I'm worried whether the right contract was actually sent."

"Well, I sent it," Gage admitted, "so I'm not sure what happened."

"Any chance that he made changes manually and then rescanned it?"

"I don't know." Gage sighed loudly. "I'll talk to him."

"Yeah, you do that, and I'll review the copy of the contract sent out," Charlie said. "Right now I'm pretty livid that he put the whole thing at risk, after all the efforts to get it right."

"So am I," Gage added.

"Did he ask to stay on as CEO?"

"No, I mentioned it recently, not him. I was going to put his name forward to the buyers to consider having Terrence stay on, but, because we haven't actually sold, I didn't get that chance yet."

"Did you tell your brother that you would give him a referral to the buyers?"

"Not before the contract went out to the buyers to sign."

"Because you realize that, if you leave, even if the deal falls through and the company isn't sold, and Terrence becomes CEO, then he stands to make a whole lot more money just in income and with legal access to the funds."

"You're thinking he's not trustworthy enough to be left

in charge and that he'd actually dip his hand into the till?"

"Right now, I think everything your brother does is suspect," Charlie claimed. "I know he's your brother, and you won't want to hear that, but it is something you need to consider. What he's already done is a pretty big scary deal."

"Crap. Check into it, please, Charlie."

"Will do."

"Yeah, make sure the buyers got the right contract."

The lawyer stopped. "You know what? That's actually not a bad idea. Maybe the wrong one *accidentally* got sent."

"Yeah, maybe. Take a look, please."

"Will do." And, with that, he hung up.

Gage sat here for a long moment, staring around at the world, wondering how things had shifted to the point that he'd come to suspect his brother of foul play. It's not how Gage wanted to see his brother, not at all. This was Gage's company; he'd built it from the ground up. His brother might have been jealous about that, and Gage could see it in a way because it's hard when one sibling did so much better than another. But it's not like Gage hadn't given Terrence many opportunities to succeed himself and to make him a lot of money in the process.

Gage frowned as he thought about it, then called his brother again but still got no answer.

Hating that, and his suspicions rising with every minute, Gage bolted to his feet and started to run down this huge long pathway. There were runners. There were walkers. There were even people using walkers. It was a huge boardwalk, but Gage was running to get away from the devil chasing him. It seemed like all it was these days was somebody after him, one way or another.

Feeling better soon, he slowed his pace, after just a mile

or so, and stood here, trying to slow his heart rate and to get his breath back to normal. When his phone rang, he looked down to see that it was Skylar. He answered it.

"Are you okay?" she asked worriedly.

"No. How did you know?"

"Is it urgent?"

"No, I'll be fine." He brushed his hair off his forehead. "Just some upsetting news."

"About your uncle?"

"Actually, no, not at all. My uncle had a heart attack."

"A heart attack?"

"At the moment the detective guesses that Jonesy snuck into the cemetery overnight and, thinking he would get caught, slipped into the broken-down mausoleum and used the bricks to hide his way in there, then had a heart attack inside."

A moment of silence came on the other end, until finally she spoke. "You know what? That actually works."

"Does it work with the energy?" He stared kindly at the bright blue sky above him, trying hard to appreciate his surroundings, with all this mess going on.

"Yeah, … it does. The question is whether it was the police he was running away from or something else."

"Was he a sensitive?"

"I don't think so, but I don't know that," she replied, "and it wouldn't be the first time that somebody who didn't think they had any type of paranormal ability went into the graveyard and actually saw more than they expected to see. There is a bit of a history about people having scared themselves to death in there."

"Well, honestly, he was a sweet old man, but he was on the more gullible side too."

"He could have met somebody there maybe."

"Or been told that a certain grave may have had the tarot cards."

"Oh, my goodness, there is a fairly common rumor about that."

"In that case, I can definitely see him having tried it."

"Oh, wow," she murmured, as if unable to get past that statement. "That would be pretty horrific if his actions caused his own death."

"Not as horrific as thinking somebody may have killed him."

"No, you're right," she agreed immediately. "That would be much worse."

"Well, if any of your ghostly friends have any insights on this, I would really love to know."

"Maybe the good news is that at least you found him," she noted, "so you can get some closure and aren't always wondering what happened to him."

"I know," he admitted. "Good timing as now I'm still dealing with a bunch of other crap too."

"Of course you are." She hesitated. "I guess this is about the traitor in your midst?"

He stared at the phone in shock, belatedly remembering her words. "You did warn me about that."

"Sorry," she said. "Remember that part about the bearer of bad news."

"I just didn't foresee who it was."

"Neither did I," she confirmed immediately. "That's not part of what I do."

"No, but, in this case, you were right," he admitted. "I just don't yet know how much damage has been done."

"Hopefully not enough that you can't correct it."

"Maybe." He sighed, then grimaced. "It does put somebody close to me in a very different light."

"Of course it does," she murmured. "And did this person have anything to do with any other disasters in your world?"

He froze. "What do you mean?" he asked, his tone harsh.

She hesitated. "Look. I keep getting some weird vibes right now. However, I'm inclined to believe them, only because I'm sure of the connection that we now share."

"I don't know what you mean."

"I don't either, not yet anyway," she muttered. "I don't mean to upset you, especially now. Let me just think about this for a bit."

"Sure," he agreed, eager to get off that whole conversation.

And, on that note, she said, "I'll go get a shower and have an early night. I don't know about you, but I'm still not quite recovered from last night." Then she hung up before he had a chance to say anything about the evening ahead.

Groaning, he stared at his phone. "What the hell just happened in my world?" he muttered.

He slowly made his way back to his hotel, picking up dinner along the way, and took it to his room. He sat out on the balcony and ate, as he thought about the crazy day. Skylar was right in the sense that he was tired too. Tired of all of it. It was a very upsetting ending to his uncle's life, and yet it could have been so much worse. That didn't make him feel any better though; it was just a sad scenario all the way around.

As he sat here with a drink, just enjoying the cool evening, he thought about her words, wondering just what Skylar was up to and what she was implying about Terrence—or somebody—involved in other parts of Gage's life.

Of course the car accident was an issue for Gage; he already knew that. But was anything else? Then he realized that she was asking if *anything else* was an issue. He frowned, as the thought slipped through his mind. What about his brother? Would he have had anything to do with that accident? No, of course not, he couldn't have. It was all about his friend Linden. And then his brother had Dr. Maddy and Stefan working so hard to keep Gage alive. He frowned at that, wondering and worrying that something else was there. Finally, unable to move on, he sent Dr. Maddy a text and asked if she was aware of any odd circumstances related to his accident.

When his phone rang a few minutes later, he wasn't surprised to see it was her.

"Depends what you mean by *odd*," she noted briskly. "We found a lot of different energy in your system, but nothing that I wouldn't have expected from somebody in a high-powered position, who dealt with a lot of people all the time."

"So, nothing suggesting that somebody tried to kill me?" he asked, only half joking.

She hesitated. "We found a dark energy, and we worked hard at getting rid of that," she shared, "and again I'm not sure that we got rid of it all. We were more focused on keeping you alive, than trying to clear out all the other hooks in you."

"Hooks?"

"When you have relationships with people, you have a back-and-forth energy stream. So generally you put a hook in the other person—and they put one in you—to ensure that the energy flows a whole lot easier. Think about relationships with ex-wives and between mothers and sons, that type of thing."

"What about my relationships with business partners and also with siblings?"

"Absolutely on siblings and on business partners," she stated, "particularly if it's a close or intense relationship. Why are you asking?"

"Because, in addition to finding out about my uncle's death here today, I also discovered a betrayal that I wasn't expecting. I'm uncertain at this point how big of a betrayal it was," he admitted. "I still don't know whether it was just stupidity and greed on his part or if something more sinister was behind the changes he made to a contract without me," he explained, trying desperately to be fair to his brother. "But Skylar just asked me if anything was off about my accident."

"Well, you already know something was off," she stated, "and no amount of nudging from her will change that."

He was stunned for a moment. "Pardon?"

"When you have something *off* like that, you have to learn to listen to your instincts," she said. "You know something was off. You just don't know what."

"Okay," he replied slowly. "I don't know what, and I guess that's been the simmering question underneath everything."

"Only you can answer that question," she murmured.

"When my brother contacted you, what did he tell you?"

"He asked if there was anything I could do to help you. Is this the same brother that you're talking about?"

"Yes. And what did you tell him?"

"That there was a chance we could help you, but there

was also a good chance that it could put you into a vegetative state forever."

"Ouch. Really?"

"Well, you had three choices. Death, coma for life—which would mean that your spirit was leaving, but your physical body was actually whole and together enough to continue its organic journey without you—or we might be able to help you. And we couldn't know how it would come out until we actually went to work on you."

"Did my brother make any comment about it?"

"No, he obviously said that having you alive and well and healthy again was the best."

Gage hated to ask, but he did. "Was there a likelihood that I would never come out of it again?"

"Absolutely." She then stopped for a moment, before speaking again slowly. "Were you not aware that you were in a coma for many weeks?"

He thought about it and then nodded slowly. "I didn't think of it as a coma as much as being unconscious and slowly recovering from all the surgeries."

"It was both," she agreed, "but that dark energy we found initially, we had thought potentially was responsible for the coma. However, so many other things in your system needed repair that, by the time we had everything fixed, the dark energy was pretty well gone."

"Would that dark energy have had anything to do with me staying in the coma?"

She took a long slow deep breath. "Honestly, yes." And then she spoke urgently. "I have to go. Somebody is calling me from the ward." And she hung up.

He looked down at the phone. "So, was it my brother or my supposed friend Linden?" He stared out from his hotel room balcony at the big bad world. Since Gage didn't think his brother had these energy gifts, he considered Terrence just guilty of human crimes. "Linden, did you want this to happen, in lieu of my death?"

An odd voice came at the back of his head.

He slowly turned to look and found a wispy white frame in front of him. "Linden?"

The wispiness in front of him disappeared.

Gage didn't know if that meant yes or no. "Linden, can you tell me what you've been doing after the accident?" Maybe this wasn't even consciously done by Linden. That was another thing Gage hadn't considered. What if Linden *was* hanging around, and his actual presence caused Gage's coma, but Linden wasn't doing it deliberately? Gage groaned. And worse, what if Linden had done it deliberately?

This stuff will make you crazy! he cried out in his own mind.

Another voice spoke in Gage's head. *Absolutely it will. Would you mind not calling out so loudly, please?*

Gage stopped and whispered, "Who are you?" He hoped it would be Linden.

I'm not your dead friend. My name is Stefan. You were just talking to Dr. Maddy, and you also have my energy because we worked so hard to bring you back to life. After a weird humming pause, Stefan briskly asked, *Now what's the issue?*

Besides someone talking to him telepathically? Nothing. He wanted to laugh hysterically but managed to control himself. "I guess I'm wondering now if somebody was actively keeping my energy suppressed, so that I either wouldn't come out of the coma or that I would die."

Possibly, Stefan confirmed, *but in the very act of doing our healing work, that negative energy was dispersed.*

"Right," Gage noted. "Is there any way to know who it was?"

No, but I can see that your brain is working just fine, and I know that you've already identified two suspects.

"Ouch," Gage murmured. "But what do you do when it's just a suspicion? How do you know if you're right or not?"

I would go with your instincts. No way you'll prove any of this done on the energy plane because it's all definitely past what the law can handle, Stefan murmured.

"I know. I know," Gage cried out, turning to see if anybody was watching. "So what am I supposed to do?"

That's a good question. I'm not sure who it is in your life that you're thinking may have betrayed you, but I can tell you it was somebody close to you.

"And that would fit either of these two I have in mind," he confirmed.

I understood that you were arguing with your friend before the accident.

"Yes."

Do you remember what the fight was about?

"No, I really don't."

That's interesting in itself, Stefan noted. *Maybe it's not so much that you don't remember as you don't really want to address it. Think about it, but do it quietly. And please, whenever you cry out in the ethers like that, once a connection has been opened up again,* he added, *don't slam all of us with your thoughts.*

"I'm not trying to," Gage said, horrified. "Christ, I wouldn't want anybody to hear my crazy ramblings right now because I don't know what the hell is going on in my life."

No, but you're getting there, Stefan stated, *and at your own speed and in your own time, and that's important. The lessons you learn now will hold you in good stead for a very long time.*

"I hope so because I don't want to go through this anymore."

Too bad, Stefan replied. *You still have a lot to learn, but, with any luck, you'll get there pretty quickly.* And, with that final thought, Stefan disappeared.

Gage realized with more clarity that he'd been having that conversation in his head. Well, Stefan's half.

Walking back inside his hotel room, Gage threw himself down on the bed. "Dear God, I'm going crazy. I'm certifiable at this point." He brushed his hands over his face. "Now they're talking to me in my head."

At that, Maddy whispered in his head herself, and he knew he was going nuts.

It's an ability we do have, she stated. *You're not going crazy, but you do have to acknowledge that some things are already in your life that you don't even know about yet. You're just beginning down this pathway. You need to let go of the past, so you can turn and face this future, which is pretty marvelous. But it does come with some drawbacks, and that's finding out the reality of the narrow and limited life you lived before.*

"It feels like a death," he murmured.

It is, she admitted. *It absolutely is. It's mourning what you didn't know. It's the death of how you see people, how you thought you knew them, finding out how they actually are or were. Not everybody has to go through this, but, in your case, I think it would be a good idea.*

"And why is that?" he asked, his voice harsh to his own ears.

Because you have the ability to do so much more that you

don't even realize yet, and all these deceptive people will hold you back more than you think. Not to mention, if somebody did try to kill you, which I'm thinking might have been in anger, I think somebody else is out there who's against you as well.

"I'm sitting here, wondering if my friend crashed the vehicle we were in on purpose, hoping that I would die with him. Plus, now I'm wondering if my brother brought you in, hoping you would kill me in the process—or at least keep me in a permanent coma—so that he would have power of attorney over my company and my estate."

After a moment of silence on the other end, she said, *I wouldn't be surprised if either or even both of those things are true, but it'll be up to you to make peace with it.*

"How the hell do you make peace with something like that?" he asked in shock. "My best friend *and* my brother betrayed me."

I can't help you with that, she replied sadly. *You're dealing with an element of the world that I try very hard to stay away from.*

"I would like to. I really would."

Then you have to find a way to get there, she noted gently. *Whatever manner it is, I suggest you do it as soon as possible because that type of thinking, that type of energy in your system right now, it'll just poison you.*

CHAPTER 11

S KYLAR WOKE UP in the middle of the night to hear the ghosts down in the shop humming like crazy. She bolted to her feet in her pajamas, then raced downstairs, unlocked the connecting door, and stepped inside the shop. She called out, "Who's there?"

An odd sound came from the back of the store. Then she heard the back door slam open and closed again. She raced there to lock it. Then realized that the siren of the alarm system was not ringing. Either the intruder had turned it off somehow—which didn't seem likely—or she'd been so exhausted that she'd forgotten to set it. She scrubbed her face, as she wandered through the store, checking to make sure that everything was secure. Why would somebody have been in here?

It was a super crazy season, busy with tourists, but she always secured all the proceeds at the end of each day either in the bank or in her safe. As she walked around, she noted the cash register was untouched. So why break in here? She soon noticed that the rack with the tarot cards had been dumped on the floor.

She frowned because anything to do with tarot cards was enough to make her heart jump, particularly now that she knew Jonesy was dead. And how it happened that Jonesy was dead was a whole different story. She didn't know where that would end up, but it was not one that she was particularly happy to hear. She also didn't know where the tarot card set he'd been seeking even was.

She wandered slowly about and picked up the scattered tarot cards, noting an unfamiliar pack just under the edge of the counter. She pulled it out and immediately felt a tingling of awareness. This wasn't just any pack; this was an *old* pack. As she stared at it, she got a horrible feeling. Not wanting to be stuck inside the shop, in case the intruder returned, she quickly reset the alarm and snuck back up to her apartment, locking the door as soon as she stepped inside.

"Elena, is anybody here?" she called out softly.

Elena appeared immediately and shook her head. "Is everybody okay downstairs?"

It was funny how one ghost was worried about the other ghosts, when nothing really could help them or hurt them, without their own consent.

Skylar nodded. "They raised the alarm to let me know there was an intruder." Then she held up the tarot cards. "Do you know what these are?"

Immediately Elena stepped back. "I do. Those are dangerous to play with."

"What I want to know is, where did this set come from?"

"Those are old, and they're dangerous." Elena faded slightly.

Again Skylar nodded. "I know. I just wish I knew how they got here."

She walked into her bedroom, where her safe was located. She opened it up and checked the tarot cards to see if a note or anything came with them, but there wasn't. She slowly placed them inside, then closed the safe. On impulse, she pulled them back out, opened them up, laid the cards out, and carefully took photos of each and every one. Some weird energy was going on around them.

As she picked up each, she quickly cleaned off the energy, put it mentally into a vat with a clean, pure love energy, and put it back into the box. Then she did the entire box and covered it with as much clean and loving energy as possible and put it back in her safe. She stood and turned toward Elena.

Almost shaking, Elena whispered, "That was a good thing you did."

"I don't know how they got into my shop." Skylar frowned. "And why would somebody have put them there if they are valuable?"

"I don't know," Elena whispered, her hands on her heart. "I really don't know. Something wrong is going on."

"Oh, yeah, I get that. I really do. I just don't know what it is."

"It has to do with Gage," she murmured, but her pronunciation of Gage's name was odd, making Skylar smile.

"You're right, a lot is going on in his world too."

"And a ghost clings to him," Elena noted.

At that, Skylar looked at her friend sharply. "You don't normally see other ghosts."

"Most of the time I don't see any," she admitted, "but an energy is attached to Gage."

"Good energy or bad?"

Elena shook her head. "I don't know. I just know it's there, and it's not letting go anytime soon." Then she disappeared.

It was three o'clock in the morning, and the thought of going back to sleep was delightful but very unlikely. Skylar crawled into bed, then grabbed her laptop and instead started researching the tarot cards. They'd been known to be in the New Orleans area for centuries. The particular set was an archaic pattern, originally designed by an Old English artist called Tab Renshaw. She found their images and confirmed they matched her set. But what she didn't know was who had them last. She had a few contacts in her world who might have that information, so she quickly sent off a couple emails, questioning whether anybody knew who the tarot cards were currently owned by. Finally, with that complete, she did a meditation and drifted off, but it was an uneasy sleep.

When she woke up again, it was not even five, but she had a choking feeling in her throat. She bolted once again from her room and raced down the block and across to the hotel where Gage was. She burst into his room to find him once again under the blackness she had seen before.

She roared, "Stop that," as the blackness tried to overtake Gage's healthy energy. She reached out a physical hand and, with a swipe of energy, brushed back the dark energy off Gage again. It bounced to the floor, stood, and then almost with a mental roar raced toward her. As soon as it came right up close, she turned on the mirror that she'd learned to create and had the dark spirit slam into itself. The energy dissipated slowly around her.

She raced over to Gage and put a hand on his neck, feeling a faint pulse, nothing more. She gave him a shake. "Wake up, Gage. Wake up!"

But there was no help for it, he wasn't waking up. She called out, not knowing if anybody heard her, "Maddy, Gage is out. Something's wrong. Stefan, I don't know what's going on, but I just pulled a black energy off him."

Immediately two voices jumped into her head. *We're*

here, they said. *Let us take a look.*

Skylar stood guard, watching as a beautiful pinkish-blue energy joined a golden energy and swarmed over Gage. Then, just as suddenly, they were gone.

Gage opened his eyes, his hand reaching to his throat, as he coughed and tried to catch his breath. He looked at her in shock.

She smiled and sat down on the bed beside him. "We've got to talk."

He looked over at her. "What happened?"

"Same thing as last time," she noted. "Only this time you were in a coma, and I couldn't get you to wake up. I had to approach Dr. Maddy and Stefan for help."

He continued to stare at her and slowly sagged backward. "God, I was so cold. It was like dying."

"Well, if that's death, it's not a normal death," she stated, "but an in-between state."

"Who the hell is doing this to me?" he cried out.

"Well, I can think of a couple people, but believe me, my world isn't exactly normal now either."

He frowned at her and said, "Explain."

She wrinkled her nose at him. "I can try, but I'm not sure it's all that explainable." And she quickly gave him a rundown of her night.

He sat up, pulled her into his arms, and just held her close. She sagged against him. "What the hell is going on?" he murmured.

"We have a saying about when things stir on the ethers. And it's not a good thing."

"Apparently not," Gage agreed. "I have a lot to learn."

"You do, but you're also getting there," she told him. "You're obviously one of those people who has to learn on the job."

"Yeah? Well, I'm okay with that, as long as I do actually learn."

"And you will," she claimed. "It's hard, but it's not impossible."

He shifted them back so they both were up against the headboard.

When she noted how cold they both were now, they tucked under the covers, and he just held her again.

"It was such a strange evening," he began.

"Tell me," she whispered, and he told her about his brother making changes behind his back in the contracts that had some very delicate time issues.

"Interesting. Obviously he wanted the deal to fail."

"That's what my lawyer said," he murmured. "And yet, never at any point in time, would I have suspected that."

"No, and even now you're still making excuses for him," she noted.

He looked down at her and then sagged against her gently. "I don't want to, but the alternative means that I've been wrong about him all these years."

"So both your brother and your friend have shares in your company?"

"Yes, and my friend was upset that I was selling the company too. But he had a lot of problems of his own."

"Like?"

"He was a recovering addict," Gage admitted. "I had put him through rehab twice already, and it looked like he would have to return again. He was very unstable and really struggling with so many things in his life. But that was a struggle that I wanted to get away from myself. If I feel guilty, it's because of that. As long as I held on to the company, he got regular income. By selling the company, he'd have a lump sum."

"And that's not enough apparently," she guessed. "Still, it was Linden's problem, not yours, and, as a friend, you could only be there as much as you could. Otherwise, at some point in time, you can't be there anymore, or you're just enabling the behavior."

He nodded. "And that time was coming. I had told Linden that I needed him to get his shit together and to figure out something on his own and that I wouldn't keep bailing him out."

"I'm sorry for asking this, but I don't suppose that was part of the conversation you were having in the car before the accident, was it?"

He nodded. "Part of it, yes, and I do now think he was trying to kill himself and possibly wanted to take me with him." Gage sighed heavily. "And that just makes it worse."

"Maybe, but, at the same time, it's also not necessarily bad to have that knowledge. If he did kill himself, he will have to deal with his healing on the other side, but he didn't succeed in taking your life, and that's a good thing."

"Maybe," he murmured. "Sometimes it feels like I wasn't supposed to survive either."

"Well, if you hadn't survived, what would have happened to your company?"

"It would depend on what order we died in, but it's likely that my shares and his would have gone to my brother."

She stiffened.

He nodded. "Don't worry. I've already been thinking about that. Maddy told Terrence that there were three ways it could go with me, if she came in to help. She would succeed, and I would live. She wouldn't succeed, and I would die. Lastly, I'd be in the limbo of a coma, where my organic body was alive, but my soul was gone."

"And in each case?"

"Two out of the three, my brother would have gotten the company."

"So, this company of yours, like how big of a deal is it?"

When he shared the selling price of well over one hundred million, she sat up in bed and stared at him, her jaw dropping.

He nodded. "It's big enough money to tempt greedy, selfish people."

"Jesus, yes," she agreed. "I know people who have killed over a sandwich."

He nodded.

"And your friend Linden's share of that?"

"He—or his estate—would get his initial investment plus five million, if the deal went through and I sold the company."

She shook her head. "Still, that alone seems like an incredible amount of money."

"It would be, except that Linden's the kind of guy who easily spends his money, given his drug habit, so it isn't necessarily a lot for him."

"And your brother?"

"Same thing. He would get back the money he initially put into the business, plus five million."

Skylar frowned. "So, if both you and Linden were gone, and the company hasn't sold yet, who is in charge?"

"Technically the board takes over, appoints another CEO."

"Right, and, if the company were under your brother's control, he could stop the sale and do so much more."

"Maybe, I don't know that Terrence is interested in

running the business without me. Now I know for sure that my brother doesn't seem to think the outright sale is a good deal for him. It's not what he wants, and he keeps telling me how I've been making the company a ton of money over the last ten years and could continue to do so for decades more." Gage shook his head. "But I'm tired of it, and I'm done with that life. I want something different, especially now."

"And you're getting it," she said, with a laugh. "You're definitely getting that."

He looked down at her, smiled, and whispered, "And now I've found something else I want."

She looked up at him, and their gazes locked. She froze.

He continued. "That is, if that particular somebody would like to have more to do with me."

When her smile came, it was slow and brilliant.

He sucked in his breath as he studied the look in her eyes.

She replied, "If you're serious?"

"I'm definitely serious," he admitted, "but it could be a little ugly getting to that point."

She nodded. "Cleansing the air and clearing out the energy can often have that kind of effect," she agreed. "You do have a history to clear."

"I know, and I'll get there. Honest I will."

She smiled, then nodded.

"In the meantime"—he slipped two fingers under her chin and tilted her head up toward him—"are you doing anything for the next few hours?"

"Well, the shop opens at eight," she reminded him.

"Perfect." He pulled her tighter and closer to him. "That means we still have two hours."

And he slowly lowered his head.

CHAPTER 12

AS SKYLAR'S MIND and heart played with the sensibility of taking him up on the offer, her body surged up tighter and closer around him, taking the decision away from both parts of her. She let herself slide into those instincts, her body warming to his touch, her heart filling with the need and the joy of being touched by somebody who cared. She didn't want this to be just a physical moment. She wanted their hearts behind it as well.

Everything she did in her world had heart, but sometimes, when it came to sexual encounters, that part was missing. And that was fine, as long as that's what everybody wanted, but when something else was involved or if one person had a different expectation, it made it much more difficult.

Still, as her body heated and her hands frantically explored the huge male body in front of her, she felt her objections sliding away. It didn't matter that they barely knew each other or that they shouldn't get involved because of all the mess surrounding them. It didn't matter that there were all these other reasons to not get involved because right now, all she wanted was to wrap her arms around him and to welcome him into her heart and soul. It was all she could do to hold back her cries of joy, as he carefully stripped the clothes off her body, laying her back down on the sheet in front of him, his gaze hot, his fingers feverish and yet so gentle, as they explored her from head to toe.

She rode the wave of shared wonder and lust in the early morning sun, their temperatures rising and falling, as the loving continued for the full two hours.

When he finally withdrew, her body sated and relaxed, a warm hum flowing through her, he whispered, "Are you sure you have to open your store?"

She trilled with laughter. "I absolutely do."

"Maybe it's time to hire staff."

"Not an option," she murmured, as she kissed him gently and then sat up. She stretched, her body warm and supple, feeling alive for the first time in a very long while. She was also still very tired from the night's attempt at healing Gage again. She yawned, and he looked at her in concern. She smiled. "I'm fine."

"Well, you're more than fine, if you ask me," he murmured. "You're downright gorgeous."

She laughed. "Well, thank you, sir." She stood, then walked to the bathroom and used the facility, studying the glowing woman in the mirror. She hadn't really expected the kind of response her own body had immediately offered to his touch.

When she stepped out, he was getting dressed. She frowned. "Just because I'm a fool and have to go to work doesn't mean—"

"I'm not staying in bed while you go to work," he stated quietly. "I'll go pick up some breakfast and coffee for you."

"Thank you." She quickly dressed, walked over, gave him a gentle kiss, and, without another word, walked out. She headed to her shop, quickly let herself in, and frowned, as she still felt the energy from her intruder. She punched in the code to disarm the security system in the back room, then opened the rear door and quickly started cleansing all the black energy from inside the store, sending it outward. It was important that she get rid of that negativity, that furtiveness of the intruder.

She didn't know how to recognize the energy, although she knew that other people could do that. She understood it had more to do with seeing the nuances in the energies, but her space was always so darn full of ghosts that she wasn't sure that system would work for her. Or maybe she was just looking for easy, and that wouldn't be as easy a solution, as some other things might be. Then again, maybe she just hadn't had any opportunity where that method could be effective.

As she quickly cleansed and refreshed the atmosphere of the store, she was hard-pressed to get the till open before tourists came flocking in. She wondered, as she watched them, if it was the fresh energy bringing them in droves. But since they were spending freely while they were at it, Skylar was quite happy to leave that thought process for now and to sort it all out later. By the time the shop cleared out after the first rush, she turned to see Gage standing there, food and coffee in his hands.

She walked over and smiled. "This looks lovely."

"I intended to come in right away, but, darn, you had a lot of business this morning. I'm really surprised."

She nodded. "And I don't know how much of that was the cleansing I had to do."

He looked at her, frowned, and asked, "What cleansing?"

She realized he needed to know more about her own intruder after midnight. Since the shop was empty, she gave him further details about her break-in earlier this morning, preceding his second choking event, but she left out the bit about finding the tarot cards.

He stared at her. "You had an intruder, and then you came to save me?"

She shrugged, as she sipped the coffee. "What was I to do?" she asked. "Ignore you?"

He muttered, "A lot of people would have."

"I'm not *a lot of people*," she stated in exasperation, shooting him a look. Just then somebody else walked into the store. For the next hour and a half she was busy with customers, sipping her coffee and working on her breakfast as she could. At some point, she noted that Gage had disappeared, and that was just part of her life; that was the way it would go. She had business to do, people to talk to, and merchandise to take care of. And she focused on that, trying to keep the energy flowing in a positive manner.

She had never attempted to influence people in terms of getting them to buy from her store because that went against all the reasons for and ethics of energy work. But it seemed like just doing the cleansing and putting fresh energy in her store was doing the job regardless. Frowning, she let it work its magic, even while she wondered how that actually worked.

By the time the day was done, she was totally ready to close and lock up, then turned around, surprised to see Gage standing there, waiting for her. "Oh my, what an insane day."

He nodded. "I know. I stopped in to see you a couple times, and it was always crazy busy."

"Crazy, wasn't it?" She shook her head.

"I had no idea what was going on, though it's good from

a business perspective."

She nodded. "It is, indeed, but, at the same time, I didn't get lunch."

"I figured as much," he replied. "That's why I'm here to take you out for an early dinner. Maybe it really is time to hire some help." He wiggled his eyebrows at the reminder of how they could utilize her free time.

She flushed. "If every day was like this, then that would be a definite consideration," she admitted. "However, this was very unusual."

"Good unusual?"

"Sure, absolutely good."

"You don't—" And he stopped.

"No," she replied instantly, frowning at the thought.

He nodded. "I didn't think so."

"You have to understand that energy has its rights and wrongs," she declared. "If you use it for the wrong thing, it can come back at you in a very ugly way."

"I guess it's like everything else, isn't it?" he noted. "You think that you're doing something to give you that edge, but it just becomes a little too tempting."

"And the line often is a little sideways when you draw it because nobody really wants to define where it rightly sits on some things."

"Right," he agreed. "For the record, I didn't think for a moment that you would misuse your gifts. I just wondered how much it would potentially affect things."

"Well, energy itself is neutral, so I should clarify that," she stated, "but it's all about motivation."

He nodded. "I get it. I really do."

"Good," she murmured. "I'm too tired to explain any-more."

"How about I go pick up something and bring it back?" he asked. "If you want, we can have it upstairs at your place."

She thought about it for a moment. "That's not a bad idea. And it would allow me to get a shower."

"Perfect," he said, as he turned to walk away. Then he pivoted and asked, "Any preference?"

She shook her head. "No, I really don't have any. I'm just too tired to even care."

"In that case I'll be back in a few minutes. Go get your shower." Then he disappeared from view.

She made her way upstairs, her feet dragging with every step. When she got inside her apartment, Elena was there, a smile on her face. "Tough day?"

"Absolutely, but good."

"Well, that's better than the other option," she noted. "And he's bringing dinner too, *huh*?"

"You heard that, did you?"

"Sure, I was eavesdropping."

"It would be nice if you weren't." Skylar yawned.

"What's the fun in that?" Elena murmured. "You know that we're all here rooting for you."

"Am I such a sad soul that everybody wants me to hook up with somebody?"

"Well, maybe it's not so much that you're willing to finally hook up but that we're interested in who it is you've chosen."

Not sure she wanted to even get into that conversation, Skylar headed toward the shower, and, when she stepped into the hot water a few minutes later, she felt some of the stress sliding off her shoulders. By the time she stepped back out again, she felt a whole lot better. She smiled at Elena. "That was definitely worthwhile."

"Good thing because he's almost here."

Skylar rolled her eyes at that. "You seem to have a sixth sense with him."

"I think I'm going to like him," she stated.

"Well, in that case you could always show yourself to him."

"Do you think he'd run? I don't want him to run."

"He talked to you the last time he was here," she reminded Elena, "so why would he run now?"

"Well, people sometimes say things they don't necessarily mean."

"Meaning that, he was saying hello to you, but he probably would react differently if he could see you?"

"That's what I'm afraid of. … Besides, I wouldn't want him to lose interest in you."

At that, Skylar stopped and swallowed hard. The ego of this woman was something else. "If that will be an issue, wouldn't you rather I find out now?"

At that, Elena tapped her fingers on the imaginary table at her side. "Maybe," she decided reluctantly. "But I really wouldn't want to do anything to mess it up."

"No, I wouldn't either," Skylar said, with a smile, "but I still would rather know, one way or the other."

"Okay, if you're sure," Elena repeated, "but I still don't really like the idea."

"I do," Skylar stated determinedly.

With that, Elena shrugged and disappeared.

Skylar wasn't sure how much she could tell Gage. Yet it would be something that she brought up anyway. By the time she heard the doorbell at the front door of her shop, she was just slipping on her sandals. She walked downstairs, flung open the door, and smiled.

As he came in, something hot, spicy, and Mexican float-ed in after him.

"Whatever that is," she stated, "I'm grateful. I am absolutely starving."

"Well, I took a chance," he replied, as she locked up, and then they both took the stairs to her apartment. As he put everything on her kitchen table, he looked around. "Is your friendly ghost not here?"

"I think she's prepping herself."

"Prepping herself?"

Skylar rolled her eyes at him. "When I told you that Elena's beautiful, I mean, she's *really* beautiful. She's afraid of showing herself—in case you fall in love with her on the spot and can't see me anymore."

At that, Gage stopped and stared. A chuckle escaped him.

"What can I say? Remember? Some people don't change, even though they're on the other side."

"Right," he murmured. "Can't say I ever considered that happening though."

"Well, adjust quickly," she noted, "because not every-body is necessarily balanced and understanding of the reality of the present situation."

He shrugged. "I think I'd rather fall in love with a flesh-and-blood female rather than a ghost that I can't even hold."

"I know, but let her down gently."

He stared at her in confusion. "It's not as if I've ever even seen her."

"Oh, I know, but I think she'll use you as a test."

He blinked and just then heard an odd sound. He looked to the side of Skylar, but Skylar didn't bother because she knew exactly who and what it would be. And, indeed,

Skylar heard Gage suck in his breath. She caught a glimpse of his gaze, wondering if Elena just had that kind of reaction on all men or if she was something that just Gage was susceptible to. Skylar studied his face, not seeing anything in particular in his reaction. Skylar turned to look at Elena, who was dressed, as always, in a beautiful dress that made her skin glow.

Gage looked at Skylar. "I really can see her." He reached out a hand to Elena and then dropped it.

Elena twinkled. *He really can see me,* she said, in pleased delight.

"Apparently," Skylar said, with a smile. She looked over at Gage, who still stared at Elena, transfixed. "So, I see the fascination," Skylar noted.

Immediately Elena cried out, *See? I told you. I told you.*

"I think the fascination is more the fact that he sees some of the details of you," Skylar explained, "versus just a glowy white form."

Gage immediately nodded. "Exactly, but, gosh, to even see this much is …"

Skylar nodded. "I know. Pretty amazing, isn't it?"

"It's beyond amazing. It's kind of … *awestriking,*" he stated, "and that's not even a proper word."

She laughed. "No, it definitely isn't a proper word, but it is an interesting one nonetheless."

"I just created it in the moment."

She smiled. "Can we eat now, or do you need to sit here and gawk some more?"

He broke his gaze free, looked at Skylar with a sheepish grin, and said, "It really is captivating."

"It is," she agreed, nodding her head, "but I'm hungry enough to not care about being fascinated."

At that, he burst out laughing. He looked over for Elena and then said, "I think she's gone."

She nodded. "I think she is too."

He frowned. "Do you think I upset her?"

"I don't know. I have been constantly amazed at her ego."

"Well, obviously it's justified. She is breathtaking," he offered blithely, as he busied himself with the packages of food he had brought. "The thing is, she still is a ghost."

"I know," Skylar replied quietly. "I'm not sure Elena has truly come to that realization though. I guess it's hard to accept that you're really not flesh and blood anymore, and that will have a very different effect on people. Particularly for her."

He nodded in understanding. "Still, it's lovely to actually see one of your ghosts. I was starting to wonder if it was something I'd ever witness." He stopped, looked at her, and asked, "Now did Elena do that, or was that from my ability?"

"That would have been her skill," Skylar confirmed. "I did suggest that maybe she would want to show you who she was."

"Why?" he asked, curious.

"Because she was hiding."

"Hiding?"

Skylar laughed. "Yes, hiding because Elena thought that you would prefer her to me, and she didn't want to mess up our relationship."

He stared at her, as his lips began to twitch, then started to laugh and laugh.

"I know," she admitted, with a shrug, "but I appreciate that she cared."

"Oh, absolutely," he agreed instantly. "I mean, that's a

very sweet thing for her to have done."

"Maybe. The bottom line is that it's a very different perspective when you're a ghost. For some of them, nothing has really changed."

"Well, I appreciate that she did make the effort because it gave me a chance to see something a whole lot more clearly than I had expected to, … even the details on her dress," he added, shaking his head.

"I know. Sometimes it's pretty miraculous. Like Thomas downstairs in his top hat."

"And he wears the top hat all the time? Even inside the store?"

"Yes," she replied, with a smile, "even inside the store. Of course he hasn't really come upstairs much."

"Can he come up?"

"I think so." She frowned. "I remember one time he started to climb the stairs, but Elena had decided that this was her space." At Gage's curious stare, she shrugged. "I don't know. I try not to get involved in their little disputes," she explained. "It would make life much smoother if everybody could just get along."

"Absolutely. Again that surprises me because you don't think of things like that."

"Nope, you don't, but why would you? But, at the same time, you also come to realize that they're still just people, and they are still as worried about maintaining their space and their identity here as they were before."

"Yet they're not even supposed to be here," he stated in exasperation.

"If I could get them to go home, I would," she said, shaking her head. "However, so far, they're pretty determined not to take that step."

"Which I find fascinating because it means that, even dead, they prefer to be here. Whereas I would like …" He thought for a moment and continued. "I would really like to think of my friend Linden being happy on the other side."

"Of course," she agreed. "All of us would prefer that. And who knows? Maybe someday I will eventually get these guys to relax enough to actually go where they belong. But, at the moment, they seem more content to live this very limited existence with me."

He nodded. "And that's exactly what it is, isn't it? They are living again but through you."

She sighed. "And that's the problem because it's this very lonely isolated world, but it's all they know, so that's what they cling to."

He tilted his head, as he watched Skylar's expressions morph from one emotion to the next. "It is kind of sad."

"It's more than *kind of sad*." She pulled out her chair, sat down, and asked, "Can we eat now?"

He nodded with a smile. "Absolutely."

And, with that, she dug in. By the time she was halfway through the first burrito, her stomach started to calm down a bit. He looked over at her, with one eyebrow raised. She shook her head. "It's good, but that's all I can eat right now."

"And maybe you're not quite so famished now that you've had a chance to plow through half of that," he said. "They are pretty big."

"It was. I used up a lot of energy today, apparently."

He didn't say anything for a long moment, and she realized that her terminology was probably strange and not what he expected. By the time he finished his mouthful, he cocked his head and asked, "Burning up energy in terms of dealing with people at the store or with the cleansing?"

"Both," she replied, "because every time I came up with something that worried me, I'd have to start cleansing things out again. Otherwise that worry would cause more of a problem."

He nodded again. "Still, it's such a fascinating concept."

"Maybe." When she had a moment, she asked a question that had been burning in the back of her mind all day. "If the deal with the company goes through, like you're hoping, what will you do next?"

He smiled. "I'm not sure yet. I've spent so much of my life figuring out how to make money, yet I've not really sat down and thought about what I would do with it."

At that, she burst out laughing.

"I'm serious."

"I believe you. I really do. I just never heard of such a thing. Most people spend money as they get it—or before, in too many cases."

"And I did spend some in the sense that I have a nice apartment and a decent car and somebody to come in and clean for me," he admitted, "but I never really blew a lot of money, just reinvested in building my own. Now I feel like the whole world is out there, and I would love a chance to explore it more, but I haven't gotten that far."

"Maybe you can now," she suggested.

"Maybe." He shrugged. "We'll see. It's a bit too early to tell."

"How long do the buyers have?"

"I think until tomorrow night."

She nodded. "And again," she murmured, "just because your brother might not be terribly happy and might have changed the dates, that doesn't mean that he was willfully trying to sabotage the deal."

"No, maybe not," Gage muttered, "but it's looking like he didn't want the deal to go forward."

She nodded. "What about your other family?"

"I have a mother, whom I don't speak to," he shared.

She looked at him. "Is that a good thing?"

"My brother and I have different fathers. He's my younger brother and had a father in his life, whereas my mother walked away from my father. So I definitely have some resentment there. I bounced from Father to Mother, back-and-forth. And that was a problem too." He shrugged. "When I finally got old enough to ditch them both, I did."

"And your father?"

"He's dead. Long dead. And so is my brother's father."

"Interesting."

"That's where Jonesy came in," he added, with a half smile.

"And is he related to your mother?"

"Yes, so my brother and I share the same mother, and we both are blood relations to Jonesy, and thankfully my mother is off in the Riviera right now."

Skylar stared at him.

"She likes the high lifestyle."

"And do you pay for it?"

He winced. "I do to a certain extent. So does my brother."

"And I would suspect that you would like to stop doing that too?"

"Oh, absolutely," he agreed.

"So, if you sell, that won't change your relationship with your mother, will it?"

"No, she'll realize just how much money I have, and it'll get worse."

She frowned. "What about your brother?"

"Well, I told him that, if he wants to keep paying for her lifestyle, that's his business, but it'll stop coming from me, along with the other changes that I'm about to make in my life."

"Maybe you could set her up with an allowance or something?"

He stared down at the food in his hand. "I would just as soon not talk about my mother, if you don't mind."

She nodded and immediately changed the subject. But, in the back of her mind, she wondered about Terrence's alliance with their mother, then just blurted it out. "How much does your brother love your mother?"

"I think he loves her just fine. They've always been way closer."

She nodded. "Sorry. I intended to change the subject, but instead the question that popped out was exactly what you didn't want to talk about."

"It's fine," he said, but he put down his burrito.

She got up and got water for both of them and asked, "So what did you do all day?"

Then he smiled and launched into a discussion of all the touristy things he'd done around town.

"See? I like to hear that. It's good to hear that you were out and enjoying life."

"I was," he agreed, with a smile. "There's a lot to do here, at least for a couple days."

"There is, even at other times of the year too."

"You seem to be rushing around, doing all kinds of stuff, including graveyards."

She frowned and nodded.

"Speaking of which, you didn't do that last night?"

"No," she murmured, "but I'll probably go some more in the next couple days."

"So it isn't every night then?"

"No. The energy in that one particular graveyard is off right now."

"Because of Jonesy?"

She nodded. "Yes, exactly."

"Understood. I'm sorry about that. … Do you ever actively try to contact ghosts?" When she stared off, not answering, he half-apologetically said, "We appear to be hitting all kinds of conversations that we don't really want to talk about tonight."

She shot him a glance and nodded. "It's all right. In answer to your question, I have actually contacted ghosts. Every once in a while, I've been asked to do so." He studied his own food again. "You want me to try to contact your friend Linden?"

"And here I figured you'd think I wanted to contact Jonesy."

"Probably him too," she agreed, "but I think it's your friend who is troubling you the most."

He sighed. "It's definitely something that bothers me, yes."

"Understood. I just don't know that I have any way to contact him."

"I don't understand. What's involved?"

"Your friend, well, he's not very friendly," she shared.

"I know he's got some issues," he replied carefully.

"That's one way to put it." He frowned and looked at her. She nodded. "Yes, he's definitely got some issues, and I'm not seeing that he's terribly warm or welcoming or friendly at this point."

"Well, I would hope he is on the other side."

"Maybe. It's not that easy to just contact them, though it typically is easier to do where they died."

"Are they always tethered to the location of their death?"

"They're tethered to people, places, and things," she explained. "So our lovely Elena here, she's tethered to this building. This apartment was hers." Gage stared at Skylar. She nodded. "Obviously a much older version, but this is where she was kept by her lover." He winced at that. "I know, but for her it was a normal life. I'm not sure that she would have enjoyed getting older though."

"No, I can't imagine she would have. So, for her, maybe this was an easier way to go, than to actually live the life of somebody who would eventually be discarded."

"Though, in her mind, that would never happen," Skylar added, with a casual flick of her wrist.

Elena immediately appeared and glared at her.

"We're just talking," Skylar noted.

I know, Elena replied, *but you don't have to talk like that.* And, with that, she disappeared again.

Skylar turned to see Gage looking at her funny. "Sorry, Elena just popped in to say that she didn't appreciate the conversation."

He smirked. "No, of course not. Still, in her heart of hearts, she believes she would have done just fine."

"And you know what? She's a survivor, so she probably would have done just fine," Skylar suggested.

"Got it," he agreed, "and that we don't know because everything was so very different back then."

"So very different." Skylar nodded.

THE CONVERSATION LULLED, and Gage wondered about the certain subjects Skylar seemed to avoid, in particular her midnight jaunts out to the graveyards. He wanted an invitation to go along again, but he also knew that wasn't likely to be forthcoming. For all that they had found in each other, and as close as they had become within a short time frame, they knew each other well in some ways and not at all in others. And he was afraid that fact would hinder their relationship as well because of whatever was going on right now in the graveyards. He hesitated about asking, and then, when he looked up, she hurriedly stood, as if understanding what he was wrestling with.

"I'm just going to clean up these dishes," she offered.

"Are you heading to bed tonight or do you want to go out for a bit?"

"No, I think I'd like to go to bed early," she said casually.

But that odd note was in her voice again. "Is there any particular time that you do your graveyard walks?"

"When it feels right," she replied immediately. When he frowned, she chuckled. "I know. That's very scientific, isn't it?"

"Nothing scientific about any of this," he grumbled, yet with a gentle smile. "I just wondered if there was any particular impetus to do it from one night to the next."

"It depends," she replied. "A lot is involved, and sometimes there's more of a push to do certain things than others."

He didn't know what to say to that, and it was obvious she wouldn't expand on this subject. "It would be nice if you trusted me more."

"It would be nice if I'd known you longer," she stated

immediately.

He winced at that. "I guess that's true, isn't it?"

She shrugged. "It's hard for me to completely open up about everything in my world just because you're curious."

"There we go on that whole *curiosity* kick again," he noted, smiling, as he got up and helped with the dishes.

"It is what it is," she said, "and, because it's all new to you, some of it's foreign."

"It's *all* foreign."

"Exactly. Some things are easier to explain, and others we should just wait on, until you're a little more comfortable."

"I would really like to be comfortable with all of it," he stated, giving her a shadowed look.

"And I get that. I really do. It's just that I'm not that comfortable with it yet."

He nodded. "I guess there's nothing I can do about that."

"No, not really."

As soon as the dishes were done, she said, "And, if you don't mind, I'll just sit here and relax a little bit, then maybe have a bath and go to bed early."

"You mean, *bed*, where you won't be woken up in the middle of the night?"

Her gaze shrouded. "I sure hope not." She studied him intently. "How are you feeling?"

"Fine, but then I was feeling fine before," he noted.

She hesitated and then added, "Well, if it happens again, we'll have to make some changes."

"Do you really expect it to happen again?"

"I don't have any expectations either way, but I hope not and yet"—she smiled—"there's really no way to know."

"I hate that," he said. "I want answers, and I want answers now."

"Which is nice and all," she agreed, with a cock of her head, "but it doesn't really help."

"No, of course not. The only person to help is somebody who *doesn't* need to have the answers."

She gave him a gentle smile and an equally gentle response. "You need to understand that—all this emotion, all that need inside you to look for these answers—it has a tendency to push away the answers."

At that, he stopped and stared at her.

She nodded. "You must be very detached or come from love. When you come from that drive or that fear," she explained, "it works against you, and it becomes something that hurts any and all progress."

"I've never heard that before." It was hard medicine to take. He'd been CEO of his own big company—well respected, feared even—and yet now, here he was, the apprentice to an unwilling master. Of course it wasn't a formal agreement between them. She was generous with her time and information, and he couldn't fault her for that. The fact that he was looking for so much more was his own problem. He'd always been driven, and looking for answers in this issue wouldn't be any different because he hadn't changed. *No.* He stopped at that thought. "I really have changed, you know?"

She glanced over at him, as she hung up a dish towel, and nodded. "Yes, you have, and you will probably continue to change for quite a while."

"Will it be in a good way?"

She smiled. "You tell me," she stated gently, "because it's all about what you create. Will this be a good change or not?"

"I feel like, if I go in this direction, I'll lose everything that I already know."

"You will. You'll lose the friends. You'll lose the family. You'll lose the people, the surety that you had in whatever field you were in before. There, you were king. You were the boss. You could make things happen, and, when you snapped your fingers, people jumped and did your bidding," she said. "*This* world isn't like that at all, and you're not a master. You have to start at the beginning. You must work your way up again in a whole new field."

"I was just thinking about that. … It'll be hard."

"But it sounds like you've made a decision."

"I think the decision was made for me," he said, with a broken laugh. "I don't know what's coming after this, but I know that something is, and I know that it's a pathway I need to carry on with."

"In that case," she replied, "this adjustment period will be uncomfortable, but you will get there."

He stared at her for a long moment. "And I know you want me to leave," he began, "and you know I'm getting there. Honestly, I am, but could you possibly share what you did before this?"

"For some of us," she replied, with half a smile, "there wasn't necessarily any *before*. I've always been like this. But growing up was not easy because I found very little acceptance."

He nodded. "I can't imagine being in school like this."

"Most of these abilities start when we're a young child, and we often block them out, until we're old enough to understand what's going on. At that point in time things happen—usually around puberty. In my case I was very active with ghosts when I was younger, and I blocked them out because everybody told me how they didn't exist. Back then I followed along just to make peace with everybody around me, if nothing else. And I stopped seeing them."

"Can you just willfully stop seeing them?"

She nodded. "Yes. And I did. Until I lost a best friend, somebody I didn't really want to lose. Before I knew it, she was there, talking to me. Actually she was scolding me." Skylar laughed. "She was telling me off for having walked away from what I could do all these years. And, by the time I was done with her, she'd walked into the light and was heading on to whatever comes after this and was doing much better."

"And do you know what comes after this?" He seemed to be a fountain of questions right now, and he knew he had to work on that, instead of overwhelming her.

She smiled. "There you go again, looking for all these answers."

"Well, if I had a ghost to talk to, then maybe I could get some of the answers without bothering you," he complained. "But it seems like you're it for getting answers."

"Maybe so," she agreed gently, "but I'm also tired."

"I get it." He nodded and immediately straightened up and walked toward the door. "I was hoping to spend more time with you tonight, but I can see that you really do need more sleep."

"I do, indeed," she replied, with a smile.

With that, he turned and walked out.

CHAPTER 13

S KYLAR NEEDED SLEEP, but tonight was also *the* night, and no way she could avoid it. Every time she tried to avoid these sessions, they got way worse and much harder for her to control the next time. Not to mention the ghosts who pounded on the door in her mind, until she could barely deal with the headache they caused. It was easy for people like Stefan and Dr. Maddy to say that Skylar had the control and that she could tell them to butt out of her life, when they wouldn't cooperate. But, with just so many of them, it took that much more time and energy to even control them.

And, of course, most people couldn't even begin to understand this overwhelming ghost problem that Skylar had, particularly not Gage. As much as she would prefer to spend the evening with him, she would have to spend it doing transfers—something that most people never even began to consider. And she wouldn't have either, except it was something she had fallen into. And now? Well, it was like she was the only one around who could even do it.

For all she knew, she was the only one to *ever* do it. And that just made it even so much harder. She wished she had somebody with like skills—even Gage at some point—to work with her to help balance out the energies, as she moved people from one etheric state to another. But, so far, that hadn't happened. Gage might get there, if this were something that he honestly wanted to pursue.

It was certainly possible that he could get there; she just didn't see it happening anytime soon. And right now she needed some sleep. These transfers always happened best between midnight and 3:00 a.m. And, because of the furtiveness of it, she had to do it quietly, without anybody knowing. If she were ever caught doing this, she would be stripped of all credibility and likely even jailed. Not something she wanted to think about.

How did one explain what she was doing in the middle of the night? There was also a good chance that Jonesy would be there because that was the cemetery she had to work tonight, and that would bring a whole new level of complexity to her problems. Not that it was his fault by any means, but it still didn't change the fact that he was an energy she would quite possibly have to deal with.

She'd seen his energy there at the time his body had been found, but it had been faint and nondescript, as if he hadn't quite figured out how and what to do yet. Which, of course, he hadn't. How could he? He was new to that world, and, just like Gage had questions here, new to the world over there took a lot longer for people who were stuck. And no doubt Jonesy was stuck.

As soon as Gage was gone, and Skylar had locked up, she headed back to her bed, where she stretched out for a nap. She called out, "Elena, don't let me sleep too late."

"I'll let you have a couple hours," she replied, but a note of worry was in her voice. "I wish you wouldn't go out and do these transfers."

"And yet, if you were one of the ones caught in-between, wouldn't you like the help?"

"Sure," she agreed, "but they can also figure it out themselves."

For the first time there was a bit of waspishness to her tone. "Are you worried about me?" Skylar asked curiously.

"It feels off."

Skylar pondered that for a moment and then had to agree. "You're right. It does."

"So you won't go then, correct?"

"Oh, I'll go," she said. "I have to. You know the lineup is getting pretty bad."

"Well, they can wait until another month has passed."

"It's not that easy though," she stated. "It'll be hard for me to keep them all at bay in the meantime, and then I'll have more to transfer next month."

"They shouldn't be screaming at you anyway," she noted. "It's not as if it's your job."

"Maybe it's not my job, but because I can do it …"

"I still think it's wrong."

And there wasn't a whole lot she could argue about that. "We'll talk about it later," Skylar replied. "I need sleep now."

And following several of the tricks that she'd learned over the years—in order to get up and to do the kind of work that she'd been doing for at least a decade by now—she closed her eyes and was out like a light. When she heard Elena calling her through her dreams, Skylar opened her eyes and remained here in the moment, listening to the sounds of the world around her. She felt the graveyard stirring. Tonight was a full moon, which made it easier in a way, but the full moon also meant more light, which, in New Orleans, would also attract a lot more attention from residents and visitors, both from those with gifts and those without any.

She'd also learned that it was still easier on her if she did these transfers during the full moon. And sometimes it was all about her. Even as much as Elena liked to think that it was never about Skylar and that she didn't take enough care about her own energy, that was wrong. She did take care of it because nobody else was out there to help her with these transfers.

After she had been injured and damaged doing this kind of work, Skylar quickly came to realize that she could do some things to maintain her own sanity and to keep helping the masses.

It bothered her a lot to think that many people were in these graveyards who hadn't found peace or hadn't found a way to move on into the life that was there and ready for them. But there were many, and—in these graveyards in particular, of course being in New Orleans—the Hurricane Katrina nightmare hadn't helped. Any kind of disaster always made these events that much worse. And that much more important.

Skylar didn't fool herself that she was the only one who could do it, though the fact was, she didn't actually know if other people were doing this work. And it didn't matter because this was about what she could do and her need to do it.

She could hope that maybe one day she could talk to others about it. Maybe there was an easier way to get it done. She didn't know because she'd never had anybody to talk to. She didn't have any friends who did this sort of thing, and that in itself was not distressing, just lonely. She got up, got dressed, and sat down in front of her mirror and started doing her face.

Elena sat beside her. She'd been here long enough now to recognize this pattern. "You do that really fast now," she noted.

"I did it really fast before too. It's just that you're seeing it differently now," she noted, with a smile at her ghost friend. "It helps that my tattoos are part of my uniform."

Elena nodded. "I'm getting better."

"You are," Skylar agreed, "but I still wish you would consider crossing over."

"Nope, not going to happen," she stated, "especially not right now." And there was that dark note in her tone again.

"I can see that you're really bothered by tonight."

"I'm always bothered," she snapped, "but tonight is even worse."

"*Hmm,*" Skylar replied. "I'm not getting the same kind of undercurrent that you are."

"You should because it's all about you and your safety."

"If that were the case, then I would like to think that I would be feeling the same thing you are," she argued, "but I'm not."

"And why is that?" Elena asked. "Have you lost touch with who you are?"

That was an interesting accusation from a ghost, who was staying where she was so she didn't have to connect with her own soul's journey. Skylar looked into the mirror, seeing her partial skeleton face, and then got up, finished dressing in her black vest, black jeans, black boots, grabbed her top hat and her beads, then stuck two rattles in her back pocket. Pondering for a moment, she then grabbed a handful of silver.

Instantly Elena nodded. "Take more silver." Then she repeated, "Take *more* silver."

Shrugging and not really caring, Skylar dipped her hand into the bowl of silver coins and stuffed them in her other pocket. Then she looked at Elena. "Keep a watch out, will you?"

"I will," she vowed, almost fervently.

It was odd to be at the receiving end of so much caring, particularly in a ghostly form. Skylar reached out a gentle hand, and, where Elena's face would have been, she pulled a strand of hair back and up and off her cheek. "I'll be fine," she reassured her, but damn if there wasn't a glisten of tears on Elena's face.

Pondering that miracle, Skylar headed downstairs and slipped outside. The partiers were reveling all around in the night. She headed through the darkness, her hat in hand, as she moved silently down the street. There was one moment where she felt something at her back.

She slipped into the alleyway and waited to see what it was. But, when nothing materialized, she checked out the energy and kept on moving. By the time she made it into the graveyard and to the back section, where it was dark and safely out of view from anyone on all sides, she crouched on her favorite spot and slowly let the energy close in around her. She could sense the ghosts standing here, so many that it surprised even her.

When she opened the door in her mind, she heard them talking. But, of course, they weren't using any manners that made things easier on her.

She immediately slammed the door closed and in a low voice warned, "Speak politely or else not at all." There were always those who didn't want to listen though, so, when she opened the door, it was cautiously because she'd been tricked before. Just because she wanted them to act with respect and patience didn't mean they would.

Since they were almost always panicked at finding some-body to talk to and some kind of a source to blame for all the horribleness going on in their world, Skylar couldn't count on it being a quiet calm energy when she again opened the door. And, sure enough, several people screamed at her. Finally she wrestled the door closed, slamming it shut again. And waited.

When she opened it the next time, she whispered, "I'll only talk to those who are quiet and in control."

Almost instantly the energy muted around her, which was good because this would be a very long night if she had to keep repeating this teaching moment for too long.

Skylar could hold on to only so much energy. She knew the universe was abundant and could do so much with the energy all around her, but when she had to direct her energy in a specific way and open a tunnel to the light, as she would tonight, that outlying energy supply was not something she could really access.

So she stored her energy greedily for each new moon of transfers.

In order to access that, she'd have to let something else go, and that couldn't happen, not when she had so many souls in her hands at the time. As she sat here, quietly letting her energy warm, she assessed the energies around her. As always there was a huge number of souls. She shook her head. "I can't help all of you," she whispered.

Immediately two stepped forward; she looked at them and nodded. "Yes, you two." She searched the crowd and pulled out another one and then two more. Could she do five? Yes, with the assessment of her own energy stores, she felt that five was doable. She wasn't so sure about more than that though. Although she may not have much of a choice, considering just how many were out here.

When one shoved to the front, she immediately looked

at him and shook her head. In a complete rage, he roared and cried out in confusion and anger. She slammed the door once again because this would be an ongoing issue. Some souls had joy. Some souls had rage. Some souls could find their own way, but so many of these souls couldn't, particularly in a disaster.

So much for an easy transfer on a full moon. Too often these lost souls got caught up in the panic of the moment or stuck worrying about others and then wandered and traipsed around, until somebody like Skylar came to help them cross over. Usually they should cross over on their own, but it didn't always work that way. Or maybe Skylar was just the odd ferryman. She'd been called that more than a time or two.

Slowly she opened the door in her mind again and realized that the angry ghost was now off to the side, screaming and yelling into a vortex of his own making, but at least it wouldn't disturb her. She sat down here and pulled out her bones, the rattles, and the silver. As soon as the sky cleared, and she felt the energy lift up around her through her own meditation, she stood and slowly began a dance as old as time.

HE STARED IN shock, and yet something primal resonated deep within him. She was eerily beautiful with her outfit, her face paint; even her tattoos seemed to glow. He sank to the ground and watched, mesmerized as she did some graceful and yet weird dance. The longer she danced, the brighter the glow from what looked almost like a halo around her. Only as he turned to look around did he note that more and more of these earthly lights came toward her, as if a circle of people were watching her—only not people, ghosts.

His heart slammed against his chest, and he was so scared of being found out and interrupting whatever was going on here that it was hard to breathe, yet his pulse pounded to the same beat that she danced to. The makeup on her face, the clothing she wore, it all suited and yet was so foreign. He wished to video it, and, even as he reached for his phone, he stopped, feeling like it was a betrayal.

In the back of his head, a voice whispered, *Good call.*

He shuddered as the voice slid into his brain again.

I'm Stefan. We registered the panic in your system and thought you were in trouble.

Gage didn't know what to say or how to say it but mentally thought out his reply. *I'm watching her. I've never seen anything like it.*

Stefan hesitated and then stated, *I'm going to do something, so don't freak.*

And then it was almost like Stefan stepped forward into Gage's brain in the front of his skull, looking through Gage's own eyes. Gage felt the jolt of surprise as Stefan watched Skylar move and flow in the light, the halo around her getting brighter and brighter, moving at a faster and faster rate, until her dance was almost a vibration, sent outward from her body.

Gage whispered to Stefan, *I don't know what she's doing, but it's incredible.*

I've never seen it done, Stefan whispered back. *I've heard of it, and I knew of somebody who could do it, but I hadn't realized it was Skylar and had no idea that she was capable of doing it at this level.*

Gage didn't know what *this* was, and, even as he watched, Skylar came to a halt, her arms stretched wide, her feet planted far apart, as she did almost a yoga pose. He wanted to say it was like a warrior pose, as her arms were up and her face shone to the sky. Immediately the energy circle tightened up closer and closer and closer to Skylar, until it blended with the energy she pulsed ever outward. *What the hell is she doing?* Gage cried out mentally.

Easy, Stefan replied, pulling his own energy to guard Gage's. *We can't interfere.*

In what?

I think the phrase in this case is transporting.

Transporting?

As in the New Age ferryman, Stefan noted.

There was such a soul recognition to the words that Gage stopped. *The souls? Is she moving them to the other side?*

Yes, Stefan confirmed. *She is, in a large quantity at a time.*

But why couldn't they go on their own?

It's not uncommon in the case of disasters.

And then Gage whispered, *Katrina.*

But he didn't even know what to say beyond that; the whole thing was just so beyond what anybody could possibly expect. It was so stunning to see somebody with such a unique way of doing things, somebody so confident, so in control. He watched as her body, her energy filled with these other souls. *Now that she's full of them, what will she do with them?*

Watch, Stefan replied. *I think we're both about to be shocked.*

As they continued to stare, she kind of shuddered, as if she were full up, leveling off, packing them in as tightly as she could, and then straightened. In a move Gage had never, ever thought to see in his entire life, she turned and faced him, her gaze lining up directly with his. Then she closed her eyes.

Stefan whispered, *Look at her go.*

As she stepped out of her body, she started to fade away, yet she was attached to all these souls, and, like a great big arc, she pulled them toward her, as she stepped closer and closer and closer.

But what is she walking to?

Can you see a light behind her?

I see a glow, yes.

She's taking them to like a, Stefan paused, *almost like … I hate to say it, but maybe a good analogy would be an airport, and the door is opening for her.*

As she stepped across this imaginary airport threshold, her energy still firmly attached to her body that stood frozen in the moonlight, the energy opened up and swooshed through her, right toward the light on the other side, taking all the lost souls with it. Then came a weird thunderous *clap*, and the door shut. She was left standing, her own ghostly form still attached to her body by a long silver thread.

I can see her, Gage whispered.

Good, Stefan noted, *and that is huge progress you've made.*

She's standing there, but what is that thread between her and her body?

It's her cord, her lifeline, the attachment to her own physical body, Stefan explained.

As they watched, she drifted back to this side ever-so-slowly, invigorated and still glowing—but maybe more like a triumphant fatigue—as she slowly slipped back inside her body. As soon as her energy and her spirit were fully one again, she straightened up, and, in an odd series, almost like tai chi flowing motions, she carefully completed several movements and then came to a standstill, her hands in a prayer position, and her head bowed. She stood like that for the longest moment, and then she stepped out and shook her arms and hands.

She turned and looked directly at him. "Gage, come here, please."

Her voice was deeper, darker than normal. Gage whispered to Stefan, *Uh-oh.*

Tell her that I'm here too, Stefan stated.

Will that help?

I don't know, Stefan admitted, *but I've just seen somebody do something that I've never imagined possible.*

Gage slowly stood and stepped forward, until he was frozen in place. She looked at him sternly; something was otherworldly about her gaze. "Stefan?"

Gage instantly gasped. "How did you know?"

"In this form, there's not much I can't see." She was silent for a moment. "Gage, I asked you not to follow me."

He nodded. "You have, and I was definitely in the wrong."

She tilted her head to the side. "Stefan, what do you have to say?"

"I came because Gage was in a panic," Stefan replied honestly, his voice an odd echo where both could hear him. "Only to find that it was his shock at the incredibly beautiful aid you just gave to those people." His voice rippled in the air in some weird way.

She lowered her head ever-so-slightly. "It's all I can do tonight," she noted, almost sorrowfully, "but so many more remain lost souls."

Gage hesitated and then murmured, "I saw this white energy all around you, low to the ground. Were they all souls?"

"I took as many as I could," she stated, "but it was really difficult."

"How many did you help?" Stefan asked curiously.

"Tonight it was twenty-seven," she said. "I was only planning to do five, but so many were crying out that I figured I should try." She gave a lopsided grin, her eyes still glowing with that otherworldly look. "And, in this case, the last ten," she added, as she turned and stared at Gage directly, "were animals."

Gage gasped. "Animals?"

"Dogs, cats, a couple otters, weasels, and ferrets—mostly pets," she told them. "Pets caught up in the same panic of their humans, affected by the human energy, caught up with that same disconnect that happened during the hurricane."

"Oh my God." Gage—now realizing he was no longer frozen, and didn't know if it was because of him or her—took a step forward.

She studied him. "You just couldn't leave me alone, could you?"

He hesitated, sensing the hurt in her own words. "I know you don't appreciate that," he acknowledged, "and I can't tell you what drove me to follow you, except that I sensed something wrong, that you were in danger. I felt strongly that I needed to be here."

"Interesting," she murmured, as she studied him.

Gage knew that he could keep absolutely nothing from her. If he lied, she'd know it. And, if he tried in any way to bluster around the truth, she would see it for what it was, an excuse.

She inclined her head ever-so-slightly. "You were not the first to express that same worry tonight."

"Who else?" he asked.

"Elena," Skylar noted calmly.

He watched in amazement as some of the energy faded from her eyes. "How often do you do this?"

"I hold off until my energy is enough that I can handle it and that enough people are here for me to make one full push," she stated. "Otherwise I'm in danger of getting caught."

"That's smart." Stefan spoke up just then, his voice echoing weirdly in the air.

Gage looked around and said, "I don't know how he does that."

"Stefan does things you could never even imagine," she said, only a tiny note of humor in her voice.

Stefan chuckled. "You're a fine one to talk," he replied. "I had no idea you were a ferryman."

"Is that even a term anymore?" she asked, her back stiffening ever-so-slightly, and then she relaxed. "I call it *transfers*."

"I've heard that term too," Stefan noted. "It's a gift and a very unusual one."

She stared at him for a long time. "I don't imagine that it's accepted by many people."

"Anybody in my world would have no problem with it," he stated quietly. "So you've spent a lifetime separated from those of us in this field, worried about judgment, worried that people would not like your system?"

"I make the souls wait," she said defiantly. "I make them wait, until I know that I can handle however many I can carry."

Skylar seemed to be blaming herself for something.

"And I need the power of the full moon."

"You do," Stefan agreed. "The bottom line though is

that, when you step up, you step up in a big way. And I can imagine that the pull the souls have on you is pretty tough and that the only way you can deal with them is to push off the event, awaiting that full moon and the promise of more usable energy."

"Sometimes they won't leave me in peace," she cried out, "even when I tell them that I will help them eventually, but that I can't help them right away and that I need my energy to build and that I need time to recover from each transfer process." She sighed. "They won't listen."

"No, because those souls are determined to go where they want to go," Stefan noted, "and it's not your fault, and you are not to be blamed when you need to take a step back and to do it your way."

She tilted her head, as if listening for a lie in his words, and Stefan, still attached to Gage, let her. And then her shoulders seemed to sag, and she whispered, "Thank you."

"You should never blame yourself," Stefan stated, even ordered. "What you're doing is incredible. I don't know anybody who can do this."

"You help souls cross all the time," she noted.

"And I only take one at a time." He laughed. "And I only help those who are ready and who can see the light. You don't wait for them to see the light, do you?"

She shook her head. "No, as long as I know that they are meant to go on the other side," she explained, "I've never yet had anyone not go, when I can take them there. Typically I take those who have been blinded by circumstances in this world, where their fear and their pain have held them back from crossing over. Then I can make it happen."

"That's incredible," Stefan said. "You don't realize what a special gift you have."

She stared at Gage now, her eyes again glowing with a weirdly inner light.

Gage felt something trickle up and down his spine, as he felt the hairs on the back of his neck and all around his arms stand on end. He looked at her and asked, "Did you just touch my soul?"

She smiled. "Of course. If you come into my world, I have a right to check to make sure that you are of my world and that I don't need to kick you right back out again."

He sucked in his breath. "I'm really hoping you don't."

After another moment of analysis, she relaxed even further.

Stefan asked her, "Have you ever had help?"

"No, and no training. I learned very early on that anybody I told was out to hurt me."

He winced. "Unfortunately that's often true," he confirmed. "I knew you were here, but I had no idea you were capable of generating that power or that you could cross over yourself, yet stay connected to here. I'm not sure you understand how absolutely unique it is that you can stand with one foot on the river Styx and cross over, letting all the souls go through you to the other side, and still return to this side, completely whole."

"Well, *whole* I'm not so sure about," she teased, with half a smile. "Yet I have learned to perfect it over time."

"How long have you been doing this?" Gage asked, dazed at the thought.

"A decade or more," she replied, with a one-arm shrug. "I don't count. I just know that I operate this way and always have."

"And nobody knows?"

"Not until tonight," she noted, tilting her head back

defiantly.

"All I would suggest," Stefan added gently, "if you ever feel you need backup or a hand or assistance in any way shape or form, you contact me and Dr. Maddy. We will never laugh at you, and we surely would never hurt you. Honestly, you belong with us, and you need to be part of our group."

"Why?" she asked, checking out his energy. "What is it that I need from you?"

He smiled. "Community support. Acceptance. Belonging."

Her eyes widened and then narrowed before she gave him a gentle smile. "Touché, you're right about that. It's the one thing I've never had. I do not have peers who accept me. I do not have anyone who supports me. I've been alone and worked alone for a very long time, never fitting in. I've always assumed that, at some point in time, I would end up in jail for this. Labeled a crazy woman and confined somewhere for months, if not years."

"And, if that ever happens," Stefan said, "I can help."

She tilted her head. "Can you?"

"Absolutely. We would do our utmost to get you back out again."

She smiled. "In that case, it would be nice to have somebody watch my back."

"The work you do is too important." Stefan said. "I mean, I can't even begin to do what you're doing here."

"And yet you seem surprised by that," she noted, with a burst of laughter.

He agreed. "I am forever surprised by things continuously happening around me that move me, especially when I have no idea that it's even done. I've never even considered that *this* was a possibility—before now." Stefan made a sound almost like a prayer, as if unable to come up with the words to describe it. "My God, … what I saw tonight."

She nodded. "I would appreciate it if you didn't share it." He hesitated, and she cocked her head, as if listening, even watching him. Yet another mystery Gage couldn't unravel. "And, yes, Dr. Maddy is okay."

With that, he relaxed. "Fine. I hope you get to the point where you are less concerned about being found out."

"I'm not sure that'll ever happen." She raised her left eyebrow at him. "Once you've been burned, it's difficult to even think about opening yourself up to that again."

He nodded. "We're not those people. Check my energy, walk through me, feel it, understand my soul, where I'm coming from, those I help, the centers Dr. Maddy and I have, the people we work with, and the people who we save on a daily basis."

She hesitated, and he urged her again, "Walk inside me and see for yourself."

Gage piped up, "*Uh,* how can she do that? Aren't you talking in my head, seeing out my eyes?"

Something moved at his side, and Gage turned to see an odd spirit form standing there, glowing in gold. "Stefan?" he asked in amazement, and the spirit nodded. As Gage watched in even deeper shock, Skylar stepped forward and stepped into Stefan's energy. Gage couldn't believe it, but the energy itself started to gyrate in a weird blending motion. He didn't understand it.

And then she separated again. "Accepted," she said, her voice calm and at peace.

"And you do realize that, having done what you've just done," Stefan began, "you've now—"

She nodded. "We're now connected in many ways," she interrupted, an odd note of humor. "I hope your wife understands."

He burst out laughing. "She does."

"I don't," Gage admitted, stepping forward. "I don't understand at all."

She looked at him and said, "Well, close your eyes."

When he did so, she stepped forward, and he felt the energy whispering closer and closer, and then he felt something cool land on his lips, and then, dear God, his whole spirit jolted, as she stepped inside his body and became one with his soul. He cried out in joy and wonder, completely in shock, and then it was all too much, and everything went black.

CHAPTER 14

"W ELL, STEFAN," SKYLAR noted, "I guess Gage wasn't quite ready for that."

"He was ready," Stefan stated comfortably. "Give him a minute to come back around again. It's a bit of an awakening."

"And yet he's so anxious for answers."

"Sometimes one is anxious for answers, until one actually understands what one is asking."

She smiled at the glowing gold ball beside her.

He asked, "It doesn't drain you? What you did tonight?"

"It is draining," she agreed, "but I'm very aware that I walk a pathway that balances energy from both sides. That's the reason for my dance at first."

He nodded. "Of course. You have to get the vibration correct, don't you?"

"Yes," she whispered, "and the energy must move and flow as intended."

"Have you ever had it not happen?"

"Not since I learned how to do it properly," she said. "There's an instinctive knowledge as to when it's all ready."

"It's stupendously amazing to realize all that you've learned," Stefan murmured, "and to think that you did it all on your own is incredible."

"Is there any other way?" she asked, smiling. She reached

down a hand, her hand that still buzzed with wild energy, and placed it on Gage's forehead.

"Will that bring him back?" Stefan asked.

"It should." She gave him a gentle smile. "Enough healing energy still runs through my system that it should be of value to Gage."

"Have you ever utilized that energy to help anybody else?"

"If you mean, anybody *physical,* yes," she replied, "but only in ways that they aren't aware of."

Stefan nodded. "I know Dr. Maddy would love to have that energy available to her."

She looked over at him. "Meaning?"

"You should be able to transfer that energy to a patient who's not here in this physical location," he noted calmly. "Which means that, anytime you have that leftover energy, she has patients who need it."

Skylar tilted her head and contemplated that thought. "There really is no physical distance when it comes to loving healing energy, is there?"

"No," he murmured. "And that type of energy is powerful."

She smiled. "It is very powerful, and I have used it a couple times, but again not in such a way that anybody would be able to recognize."

"You must have had a fascinating life," he murmured, "to have become so independent and so capable on your own."

"I always wondered what it would be like to have people," she added, with a smile, "people who cared, people who were there for me, people who were supportive."

"You may not have had it before," Stefan noted, "but

you will now."

"Nothing will really change though, will it?" she asked.

"Except maybe just knowing that you're not alone?" he stated, "Hopefully that will put a smile on your face, a smile that hasn't been there very much, I suspect."

"No, not near enough."

"And now it can be," he said.

At that, Gage groaned, opened his eyes, and stared up at her. "Did you just walk inside me?"

"Is that even possible?" she asked, immediately turning the question around and looking at him, all with a big smile.

"I would have said no," he began, "but you've given me a glimpse into another world. It seems like a parallel universe, so foreign to the world I lived in before that my other world means absolutely nothing to me now."

"And it will be that *absolutely nothing* determination," she explained, "which will allow you to take whatever offer you're given on your company and just walk away."

He stared at her, as he slowly sat up. "You know what? Right now I agree." He looked around the graveyard. "Jesus, I can't believe what I just saw."

"Well, I suggest you get on your feet," she suggested. "I had a ton of energy, but it will fade quickly."

He nodded. "What about Stefan?"

She looked around, but that sense of loss was here already. "He's gone. And now we need to get moving too." She helped Gage to his feet.

He immediately wrapped an arm around her shoulders, tucked her up close, and whispered, "My God."

"Yeah, well hold all that shock for a little bit later," she noted, feeling an inner sense of panic rising. "We have company, and we need to get out of here fast."

"Company?"

"Yeah, and it's not friendly." She immediately ducked and raced toward the open gate. He followed, and, by the time they got to the other side, she closed and locked it.

He looked at her. "Ghostly or human?"

"Both. And I'm not exactly sure why."

She moved away from the gate itself, but looked back at the graveyard.

A man in a loud, cranky, almost angry tone yelled out, "Gage, you can't escape."

Gage froze, turned toward Skylar.

She faced the ghost and asked, "Linden, by any chance?"

GAGE STARED AT the strange apparition in front of him. According to Skylar's words, it would be his friend. The one who had died in the car accident. "Linden?" he asked hopefully. "Is that you?"

"Yes."

So much anger, almost hatred filled his voice.

"Yes, it's me, not that you care. Of course you lived. Of course you'll do very well out of all this. Look at you, and yet I'm the one who's dead. I'm the one who doesn't get to live and do anything that I wanted to do anymore. I had dreams too, you know?"

"So why did you kill yourself?" Gage asked him.

At that, Skylar grabbed Gage's hand. Turning to Linden, she stated, "You need to take that anger out on someone else. And you can't stay in that agitated state for long. It's draining you of all the things that you need to do with your life."

"What life?" he roared. "My life is over because of him."

"Are you sure about that?" she asked, her gaze scanning the area for the evil human she had sensed.

"Yes," he snapped, "I am. He's the reason I'm dead. I'm sure he told you something else," he yelled, with so much bitterness. "But he's wrong. He's lying. He is the one who caused the accident. It's his fault. He tried to kill me."

Gage felt like his heart had just been ripped out of his chest at the lies spouted by his friend. "That's not true," he whispered, hoping nobody else could hear Linden speaking. "You know it's not true."

"Do I?" he snapped. "All I know is, you got the money, and you got life, and look at me. I'm dead. I'm not even on the other side, where I belong. I'm here, stuck in-between."

"That's because you chose it," she stated instantly. "Now you could choose to go follow the light on your own. You could choose to walk away from this half existence."

He laughed. "Says you," he muttered, with such disdain.

"Yes, I do. I do understand, whether you acknowledge it or not," she explained, "but your anger and your hatred keep you anchored where you are."

"And why am I here?" he asked. "That's what I don't understand. I didn't die here, and yet Gage is here."

"That's because you're not tethered to where you died. You're tethered to Gage himself."

"It doesn't matter," he roared at her. "You will not stop what I'm here to finish."

"And, if you're here to finish something, why haven't you already done so?" she asked, inciting further rage from Linden.

Gage looked over at her in shock, and she just shrugged, then spoke to Linden. "All I see right now is somebody who's so angry and so incapable of accepting what he did to himself that he can't let go. You wasted your human life here, indulging in your addiction, then cutting short your own life. And now you're wasting the in-between time you have to think and to figure out how to fix your next world," she said. "You have a chance at a second life, an opportunity to do so much good, to learn from your mistakes in this life and to come back and to live all over again, but better and differently and learning other lessons."

"You lie," he growled. "There's none of that for me. You know it as well as I do. Gage must pay for what he did."

"And why is that your decision?" she asked, looking at Linden. "Why do you feel that you have the right to say what he has to pay for or not?"

"Because it's not fair," he roared, the sound splintering into Gage's eardrums.

Gage clapped his hands over his ears. As Skylar placed her hands over his, almost immediately the tone went down. "Thank you," he whispered to Skylar, then looked back.

Only Linden's ghost was gone.

"Dear God, what the hell was that?" Gage asked.

"That is an angry ghost," she stated calmly. "It won't be the last one you see, and unfortunately it happens to be your friend. However it does feel like it's gone for now."

"You have to believe me," he said, looking her in her eyes. "I did not kill him."

"I know."

"How do you know that?"

"Remember when I walked through you? You have no secrets from me now." Her eyes once again gained that weird glow. "I can feel and sense the heart of you," she murmured, "and you did not lie."

He felt the relief wash through him, even as her words

stunned him. "So, like, you know everything?"

"If I wanted to, I could access everything, yes," she admitted. "And, if you don't like it, well, that's too bad because there are repercussions for your actions too."

He winced. She was talking about him following her. "I really did feel like you were in danger."

"You did when you saw me walk out of my building," she shared calmly, "but that is not why you initially came after me."

"No, because, when I saw you in that outfit," he replied honestly, "I was afraid that you had a partner that you hadn't told me about." She shot him a look, and he smiled and added honestly, "And you can tell the truth from this. I was jealous."

She smiled back at him. "And I can tell that you're speaking the truth, so, in this case, I forgive you. But, when you lie, I will know," she stated, "and I will not tolerate it."

He figured there would be consequences for lying too, because obviously she was an incredibly powerful woman, and he had no freaking clue how to combat that. The good thing was that he had no wish to either.

She was damn special, and he felt blessed to have her in his life. He just had to convince her to keep him there.

CHAPTER 15

THE WALK HOME was swift. Gage insisted on walking her home, even if that was all that was involved. By the time Gage and Skylar reached her shop, they both entered her store, as she went to disarm her security system, while Gage locked the front door behind them. They each checked the energies inside. She turned to say good night, but the energy still crackled between them.

She hated to end the evening now, while her energy still flashed and sparked. Something was so very primitive about the energy work that she did. And, of course, with every dead person that she helped into the light, there was always that spark of life left behind. She knew it was a dichotomy, but it was hard for her to explain. As she looked up at Gage, he leaned down and kissed her ever-so-gently.

"I want you to know that I'm really proud of what you did tonight."

She raised her eyebrows.

He nodded. "I know that's probably not what you expected to hear, but I mean it. There's something very special about a woman who puts herself in a position to help others, regardless of the consequences to herself."

She frowned and went to say something, but he placed a finger over her lips.

"No arguing."

She smiled and gently kissed his finger, feeling the rough skin against her soft lips.

He sucked in his breath. "You know that I really hope that more of that could be on our agenda tonight, but I understand if you're tired."

She murmured, reaching up to kiss his chin. "I might be tired, but the energy is still humming through me. Of course I still have all my makeup on…"

"And it's beautiful. You're beautiful." He wrapped his arms around her, pulled her up close, and whispered, "As for the fatigue and energy… we might be able to do something about that." And he lowered his head again.

But, if he thought that it would be a soft, gentle coupling, he was in for a shock. She kissed him, hot and passionate, with some of the raging energy still fueling her blood also making him vibrate within. Even though she was tired, still these vestiges remained from the energy work she had just done.

She wrapped her arms around his neck, pressed her body from pelvis to chest tight against him, and let loose. He shuddered in her arms, clenching her tightly around her rib cage and holding her close. When she finally stepped back, he leaned up close, trying to regain that proximity.

"If you're ready for that," she said, in an attempt at a normal voice, "follow me."

And she dashed to the stairs, with him following quickly behind. She laughed and raced upstairs, unlocking her apartment door, then heading straight for her bedroom. She tossed off her vest, kicked off her boots. The hat went flying onto the floor, and, by the time she pivoted to face him, she was already down to her panties and bra, standing beside her bed.

He sucked in his breath, trying to shuck off his clothing as fast as he could, already toeing off his boots.

She didn't wait. She reached over, stripped the belt from his pants, and pulled down his jeans, so he could step out of them. By the time he was as naked as she was, she had her hands wrapped around him, making him shudder in place.

"Oh my God, is this what happens afterward?"

"No idea," she admitted. "I've never actually had a partner with me before."

She stood up and pushed him onto the bed and proceeded to mount him. What followed was a tempest of hot sexual fire that needed to be appeased, a reaffirmation of life, proof that it wasn't their time to go through that doorway with the light. That this was their moment, this was their time right now. And nothing but absolute surrender would be enough.

By the time she collapsed on top of him, both of their bodies slicked in sweat, he whispered, "Dear God, you may have killed me, but, if you ever have somebody else making love to you on a night like this, you'll break my heart."

She murmured, "Then don't let it happen. I've always been alone before. To have you there tonight was very unique."

"Yes, that's a good word for it."

"Did I scare you?" she asked, as she slipped to his side, lying on her back, her arms flung wide, as she let her body cool and the sweat dry on her skin.

"I was fascinated, never scared," he replied. "I didn't quite understand everything, but, when Stefan stepped into my mind, he explained a lot of it."

"Stefan is a very knowledgeable person," she said.

"He seemed quite surprised at what you could do."

She shrugged. "I've never shown anybody," she admitted, "and I don't know how many people are really aware of what can happen."

"Well, Stefan seemed to be pretty surprised, and I don't think he thought anybody could do what you did tonight."

She laughed. "Well, I'm glad in that case that you both were there. It's not that I did anything to show off. I was doing something that I do on a regular basis."

"And I think it was that matter-of-fact precision and the absolute ease with which you slipped in and out of whatever persona you were in," Gage suggested, "that surprised him the most."

"It comes with long years of experience," she murmured.

"Exactly, and he knew that. I think he appreciated that the most."

She nodded. "I can see that in a way. He's been doing this for a very long time himself. I don't know if he realizes how many people are out there with similar abilities."

"I think he was happy to have found another one."

"Maybe," she murmured, as she yawned. "As long as he knows I didn't do it to show off."

"Oh, I think he knows that." Gage laughed. "We were both stunned."

"Well, I wasn't stunned as much as I was irritated that you were there, but I couldn't stop the transfer. I had to put you in your place mentally, so you didn't distract me."

"I'm sorry for that," he said. "I recognized when you saw me, but it almost wasn't ..." And then he stopped.

"Almost wasn't me, yes."

"Exactly." He leaned over and, propping himself up on one elbow, looked down at her. "It's like you had become someone else."

"No," she corrected, "not someone else. It's just another aspect of my personality that you saw."

"Is it that simple?"

She nodded. "We're all combinations of various personality aspects," she murmured. "You just saw the part that I needed to do this type of work."

"It's like your soul shone through your eyes."

"It was," she admitted. "That's why I step out of my body because I grow so big and so full of energy that my physical body will get damaged if I stay within its confines. Besides, the work I have to do has to go much bigger than that."

"And you did," he noted in awe. "The fact that it was just so blasé for you was one of the biggest surprises."

She shrugged, not really understanding why that was a shock. "When you do something over and over again, you become proficient. And, with that, comes not complacency, because it's always different, but you become comfortable with those adjustments to be made."

"I guess that's it. And you're right. Something like this is never the same, is it?"

"No," she agreed. "Souls are always different, and, because they're always different, the reactions, the things that happen with them, all are always different. You can't ever really count on any two being the same. Some are a little rough around the edges. Some are angry. Some are friendly. Some are whimpering. Some are crying." She shook her head. "You'll get the whole gambit there."

"And yet still you show up."

"Because anything else is less than what I can do," she stated, "and that's not acceptable."

"Is it always about honor and doing what you can?"

"It's always about helping. It's always about coming from love," she murmured. "It's always about being the best that you can be and taking the high road in all things. Just because a ghost insults me or laughs at me or makes a comment that I don't like"—she sighed and showed both palms—"that doesn't mean that I sideline him and don't carry him across."

"No, of course not," he agreed. "Yet I know a lot of people who would make that delineation though."

"And that's sad for them," she said. "However, do you really think—now that I know what's on the other side and what is required to cross over—that I won't be very careful about how I act on this side?"

He slumped back on the pillow. "I never thought about it that way, … but I guess taking the high road does become the easiest thing, doesn't it? Because anything else hinders you from crossing over."

"To a certain extent," she noted, "but you do realize that angry people over there are still angry? They still have things to work out. It's not as if you magically become this perfect person. You become whatever accumulation you have accrued, both of good and bad things," she murmured. "So being the best that you can be here makes for easier and faster growth over there." She smiled. "And now I'm just about done," she explained and yawned on cue.

He murmured, "Go to sleep. I'll watch over you."

"Not needed. I am going to sleep deep."

"Is it okay if I stay the night?" he asked hesitantly.

Her eyes flew open. Then she looked at him and smiled. "I don't generally let anyone stay overnight, particularly on the evenings that I'm going to the cemeteries. It's a little unnerving to try to sneak out of bed, without letting them know that I'm heading off to graveyards."

He smiled. "Well, if you're not planning on going any-where else tonight, then how about we get some rest?"

She closed her eyes and, within minutes, was sound asleep.

WHEN GAGE WOKE up the next morning, he found himself all alone. He stretched in bed and rolled over to see a note on her pillow.

Had to open the store.

That was it. He was not sure what he had expected, but, so far, she never acted or reacted in any manner that he expected since the moment he had met her. He got up and wondered if she'd mind if he had a quick shower, then realized that she probably wouldn't. So he availed himself of the opportunity and then got dressed and headed down to her shop.

When he got there, the store was full of people, as in seriously full.

She looked at him over the crowd and waved, and that was all she could do. He couldn't believe it and didn't know why it was so terribly busy. He waved goodbye and headed to his hotel room, where he changed into fresh clothes. Just as he was about to return to her shop, his brother called.

"Hey. Any news?"

"Outside of the fact that we found Jonesy's body and that his cause of death is a heart attack, I haven't heard anything else back from the cop yet. Nothing to really find out," he said.

"I tried to call you last night, but you didn't answer."

"Yeah, I tried you several times too. I went to bed early."

"Are you doing all right?"

"I'm fine," he replied. "Look. I've heard some weird rumors about this chick you're hanging around with."

Gage winced at that. "Well, I don't know why you're listening to rumors, but New Orleans is full of that."

"I don't know. It sounds like she does voodoo and all kinds of stuff."

Terrence tossed off the words with such a casual dismissal that it almost made Gage angry. "I wouldn't worry about it." Gage yawned.

"Is that who you were with?"

"I was with her a little bit, but I was off on my own most of yesterday."

"Good," his brother said, with some relief.

"Any news on the contract?"

"Well, your lawyer contacted me," he noted in disgust, "and seemed to feel that I was trying to sabotage things. He contacted the buyers on *your* behalf apparently."

This time the hurt was evident in his brother's voice.

"I wasn't trying to do anything to damage the sale, you know?"

"Glad to hear that," Gage replied, a slightly false note in his tone because it was hard to even give a shit anymore. Skylar had been correct last night when she had said that his old world was over. "I want the deal to go through, and I want it to be done fast."

"Well, today is the day," his brother said.

"Good, hopefully they'll sign, and we can carry on."

"Do you really think they might keep me on?" his brother asked.

"I don't know," Gage admitted. "That would have been

my recommendation, if we got that far. It probably depends on whether they feel like you messed up on the contract, and if so, whether on purpose or by accident."

"Well, shit," his brother said. "I didn't know you were going to recommend me for the post."

"Of course I would," he retorted. "That's always been my intention, if we get to that point. However, your actions should have been the same regardless."

"I figured you didn't think I did a good job."

His brother obviously didn't believe him. "Why didn't you just ask me, straight out and up-front? I never said that," he replied, trying for patience. "I don't have anything against the work that you did. Yet I'll be pretty upset if anything goes wrong to make this deal collapse though."

"Well, it wouldn't be because of me," he groaned.

"Good, let's keep it that way." And, with that, he hung up on his brother. Then he called his lawyer. "Any news?"

"Yeah, I left you a message," he noted. "I expected to hear from you first thing this morning."

"And do you expect to hear from the buyers too?"

"Yes, I do."

"Any problems?"

"Not that I'm hearing so far, but I'll tell you that they were pretty pissed at your brother. They weren't even going to look at the contract."

"Shit, because of the changes he made?"

"Yeah."

"That's not good."

"No, it isn't. When I explained that your brother had gone around your back on it, they were appeased—but only temporarily. This needs to come to an end, and I still don't know that this won't have some kind of ill effect."

Gage sighed loudly. "My brother says he didn't do it on purpose."

His lawyer didn't say anything.

"You don't believe him, do you?"

"It's hard to call something like this as not done on purpose. You've been covering up for your brother for a very long time, Gage. I'm just not sure why you even bother."

"I want this deal to go through."

"You and me both," his lawyer confirmed. "I put a lot of time and effort into this to have it all blow up at the last minute because somebody decided to make some changes on his own behind your back for God-only-knows what reason."

Such disgust filled Charlie's voice that Gage winced. "Sorry about that and thanks for trying to keep the deal viable. I'll talk to you soon."

"Yeah, I'll let you know if I hear anything."

"Okay." Gage hung up with his lawyer and headed out of his hotel and down to the street, his feet almost having a mind of their own as they headed to the water. He walked the pathway along the river, his mind consumed with everything that had happened. One of the things that was definitely clear, particularly after those two phone calls, was that Gage no longer gave a shit about anything to do with the company. The sooner this was over, the better. He just wanted to be free of that life so that he could pursue whatever the hell this life offered.

He knew nobody from his business world would understand, not a one. But he'd made them all very wealthy in the process, and he didn't owe them a damn thing more. That was what he had to hang on to. He wanted to do something for himself for a change. It would be hard potentially, but maybe not. Maybe they would automatically drift away from his life as he changed his vibration—at least he thought that's what it was called.

After enjoying the fresh air and a breeze, he turned and headed back, where he picked up breakfast and coffees and headed to her shop. He was stunned to see that it was just as busy as it was before, and she was running her feet off. Automatically he went to the cash register and assumed the role of her assistant and manned the till. It didn't take him very long to pick up on it, as his first summer job had been doing exactly the same thing, and her equipment wasn't much newer. As a matter of fact, she needed an upgrade. But, with that in mind, he just worked alongside her. She never spoke a word to him, just smiled at him as he stepped up.

By the time noon came along, and the rush died down, she turned to him. "Thank you," she said gratefully. She sipped her cold coffee.

He looked at his and winced. "I think I'll go get us some fresh coffee and food."

"Hey, I'll take that right about now."

"Why was it so crazy busy all of a sudden?" He walked to the front door, turning to look back at her. She looked at him sideways, and he realized something else going on. "What?" he asked. "What am I not getting?"

"It's because of the energy," she murmured, "from last night."

He stopped and stared.

She shrugged. "I find it a side effect of my work every time."

"Well, it certainly keeps you in business."

"Yeah, but I don't know if it's ethical or not," she murmured.

"Are you doing anything to attract it?"

"No." She shook her head and laughed. "No, they're coming for the energy."

"Then I wouldn't worry about it. This is crazy busy though."

"It is sometimes, but it's also good." And she was humming along quite cheerfully. "Hard to argue against the improved sales."

He realized just how much she could benefit from somebody helping her out financially. With the energy work she did, it wasn't like anybody would pay her for the energy, her time, or the risks she took. There was absolutely no monetary assistance for her. "These people should be helping you."

"What people?" she asked, with a laugh. "The dead ones?"

He sighed. "Can't Thomas or Elena or any of the ghosts around here help you out so that you're not so cash tight?"

"I think, if they could, they would," she noted, "but what do I know?"

At that, Gage nodded. "I'm hungry. I'll go grab food."

And, with that, he disappeared.

CHAPTER 16

S KYLAR WATCHED GAGE leave and smiled at Thomas, standing by her side and watching the exchange.

"He's learning. And you've never asked us before," he noted. "I don't know if there's anything we can do or not, but Gage's right. So many souls benefit from you, and yet they don't pay you."

"And there's nothing to pay me for," she argued. "And it's not as if you guys have money."

"No, no money," Elena replied, stepping up to join them.

Skylar was surprised, as Elena almost always stayed upstairs.

Elena added, "I wish there was something we could do."

The ghosts looked at each other and faded away.

Skylar shrugged, not sure what she was supposed to do with their assistance, but added, "Thanks for the thought, guys."

When Gage returned, he had several muffulettas. She tucked into hers, without even thinking.

He ate his, as he silently watched her finish it all and then nodded. "That energy of yours is one of the reasons why you eat so much?"

She nodded.

"And again we're back to the fact that there's a cost for

you doing what you're doing."

"But not everything has a monetary value," she argued, right back at him.

He smiled. "Let me think about it."

"No, don't worry about it," she said. "This is my world."

"I would like it to be my world too, if you will let me."

She looked at him and then frowned. "Seriously?"

"Yes, seriously. I'm thinking about moving here." He smiled. "I really love the energy."

She laughed. "That's actually why I moved to New Orleans, for the energy. Besides, I could hide here."

"I needed to be here obviously," he said, with a wave of his arms. "Have you ever lived anywhere else?"

"I was in San Francisco for a while."

"Oh, right." He stopped, winced, and asked, "Don't tell me that you did the same thing there?"

She nodded. "Until I got caught."

"Oh, crap," he said. "How bad was that?"

"It was pretty bad," she replied cheerfully. "I got away on a technicality, but my lawyer also told me that I better scram and not come back. They figured I was desecrating graves."

"But, of course, you weren't."

She shook her head. "No, a lot of people needed help there to cross over. I also spent some time in Japan and various other parts of the world."

"Oh, boy." He frowned. "So, if you were to stay here, any idea how long before you actually transferred over all the stuck souls?"

"Decades," she murmured. "And the stronger that my presence becomes in one location, the more spirits can come to me to work from this space."

"So, if you actually set up this as a home base, you could stay here?"

She nodded. "That's the hope, at least."

"Wow. We don't even think about things like that, do we?"

"Not normally, not unless you're in this crazy business."

He shook his head. "And the store is right up your alley."

"Well, it seems that people are attracted to the energy," she noted. "And I desperately try not to do anything to encourage them to buy things. That would be unethical."

He nodded. "That obviously bothers you, as you have mentioned that several times now. I think, because you are working solo, that you question that part too much, that you are too critical of yourself and question your own handling of your gifts. You don't need to do that. Like you told me, as long as you are coming from the heart, your motivation is pure." When she remained silent, Gage added, "And I bet, if you asked Stefan and Dr. Maddy, that they would agree with me too." He paused. "You really are in a place now where you are accepted. Believe that. Stop worrying about your motives. You have been very generous with me and these ghosts in your shop and the poor souls in the cemeteries." He stared at her for a long moment. "Okay?"

She hesitated, then nodded. "Thank you. ... I should let that worry go. I found out very quickly that I don't need to do anything because that energy is what they're really buying."

"Of course they are," he agreed. "And, for some of them, it's probably incredibly healing too."

"Considering that some of the healing energy is still around, I would say that is true."

"Is it still around?" he asked. "Even after all this time?"

She nodded. "Yes."

"Wow."

She shrugged. "You get used to it after a while, but the buzz from the last night is still there."

He looked at her, and his eyes gleamed.

She laughed, seeing his instant interest. "I still have the store open."

"But if you had an assistant …" He waggled his eyebrows in a suggestive manner.

She smiled. "Oh, yes, thank you for stepping up and being my assistant this morning," she teased. "You took to that very well," she noted, with sincere admiration.

He grinned. "I wasn't always a successful businessman, you know?" he added, turning serious. "I started doing summer jobs as a cashier in local grocery stores," he murmured. "It actually brought back a lot of memories."

"Good, I hope they were good ones."

"They were … and also reminded me of my beginnings."

"That's not a bad thing," she said gently. "Sometimes we forget all about where we've been because we're so anxious to get to where we think we're going."

He stared at her, and his gaze darkened, and then he nodded. "You know what? That's very prophetic. I did talk to both my brother and my lawyer this morning."

"Oh? How did that go?" She moved about, cleaning up the remains of their meal and then the store, as they talked. Something about having a large rush of people come through always seemed to leave it dirty. She also had to cleanse the energy out in preparation for the next tourist wave. As she busied herself, she listened to him talk.

"It does feel like my brother deliberately tried to affect the outcome of the sale."

"But he didn't, right?"

"Well, we're still waiting to see. It is possible that he did some damage, though my attorney may have headed it off. Certainly the trust factor has shifted though."

"Well, trust you can repair it, or at least maybe help them with it," she suggested, looking over at him. "Making sure that your brother has nothing to do with it, of course."

"I had planned to recommend that they hire him and keep him on for a few months."

"Interesting. Why?"

"Just for ease of transition."

She nodded. "They won't want him now, will they?"

"Not at all," he stated. "And that's too bad because my brother generally would have been good for the job. I honestly don't know what he was thinking."

She looked at him, smiled, and said, "Fear. That's all it was, fear. Afraid that you wouldn't need him anymore, that he wouldn't get the interim job, that he wouldn't have any future income, and just generic fears of the future and the inevitable changes. So many people sabotage themselves and those around them because they can't handle even the idea of change."

He stared at her. "You are a very wise soul."

"I've just seen a lot," she replied, shooting him a brilliant smile.

He nodded. "Well, if the deal goes through, I should hear about it today."

"And if it doesn't?"

"I'll instruct my attorney to sell it anyway, even if for a lower price." He shrugged, while shaking his head. "Obviously my world has shifted, and I didn't really realize how much, until you brought it up."

"It's a paradigm shift," she noted, "and, once it's happened, it's almost impossible to reverse."

He nodded. "I'm not sure I want to reverse anything at this point."

"No, of course not," she agreed. "you've experienced something so different, something that most people will never get to see in their life."

He nodded. "And it's fascinating. I want to know and to see so much more."

"And you'll get to," she confirmed. "Every day you're learning more and more."

"Only because of you." He shook his head. "It's unbelievable how much you really do know about this stuff."

"It's not even that I know about this *stuff*, as you call it," she explained. "It's not so much about *knowing* as I've been *living* it. Meanwhile, in comparison, you've been living under a rock."

"Apparently." He laughed. When his phone rang, he pulled it from his pocket and looked at the screen. "Well, this is my lawyer. Wish me luck."

She smiled and said, "It'll all be just fine."

As more tourists walked into her store, Gage stepped outside for a minute. She watched his energy as he answered, and then he turned to look at her, a beaming smile on his face. She grinned back and knew it would all be okay for Gage.

His brother might have some challenges ahead, but the sale of Gage's company would go through. And, for that, she was happy for Gage. At least he would have the freedom to do what he wanted with his life, and that was something most people never had a chance to experience, so he truly was blessed.

Then she focused on everybody around her, as the store filled once again.

PUTTING AWAY HIS phone, Gage stared up at the sky, leaning against the front of her store, and he felt like a weight had literally come off his shoulders. The deal was done, signed and sealed. There would be days of transition paperwork, legal stuff that his lawyer was thoroughly excited about, but then Charlie also stood to make a couple million off this deal. And Gage was more than happy to share. His lawyer had been a godsend throughout these last few years.

Gage now had to tell his brother, and that was a phone call Gage didn't really want to make. He pulled out his phone and called, but, when it went to voice mail, he frowned, as he left a message, asking his brother to call him, then put away his phone.

Seeing that Skylar was at the tail end of a lineup that he couldn't help any faster, he headed down to the river. He felt so much better. Just as he reached the water, the detective called him.

"Your uncle's body can be released now."

"Perfect. Thanks."

Now he had to make arrangements for Jonesy's body. Gage still didn't understand anything about the tarot card business that his uncle had been so focused on. But, after what Gage had seen in the wee morning hours at the cemetery, he wasn't even sure that mattered anymore. Slowly he drifted back toward the store. Seeing just a couple people were left, he stepped inside and went to the back room and made coffee.

When it was done, he grabbed two cups of coffee. He came back out, sipping his brew, feeling more at home in her store than he had felt in his own company this whole last year. When the last person left, he smiled at her and handed her a cup. "Well, the merger went through."

"That's wonderful. Congratulations."

"And my uncle's body has been released."

"Even more wonderful," she said, with a gentle smile. Then she turned and stopped. "Wait. I forgot to tell you something. Well, I mentioned part of it, but life has been crazy since."

He faced her. "Now what?"

"Somebody put the tarot cards in my store," she whispered. "I haven't had a chance to check my emails to see if anybody answered my questions about them."

He stared at her. "The tarot cards my uncle was after?"

She nodded. "I've got them hidden right now."

"Is it possible?" he asked.

She shook her head. "I don't know. I'm wondering …" She hesitated. "I'm wondering if your uncle may have found them and then worried about his life and hid them in my shop."

"But … that would mean he knew he was in danger."

"Then you kind of knew that anyway, didn't you?"

"Well, I knew he was here, and I knew he was worried about something," Gage noted, "but I didn't know what."

"But who would be after him? What were the tarot cards for?"

"His collection," he said instantly. "I don't know that he actually believed any of rumors surrounding it, but the deck was for his collection."

"And other than that?"

"I don't know." Gage frowned. "That's not something I have the slightest idea what to do about."

She nodded. "I know, just from touching them, that they're very high energy. I just don't know whether they're dangerous or not. Somebody ..." She hesitated and then continued. "I'm also not necessarily sure that Jonesy wasn't murdered."

He grimaced, shaking his head. "There was no sign of injury to his body. The detective said it was his heart."

She nodded. "And I get that. I really do. I'm just not sure what we're supposed to do with that."

"I don't understand."

She shrugged. "He wasn't at the graveyard last night."

"And did you expect him to be?"

"I wondered if he would be," she noted. "I just wasn't sure."

"And he wasn't. So what does that mean?"

"Maybe nothing," she admitted. "I just know that it's something I still don't understand and that it troubles me."

"*Okay.*" He raised both hands. "When you figure it out, do you want to clue me in?"

She burst out laughing. "Of course I will. I'm just not sure that I'll have all the answers."

He stared at her and sighed. "It would make sense, him hiding both that bone and that tarot deck here, as we have video proof that he was here. Did you say he was at your shop at the end of the day?"

"The detective did, but I remembered him, after seeing his photo." She nodded. "So there is a good chance Jonesy may have been killed not long afterward. And then I had a break-in at my place after Jonesy's body was found."

"And the intruder didn't find the cards, did they?"

She shook her head. "No, they didn't, but, at that point, I didn't even know the deck was here. I also don't know who my intruder was."

"And it had to have been someone who knew Jonesy had been here."

"If somebody was following him, they would have known."

"What are the tarot cards worth?" he asked.

She guessed at what they might sell for, and Gage's expression reflected his surprise. "One-half-million dollars?"

She nodded. "Thereabouts. So, yes, anybody who's looking for money could be a suspect—or someone who is after them for what they can supposedly do."

"Which is what?"

"To live again," she shared, with a doubtful shrug. "The rumors talk about them being used to forecast several murders. Then maybe were used in rituals to bring the same people back to life again. I don't know the true story. I think it's all just legend, but given what I do …"

"Perhaps a legend, but legend matters," Gage stated. "I don't know who else Jonesy might have spoken to. No telling who he might have had something to do with."

"I know," she agreed.

"It's likely just a matter of whether he triggered somebody here in town with his questions."

"And that could very well be, and maybe this person hasn't been back because of the energy of the store."

He looked at her sharply, and she shrugged. "I was unsettled for a couple days, and I was doing constant cleansing, but obviously I wasn't necessarily doing a good enough job since that intruder got in. But, since the full moon, it's hard to walk into my store if you're full of negatively."

"More for me to learn," he muttered, in an almost absentminded way.

She smiled. "You'll get there."

He realized for the first time in a long time that he probably would get there. And, best of all, Skylar would be with him, by his side. "First, we have to figure out what's going on with these cards."

"With your uncle's death, what happens to all his property?"

"I didn't want anything to do with his collection, so I think that goes to my brother," he guessed, "but honestly, I haven't spoken to my lawyer about that."

"Is it the same lawyer for you and Jonesy?"

He nodded. "It is." He pulled out his phone. "Hey, Charlie. I've been allowed to get my uncle's body back, so I'll be making arrangements. Have you pulled out the will yet?"

"I haven't actually. I need to do a read-through and then bring in you and your brother."

"Okay," Gage said. "Is anybody else in his will?"

"I think a few bequests were made, but I'm not sure there's very much. The bulk of the estate goes to you and your brother. But Jonesy did make a few changes recently. And I have that letter here for you. I can put it into an email for you."

"Sure. Thanks for that. At least Terrence shouldn't mind the actual sale of the company then, as he still gains through Jonesy's estate."

"As it turns out, your uncle didn't have that much at the end of the day. Outside of his collection."

"What do you mean, he didn't have that much?"

"He spent a lot of money enhancing his collection,"

Charlie explained, "and he paid some pretty steep prices."

"Right, so then maybe there isn't all that much to split?"

"Not once the charities get theirs," Charlie noted, "and Jonesy made it very clear that the charities get theirs first."

"Well, it's not as if my brother and I needed the money anyway."

"No, but, in this case, maybe your brother needed it more."

"Maybe, but he'll still be fine."

"I would think so." With that he ended the call.

Gage grimaced, as he turned to Skylar. "I just need some air, but I'll be back soon, okay?" She nodded, and he wandered around outside for a while, feeling just a little unsettled. As he looked around, he saw a woman he thought he recognized. He blinked, and she was gone. He frowned. Feeling oddly out of sorts, he called his brother again.

"Hey," his brother answered.

"There you are," Gage said. "I was expecting you to call me back."

"Whatever. I just now talked to the lawyer. Charlie told me the deal went through."

"Yes, it did," Gage replied, buoyed by the news all over again.

"Well, good for you."

"Hey, you're getting five million plus your money back. That's nothing to sneeze at."

"That's fine, but I'm sending Mom over to you from now on. I can't afford to help her out."

"Won't do any good," Gage noted. "I'm cutting her loose too."

His brother was silent for a moment. "Seriously?"

"Yep, seriously, and I told her that before I left to come

here."

"Why?"

"Because she has been bleeding me for money for far too long, and I'm tired of it. I don't owe her anything," he murmured. "I'll set her up with a one-time fixed amount that I think is fair to cover her life expectancy, and that's it. One and done. If she invests it wisely and lives off the interest, she should be just fine. She's gotta learn to budget. I don't want her hounding me for handouts constantly. I don't want to speak to her or to deal with her afterward."

There was a shocked silence for a few moments, then his brother laughed. "I bet that was a surprise to her."

"I don't think *surprise* is quite the word. She was angry, horrified, furious, all of the above."

"Of course she was. You've been looking after her for a long time."

"For the longest time, I convinced myself that we equally supported her, but you're right. It's been me all along. Well, maybe it's your turn now."

"Nope, not happening," Terrence argued. "Not on the money I'm getting from the company. I don't have that much left."

"You'll have lots left. Besides, she needs to be a little smarter with her money. It's past time for her to be the responsible adult," Gage explained. "It's not as if she's destitute or anything."

"No, but somehow she sure always seems to be broke."

"That's just how she makes you feel to get money out of you," Gage noted. "I'm not playing that guilt game anymore."

"Well, do me a favor and make sure she has enough to keep herself alive and well."

Gage huffed, then replied, "I will but not at a level where she'll get designer suits for every day of the week."

At that, his brother laughed. "Nope, and I agree with you. She blows money like crazy, and it's high time for her to stop." He spoke firmly, then he hung up, leaving Gage thinking his brother should take his own advice.

Only a few moments later the email arrived from Charlie, with his uncle's letter attached. Gage walked back to his hotel room, where he sat down and read it. Emotions roiled within as he read his uncle's last words. They were caring and so *Jonesy* that it brought a heaviness to Gage's chest and tears to his eyes. But one line in particular would cause all kinds of trouble. He so didn't want that conversation when his brother found out.

CHAPTER 17

IN THE WEE hours of the morning Skylar woke with
something clamoring inside her brain. She bolted upright
and looked around in confusion. She'd broken yet another
rule. She'd fallen asleep in someone else's bed. She couldn't
even remember the last time she'd done so. She looked down
to see Gage, snoring gently at her side. And, of course, that
explained it. The lovemaking had been hot and furious,
seemingly never-ending. She slipped out of bed and quickly
dressed, the clamor inside her brain getting ever louder by
the minute.

As she bolted for the door, she heard Gage calling out,
"What's the matter?"

She turned to look at him. "Something's wrong at the
store." Then she slammed the door shut behind her and took
off running. She heard him calling out for her to wait, but
there was no time. She raced down the stairs, out the front
door of the hotel, into the darkness before the dawn, and
onto the street. Some celebration was still going on down at
the other end, yet she heard her shop-specific noise through
the chaos in her mind. It wouldn't be so bad except she knew
the noise of the celebration also served as a hell of a cover for
any noise and chaos going on in her store.

She raced to her store to find the front window broken,
and, of course, the sirens of her alarm system were going off.

Swearing, she quickly unlocked the door, snuck inside, and moved silently to the back room. Nobody was in the store; she would have been able to see them. At least she would have thought so, but, with all the ghosts clamoring around and filling up the space, she immediately waved her arms to get rid of their energy, so she could see what the hell was happening.

She noted grimly that the container of tarot cards was again tossed on the floor, so possibly her first intruder was the same one who broke in this time too.

She slipped to the back door, but it was open, wide open, as if intentionally left that way to encourage anybody else to come in and to help themselves. She hated that mentality. But she found nothing here, no sign of anybody—at least she didn't think so.

Soon she heard Gage calling out, "Skylar, where are you?"

She raced to the front. "I'm here," she said, as she flicked on the lights.

"What happened?" he asked.

She pointed to the window and then at the tarot cards scattered about.

He leaned in and whispered to her, "Shit. You need to get rid of that set."

"Well, that would be nice, but I need a place to do so." She motioned toward the back. "He went out the back way again and left the door wide open."

"You think it's the same intruder?"

She shrugged. "I would think so, with the tarot card rack turned over both times. Regardless, I'm getting damn tired of this."

"So am I," said a man with a harsh voice. "Don't even

try to look at me. Turn toward the storefront and get your hands up."

They looked at each other, then slowly faced the front of the store, refusing to raise their hands.

The guy had masked his voice somehow, maybe with something in his mouth, making it hard to distinguish his true voice. "Now, where are the tarot cards?"

"All over the floor, as you can plainly see."

"Stupid bitch, don't give me that shit."

"Why not? It's true," Skylar said, perturbed.

"You know what deck I'm talking about. Everybody is looking for them."

"All I know is a guy was in the store asking about them, and he turned up dead later."

A moment of shocked silence came. "He didn't buy them off you?"

"Hell no," she snapped. "If I had had them, I would have sold them in a hot minute. Do you think I want to sit here and run this store for the rest of my life?" She managed to get enough of a caustic tone into her voice to make it believable.

Muffled noises came from behind them. "Don't turn around. I mean it. I don't have a problem shooting either one of you."

And then there was silence.

"What do you want the tarot cards for anyway?" she called out. When no answer came, she shifted ever-so-slightly.

Gage immediately grabbed her hand. "Don't."

She glared at him and then turned around, noting absolutely no energy, other than the ghosts standing back within the protective boundary she'd given them. "He's gone."

Gage turned, looked at her, and then tore out the back of the store, running flat-out.

Surprised that she hadn't even thought to do the same, she tore out after Gage but found no sign of anybody. At the corner he looked left to right, and then he booked it right, so deciding that the smarter move was to split up, she headed left. She didn't know what she was even looking for. No sign of anybody out here, and it was pitch-black.

As she turned and headed back toward the main streets, the streetlights shone a welcoming warmth. Yet also an eerie light beamed because this part of town—especially in the middle of the night—was not exactly encouraging. New Orleans hosted an awful lot of nightlife, but also an awful lot of people were out at night, who weren't there for good reasons.

Finally she reached her block and circled around her shop, not seeing Gage anywhere yet, coming to the front of the store again. Glass was all over the sidewalk. She groaned as she thought about how she was supposed to shore up that broken window. It wasn't a massive hole, but it was enough that she would struggle to find a way to keep anybody out. She stepped in through the front again, then went and closed and locked the back door. She rummaged around in the back, looking for something she could use to cover up the hole in the window.

Finding a piece of plywood, she pulled it to the front and tacked it in place. As a deterrent it wasn't much. It would only deter those who had no intention of breaking in anyway, maybe kids or something. But any real intruder wouldn't give a shit. And that was the story of her life. Nobody understood what she did, why she did it, or how she did it. So, therefore, she was just as susceptible to the nuances of society as anybody else.

As she stood here, staring at the window, wondering how the hell she would clean up all the glass inside and out without cutting herself, she realized that it was probably just as well that they—good guys or bad—didn't know what she did. Nobody would understand. Nobody would like that she could talk to the dead. Just imagine all the people who would think she might uncover their secrets. The truth is, in all the times that she had worked with ghosts, she hadn't found anybody who had anything to offer to help solve their own deaths.

In many cases the crimes were simple, like taking a bullet. Yet the ghosts of the dead had no clue who had killed them, holding no memories of the people involved or no emotions about it anymore. Even the angriest ghosts that she'd seen couldn't tell her who had killed them, not to mention how or why. And Gage's friend Linden? Another angry ghost, Linden had blamed Gage, but Linden couldn't really see how his own death had come about, not until he crossed over. Then he would see that he had been driving.

Of course he was trying to say that Gage was driving. In which case Gage himself should have been the one who was killed. Gage had shown her a picture of the vehicle after the accident and how absolutely destroyed the driver's side was. As proof, it went a long way toward making the ghost sound like a young, immature person, still not capable of accepting responsibility for his own actions. And unfortunately she saw too much of that in all ages of people, among the living and the dead.

She walked over to where she kept the broom and dustpan, and, leaving the front door open, she started with the street outside and quickly swept up as much glass as she could. She dumped it into a garbage can, then stepped inside and worked on cleaning off the window ledge, sending everything to the floor.

Thankfully not too much glass fell on the table of curios adjacent to the window. She quickly removed everything, took off the tablecloth that she used to hide the open space underneath, dumped it into the trash can, then wrapped it up to go into the laundry. She moved aside the table and started sweeping up inside and was lost in thought when Gage returned, his voice disrupting her.

"Hey, I can help you with that," he offered, reaching for the broom.

She shook her head. "I'm almost done. Any sign of him?"

He shook his head. "No. And I don't suppose you want to call the police and add their negative energy to your shop, right?"

"Not now, not if we don't have to."

"So we put it off a bit," he agreed, but something was hard about the look on his face.

"I'm okay, you know," she said, trying for reassurance.

"*You're* okay, and that's only because you weren't here. And you bolted out of that hotel room without me," he stated, his hands on his hips and a glare on his face.

She shrugged. "I'm used to being alone, to acting alone. I'm used to having only myself to depend on," she explained. "It's not as if I could ask Thomas to help."

He glared around at the room. "Can the ghosts do nothing?"

She snorted. "They can talk, and they can see some things, but I have yet to find one who can do anything other than that."

"It's too bad Thomas can't pick up a baseball bat and whack your intruder. And I get that he can't," Gage said in frustration, still glaring at her. "It just would be nice if, with all this nastiness going on here, somebody human could do something to help."

"Isn't that your job?" Elena asked a little delicately.

He turned and glared at her too.

At that, Skylar started to chuckle. "Well, I'm really glad to see you crossed over on another area of skill," she murmured.

He frowned at her. "What are you talking about? I missed the intruder," he snapped, the rage obviously still pouring off him.

"And maybe that's a good thing," she agreed. "You probably would have pounded him into the ground."

He nodded immediately. "You're damn right I would have, and he'd have been lucky if he got off that easily."

Thomas nodded emphatically on the other side of Gage.

She smiled. "Even Thomas is agreeing with you."

He looked over, glared at Thomas, and added, "Right, that's what we should be doing to these guys."

Thomas immediately gave a firm nod.

"So, you have no trouble seeing Thomas right now, *huh?*"

Gage stared at her, then at Thomas. "I told you before that I could see him. But to hear him…"

"Well, you told me before that you saw a ghostly apparition, like a wispy cloudy kind of thing." She motioned beside him with her hand.

He nodded. He turned in the direction she pointed, and his eyes opened wide. He took a step back, his hand going to his chest. "Jesus Christ. That is no wispy thing any longer."

"Yeah, Gage meet Thomas. Thomas meet Gage."

Thomas reached up, cocked his hat to one side, and said, "A pleasure."

Gage shook his head at her and slowly let out his breath. "You're right. How the hell did that happen?"

"Necessity and rage," she noted in a calm manner. "What about Elena?"

He pivoted to look at the buxom lady beside him. "Yes, I can see her too."

Skylar laughed. "You can talk to them and can hear them too."

"Oh my God, I can," Gage realized.

Elena dimpled in delight. "Somebody else to talk to," she murmured. "Thomas, isn't this wonderful?"

Gage frowned at Thomas. "So you two can see each other?"

"We can," Thomas confirmed, "but we've been here longer."

"Does that mean ghosts develop skills over time too?"

Thomas laughed. "Well, I couldn't talk to Skylar here in the beginning, and now I can. I can also see other people. I can wander freely around the store. I can follow Skylar out of the store too. I can see when people are stealing from her." Thomas pointed a finger at Gage. "See? There are bits and pieces that we can do, and we're working on it. I could always sense that Elena was here, but I couldn't actually see her form. Somewhere over the last couple years it changed, and I could." Turning to look at Skylar in a contemplative manner, he added, "It must be Skylar's energy augmenting ours."

Skylar laughed. "To a certain extent. Thomas, can you also see Jackie?"

He smiled and looked down at the little boy, who sat at his feet.

Gage followed Thomas's line of sight and sucked in his breath again. "Good God." And then he slowly turned and looked around in the store. "How on earth," he whispered, "can all of you fit into this space?" As he watched, they all slipped in front, over, and through each other. "Good Lord," he murmured, completely stunned.

Skylar laughed and laughed. "Well, I'm really happy for you. Welcome to my world."

He looked at her with a shocked gaze and nodded. "Is this what you always see? My God."

"Right, it's a busy world, and is there any wonder I like the peace and quiet of living alone?"

He shook his head. "It's just amazing."

"Well, the energy here is attracting the ghosts," she repeated. "What I can best figure out to date is that, anywhere within a couple blocks, are ghosts tied to various spots—people who have died in accidents out on the street, one guy knifed on a sidewalk. Mary over there actually had a heart attack in the little tea shop that used to be a couple storefronts away, but they all seem to collect at my store."

Gage nodded. "Well, it's no wonder. They actually have a ..." He stopped. "I guess it's the wrong word, but I'm trying to say they have a *society* unto themselves. You know that in business we would say, *Find your own tribe*. And it looks like that's what they've done as well. They found their own tribe, ... just a ghostly one."

Thomas spoke up in an accepting voice. "Of course because we are ghosts, but Skylar is part of our tribe too. She isn't a ghost, but she is what keeps us all anchored here."

"So that answers that question." Gage stood, his hands

on his hips, staring at her. "I guess I'm moving here."

She looked at him and nodded. "Well, you mentioned earlier about making New Orleans your home."

He nodded. "But I mean, all these ghosts, they are part of your family, aren't they?"

At that, Thomas faced Skylar. Elena turned and stared; even little Jackie lifted his head to look at Skylar.

They all waited expectantly, as she smiled and replied to Gage. "Exactly. I'm glad you understand."

And, with that, all the ghosts beamed.

Gage, with his new ghost sight, gazed around the room at Skylar's tribe. He shook his head in awe. "That is absolutely stunning. I get it," he said. "I really get it."

And, for the first time since waking up with that feeling of panic and knowing something was wrong in her building and flying out Gage's hotel room door, Skylar relaxed.

"YOU KNOW SOMETHING? I think I finally found *my* tribe," Gage murmured.

Skylar looked up at him, with a shy smile.

He tucked her closer, then leaned over and kissed her gently on the lips.

She caught sight of her ghosts turning around, giving them some privacy. "And I thought that big old business was your tribe."

"You know what? It *was* my tribe back then, when I was driving and pushing to make something of myself, to be somebody," he admitted. "I realize now that the years of feeling incomplete, even as a young child, without a mother's affection or a father's pride, it makes you work harder to fulfill that need for respect and approval from someone. And

I did all that. I built a big business, and now I've successfully sold it." He paused, felt no stress over this huge change he had just made in his life. "And that's just not who I am anymore. My accident changed me."

"It did," she agreed, with a gentle smile. "And I think for the better."

He looked at her, cocked an eyebrow, and asked, "Are you saying you wouldn't like me, the old me?"

"I don't think the old you would have stepped foot in my store," she noted, with a trill of laughter.

He winced. "You're probably right." He studied her shop. "Back then, I would have said it was all a sham, and I wouldn't have understood any of the nuances."

"It's a whole other world out there," she stated gently, "and most of the *normal* world, the society that you lived in, wouldn't have seen it."

"That's the thing," he replied. "The part that just blows me away is that 99 percent of the world is asleep to this. It's like finding a magical, mythical world right under your nose, and realizing that other people knew about it, and they didn't tell you."

"Well, I didn't know about you then," she noted, "but you're right. I wouldn't have told you either."

He stared at her with a frown, and she laughed. A grin peeked out as he acknowledged her point. "And with good reason." He nodded.

She added, "And, if you had ventured in my store, before your accident, I probably would have tossed you right on your ear, due to all the bad energy."

"Probably."

"It's a hard thing for some people to acknowledge that some things have been under their nose the whole time that they didn't see because they simply weren't willing."

"Is it that easy?" he asked, pondering her words. "Is it because I wasn't willing to see it, or was it because I didn't yet have the ability?"

"Well, I'm sure Stefan and Maddy could give you answers about that," she stated. "What I understand is that, in many cases, those two would say everybody has some ability, but, for whatever reason, we block it. You hear stories about children, who talk about coming back reincarnated, and, if you listen while they're young, they will tell you where they came from. And some cases obviously are much more defined than others. Some have verifiable facts that you can go back and take a look at," she noted. "And, for others, it's a matter of going on blind faith, which, in your case, you don't have much of."

"No, but I'm getting there because I believe in you." He knew that pleased her because she beamed at him. He smiled and added, "I mean it. You've opened my eyes to something I had no idea existed."

She shook her head. "I didn't open your eyes," she argued. "That was you. Or maybe we should blame Maddy and Stefan for it."

He looked at her, remembering something. "You know what? That just might be the reason why, … why Maddy and Stefan said something about leaving some energy behind to keep the healing flowing and to keep me alive or to stay connected to them or some such thing," he muttered, with a wave of his hand. "It was to counter the dark energy, they said. And they had wondered if they had brought something else into my system. I don't remember their exact words. But I was scared at first. Now I think it was my own dark energy, my pre-accident mentality. If so, I'm glad to be rid of that."

"And it could be just that simple," she agreed. "Still, the fact that you were actually helped by them is an absolute miracle in itself."

"And why would that have happened?" he muttered.

"I don't know, but I guess you owe your brother thanks for that."

He smiled. "Maybe I do at that. I'll have to talk to him about it some more."

"And here I thought you were considering whether he might have had ulterior motives, hoping that you didn't live."

"And maybe he did, but you know what? I just don't understand him anymore," he admitted quietly. "Right now, everything in that whole side of my family life is beyond confusing."

"I get it." She nodded. "I don't think anything is quite so puzzling as family, and that's on a good day."

He smiled, looked around, and asked, "So, can we finish locking up and go back to bed?"

She checked her watch and nodded. "I might be able to catch a few more hours before the shop opens."

He nodded. "Upstairs or back to my place?"

"Upstairs. It's closer, and, if I can grab a couple hours of sleep, I really need to." And, with that, she locked the front door and then stopped. "I don't even know why I bother to lock up, since it seems like these guys can get in without any trouble. I'm not too sure how or why, but maybe it's not that difficult to be a thief," she noted. "I mean, this time they broke a window, so it's not a crime that required any particular skill."

He nodded.

"And, like last time, I actually wondered if I'd forgotten

to lock and set the alarm," she murmured.

He stared at her, and his gaze narrowed. "I know. I know," she admitted, "but I was a little tired."

She used that word rather than saying *rattled* or anything else, he figured, trying to think back to when it had happened and realizing that he hadn't known her well enough the first time someone broke in for her to tell him more.

He nodded. "Well, let's hope it doesn't happen again."

Thomas spoke up. "Perhaps we can try to scare the next intruder."

Skylar and Gage shared a glance, not sure how to address that. "Only if you can trip him or something, like an accident, not like a ghostly visitation," Skylar suggested.

Thomas gave it a thought and nodded. "Good night."

Gage led the way out of the store, and, once it was secured under his watchful eye, they headed to her apartment upstairs.

As they got closer, Skylar waved at Elena and said, "We're heading to bed. It's been an eventful night."

"I knew you'd sort it all out."

Gage just stared at her in shock, and, when they got to Skylar's bedroom, he whispered, "Dear God, she's gorgeous."

Skylar's laughter peeled out and surrounded the room, as he flushed.

"I get how you are used to seeing Elena," Gage began, "but you don't really realize it until you see her, as she just sits there and shimmers."

"*Shimmers* is a good word for it," she agreed, with a smile. "And don't worry. I don't take it personally."

"Good," he replied, "because I'd rather have flesh and blood any day."

He joined her on her bed, grabbed her in his arms, and

pulled her close. Only then did he note she was lying on top of the covers, fully dressed. He frowned. "Are you sure you don't want to get undressed and actually get some quality sleep?"

"No, that's not even close to possible tonight—this morning." She yawned. "If I can just catch a few hours, I'll be grateful." And, with that, she closed her eyes.

He wrapped her up, pulled her closer, and just hung on, before falling asleep himself. His last thought as he went under was how different his world had become. Now if he could only get to the point where he could help her with some of her work and could make things easier on her, then he would be a happy man.

And that reminded him of something else he needed his lawyer to do. He'd take care of it first thing when he woke up—in just a couple hours.

CHAPTER 18

LATER THAT SAME morning Skylar stood in front of the broken window, contemplating it, with Gage at her side.

"Insurance should cover this," he noted.

"Yeah, it sure will, and I'll pay the deductible, and they'll probably jack up my premiums for like three years for having made a claim."

He muttered at her side, "Probably longer."

"Right, so I don't know. Maybe I can just get a quote from somebody I know around the corner, who does glass."

"Why don't you give me his name and number, and I'll go talk to him?"

She looked at him, contemplated the idea, and then nodded. "Sure, why not?" She told him about the little glass store on one of the back streets. Gage took off, as if on a mission, and she opened up her store. The first couple customers who came in exclaimed over the broken window.

She just smiled and said, "It's all right. It's all being handled. New glass will be in shortly."

"Oh, good." They bustled about, looking at her wares.

Skylar should clean the energy again. Grabbing the broom, she opened up the front door to let some of the brighter energy in, and she did her best to smooth it all out. Yet already she felt an odd sense to it. The women obviously felt it too, and they left without buying anything. And that was enough of that.

The only reason she kept the business was so she could keep herself going in terms of paying the bills. As long as the money flowed, then she was good. When the money didn't flow well, then things got ugly, and she'd have to find another way to make a living. She didn't want to return to reading palms or to doing online psychic readings. She could, and she had when times were tough, but that should be the least of her worries right now.

As soon as she had the broom, she cleaned out the front and then moved to the back, opened up the rear door, and started smoothing the energy out that way too. A few people came in, wandered around, then left again. By the time she finished in the back, she noted still more of the negative energy in the front. Groaning, she swept out more and more and more. By the time Gage came back, she was flustered.

He looked at her, frowned, and asked, "Problems?"

She just shrugged and smiled at the workman at his side.

"I sure hope you can give me a reasonable quote for this," Gage told him.

The man looked at the window and shook his head. "This used to be a nice town."

"Yeah." She grinned. "When was that?"

He rolled his eyes. "Before the tourists."

She wouldn't say anything to that because they all needed the tourists.

He quickly measured the window and nodded to both of them. "I'll send you a quote later today."

"You can send a text, if you like," she suggested, giving him her contact information.

"Good enough." And he took off.

Gage added, "He'll see if he can patch this up later today

as well. Meanwhile, I'll go get some food. Do you want anything in particular?"

"Yes, I want it all."

He laughed. "Good thing I've got lots of money, and I can feed you, *huh*?"

She immediately frowned.

He frowned right back, wagging a finger under her nose. "Oh no you don't. Don't you even start with me."

She glared at him. "I can pay my own way."

"No, stop it. I have so much money that it's ridiculous. And that was before the stupid sale went through."

She shook her head. "I thought you needed it in order to live the life you wanted."

"And I was a fool," he stated shortly. "Believe me. I've had a few paradigm shifts and realizations since this all started. It definitely won't break me to feed you, and, if you'll be difficult about this," he stated, "I'll just show up with food and not even talk to you about it."

She frowned, not liking the tone in his voice. Then she realized that getting upset was mostly due to her lack of sleep and the added irritation over whatever was happening in her space. Plus, she needed time to adjust to this new life of hers, now that Gage was in it. "Fine," she said, with a wave of her hand. "Just go get food. Maybe it'll make me less cranky."

He smiled. "And, for the record, this is the first time I've really heard that term apply."

She lifted the broom in a half-threatening manner, but he laughed and took off. She smiled, as she watched him disappear down the block.

She turned around and headed toward the counter, thinking she'd sit until the next tourists came in. Hearing the back door, she walked to the rear of the store and came face-to-face with a man dressed all in black, though that wasn't the issue.

The snub-nosed revolver in his hand was.

He looked at her, smiled. "There you are."

"Who are you?" she asked, backing up slowly.

"Don't move," he snapped, waving the revolver around. "Now that your lover boy is gone, you and I will have a talk."

"Yeah?" She was already judging the distance to the front door, wondering if she could dodge the bullet, by running through the store around the shelving.

Thomas whispered in her mind, *Don't be foolish. I'll go alert Gage.*

"Don't even think about it," he ordered. "You can't out-run a bullet."

She studied the gun in front of her, wondering just what her options actually were. Energy maybe, but she'd never used it to hurt anyone. "What do you want?" she asked, furious that her gunman had waited for Gage to disappear, and what if Thomas didn't find Gage soon enough? They wouldn't be back for quite a while now.

"I want the tarot cards."

She raised her eyebrows. "Why is everybody after the tarot cards?" she asked, infuriated.

"Because they're worth a lot of money," he replied.

"Is that the only reason?" she asked, turning her head to look at him. Because, if it was only about money, she'd be tempted to give the deck to him.

He frowned. "Is there any other reason?"

"There are rumors about them being magical. Or evil, rather," she corrected herself, with a casual hand motion. And, with that simple motion, she tried to move some of the energy around her. But she found that it wasn't very open to being moved, realizing that this was the source of the energy she had been trying to clear out of the store. She glared at him now, more pissed than ever because he was responsible for her losing what looked to be a full day's worth of sales.

"I don't believe in that wacky woo-woo stuff," he declared. "I know somebody who spent way-too-much money on all that crap, blowing it just as fast as he could get his hands on it."

At that, she froze. "That's just your opinion. Some collectors are pretty crazy when it comes to whatever they're collecting."

"Crazy obsessed," he added, "he blew so much money."

"And I get the impression that you feel like that money was yours."

"Well, some of it was coming to me," he confirmed. "And it's not even so much that I care, but it's a means to an end."

She frowned at that, not liking the suspicions in her mind. "Money should always be a means to an end," she stated. "Like for housing, food, clothing. Money only becomes a problem when you start clinging to it, worrying about not having enough. Hoarding money is always associated with fear."

She was just warming up to a subject she hadn't really had a chance to talk to Gage about because he had so much of the damn stuff. "It's really sad the way the world is right now," she muttered. "Just so many things out there in life could be done so much better, yet everybody is hung up on greed instead."

"Well, it's obvious that you don't have any money," he declared. "From the looks of this store, you're pretty poverty-stricken yourself."

She stiffened and glared at him. "There's nothing wrong with my store," she snapped, "just because it's not up to whatever Taj Mahal level you seem to think it should be." She glared. "It's my livelihood."

"Yeah, little trinkets and scummy shit," he sneered. "You're just capitalizing off New Orleans."

"Everybody has an opinion." She refused to get dragged into an argument with a gunman over what she sold in her shop. It was hard enough to find things that the tourists wanted to buy without having to deal with criticism from an asshole like this. "And I don't have your damn tarot cards. Some guy came in here a few days ago and looked for them. He asked me about them too. I'll tell you the same thing I told him. I don't know anything about it."

"But you do, don't you?"

She frowned. "What do you mean?"

"Well, you know something about them."

"Sure, I know that they existed. I don't know if they still do, and, for all I know, the old man was chasing a dream, and it had nothing to do with anything," she told him.

"As far as I'm concerned, he found them, and he bought them."

"Then why the hell would I have them?" she asked.

"They're worth one-half-million dollars," he stated, stepping forward and glaring at her.

She feigned shock, her jaw dropping. "Good God. Half a million dollars and you think I sold them to him?"

He took a step back and looked a little confused.

"If I had that kind of money," she huffed, "do you think I'd still be here?"

He looked around the shop, as if to assess the sense of

her words and then nodded slowly. "Then I need to know who has them."

"I don't know," she cried out. "And if you're the asshole who broke my window earlier, thanks a lot. It'll cost me a pretty penny to get it fixed," she muttered.

"Why? Don't you even have insurance?" he sneered.

"Sure, and then I have to pay the deductible, and then they'll raise my insurance premium for God-only-knows how long."

He frowned at that, shrugged, and quipped, "Jeez, you'll just have to sell a little more of this shit then, won't you?"

"That would be nice if it wasn't for people like you in here stopping me."

"Look at the store." He pointed the gun around behind her. "Nobody is in here."

Well, that was mostly because she was putting up a blind, telling people to stay away, which she would find damn hard to clear after this, and that was just making her mad all over again.

Stefan spoke in her mind. *I'm sending Thomas back to you, while I locate Gage.* Then he disappeared from her mind.

"Just take off," she snapped. "I don't have a clue who or where or what has those stupid cards. I wish I did know, since I could sure use a half-million dollars myself."

"Well, that's too bad because they're mine," he snapped. "Look around town and find out who has them. Last I heard, the collector was coming in here to buy them."

She stiffened again at the mention of Jonesy. "If you're talking about that old guy who came in here, he's dead," she stated flatly. "As far as I know, somebody killed him in the graveyard for that deck."

He sucked in his breath.

"What?" she shrugged. "Haven't you heard the latest rumors?"

"No," he said, frowning. "At least not that kind of rumor."

"I don't know if it's real or not," she added. "I wouldn't be at all surprised though. This place is a mess."

"What do you mean, this place is a mess?"

"New Orleans," she said. "Everybody's out to make a buck, so who the hell knows if anybody is telling the truth about that tarot deck?"

He waved the gun around, obviously agitated by her theory. "You have one day, and that's it. One day to find out the truth and then I'll be back, and you better have it."

"And if I don't?"

He gave her a smile, and it was not a smile she ever wanted to see again because it literally made her blood freeze.

"I'll be back, so have them or else." And, with that, he raced out, closing the door behind him.

She tried to open the door and fumbled with the lock, and, by the time she got it open and raced outside, he was gone. She stood here trembling for a long moment. "Thomas, can you go out and find him?"

"I've already looked," he noted quietly from behind her. "I can't go as far as he can."

"No, of course not," she agreed. She bowed her head for a long moment and then stepped back into the store. "Stefan, do you know how to protect my store?"

Is that what you want to protect? came his calm voice.

"This is the only livelihood I have," she murmured. "It would be nice not to lose it."

There was a moment of silence. *We can put up an energy guard, if that would help. But you know he'll find you some-*

where else.

"You heard him?"

No, I only heard you processing his screaming in your mind, but I'm not sure. It seemed like that was mostly rage.

"Yes," she said, with a broken laugh, "part of it definitely was rage."

And why?

She shook her head. "You don't have time to deal with people like me."

I will always have time to deal with people like you, he stated in that same calm manner of his.

"Fine." And she told him what had just happened.

Tarot cards worth a ton of money?

"Yes, do you know any collectors who would pay for them?"

Yes, I probably do, if only to get them taken off the streets.

"Do they really have that kind of energy?"

They do, at least I've heard rumors that they do.

She hesitated.

You have them, don't you? he asked, with a note of amusement in his voice.

"Maybe, but I'm not sure whose they actually are."

Did you find them in your store?

"Yes," she admitted.

Then I would say they're yours.

"But I think they belong to Gage's family. And he knows about them."

Well, you'll have to figure that out later. In the meantime, you need to move them out of there.

"Yeah. Have you got somebody who can come and collect them?"

Do you want to donate them or do you want to sell them?

he asked calmly.

"Again, they're not mine, so it's not my decision."

He hesitated and then said, *Well, Gage is on his way back to you, so explain it to him and then let me know. We do have a way to secure them.*

With that, he disappeared from her mind. She turned to see Gage walk in with a tray of coffee and something that smelled absolutely delicious.

But, when he caught sight of her face, he frowned and asked, "What happened?"

"Yeah, I just had a visitor, probably the same guy who broke my window." She explained what happened. "It's all about those damn cards."

"Get rid of them," he muttered instantly.

"Well, I think that they probably belonged to your uncle," she whispered.

"But you don't know that," he whispered back. "You don't know anything about that. They were in your shop, so you keep them." After thinking for a moment, he added, "It seems like we just need to get rid of them." He frowned and looked around.

She stepped closer to Gage and kept her voice low. "I talked to Stefan, and he has a way of keeping them secure."

"Are they dangerous?" he asked, looking at her.

She shrugged. "According to Stefan, they are."

"Interesting," he murmured. "Then take him up on the offer."

She hesitated. "It's because of you that I haven't."

"Why is that?" He stared at her, frowning.

"Because it doesn't feel like they're mine."

He gave a wave of his hand. "Well, a lot of Jonesy's inheritance is coming my way anyway," he noted. "If nothing else, I'll say I took those as my portion of it." She hesitated still, but he shook his head. "Look. You need to get rid of those things, and, if you need permission from my family, that's your permission."

"But you only inherited half of Jonesy's estate, right?"

"Yes, but there's no proof they were my uncle's either. I'm more than happy to make the tarot card set the half that I get."

She frowned and then reluctantly picked up the phone and called Stefan. When he answered, she said, "Fine. Do you have a way to get them out of here now?"

He replied, "Yes, sit tight, and somebody will come and collect them." And he hung up.

She turned to look at Gage. "Somebody is on the way to collect them."

"Interesting. Did you ask him what he'll do with them?"

She shook her head. "I did not." She wasn't sure if she should or not.

But Stefan answered in her mind. *They'll go into a museum for safekeeping, where we keep a variety of esoteric items that are dangerous.*

She murmured to Gage, "Apparently he has some hand in protecting other dangerous items. A museum of some kind."

"Now that would be one hell of a museum to see," he murmured. "Do we get to see it at some point in time down the road?"

She nodded. "Stefan says yes."

"Good. The sooner, the better."

She nodded. "Except that this guy will still be back."

"Which just means that I'm never leaving your side, until he does."

She frowned. "He seemed to know an awful lot about Jonesy."

"Well, I'm sure that, in his enthusiasm searching for the deck, Jonesy contacted an awful lot of people."

She winced. "I'm afraid that could be true. The guy also said the cards were more of a means to an end."

"And that could just be the fact that the rumor on the street is that they are worth a lot of money."

"That actually makes sense. However, money in itself isn't an answer." She smiled, walked closer, and asked, "What did you pick up for food?"

"Anything and everything." He laughed, and he handed over the tray with coffee and some breakfast sandwiches. She immediately dug in, filling her empty stomach like an open empty cabinet in front of her. By the time she was done, she had finished his too. She stopped and stared. "Oh my God."

"No, it's fine. I'll just go get more." Then he stopped. "No, I'm not going anywhere, not until these things are collected."

"And then what?" she asked, in a teasing voice. "You can't be here all the time."

He frowned, pulled out his phone, and stepped up to the front of the counter, where she couldn't hear him quite so well. And, before she knew it, a delivery person came inside the store.

"Two breakfast sandwiches?"

"Two?" she asked, looking at the delivery guy.

He looked at the order and said, "Nope, sorry, four."

And he handed it to her and took off.

Before she turned around, Gage took the bag from her.

"It's called delivery, and we'll be doing this for a while now."

She frowned. "And you bought four for yourself?"

"No," he corrected her. "I bought two more for you. Stop always being so hungry. Fill up for once, will you?"

She grinned, grabbed one more, and ate it. And that made three total. And three was enough. She handed the last one over to him, the one still in the box.

He smiled. "Oh, would you look at that? We're finally getting you full."

"Well, I wouldn't count on it," she admitted, with a smile, "but I am feeling better."

"Good."

Just then somebody else walked into the store.

She looked up, smiled, and then it fell away. Whoever the hell this tank of a man was, he radiated power and strength on another level altogether. "Hello," she said, stepping forward, her energy guarded.

He looked at her and smiled. "Hi, Stefan sent me."

She studied him a moment and then asked, "And how do I know that for sure?"

He gave her a quick scan and then stepped out of his body in front of her. *We can talk this way, if you want.*

Jesus, you can do that at will too? She stared at him, intrigued.

"I can," he confirmed out loud, "but I understand you have some pretty fascinating skills yourself."

She nodded. "I'm Skylar. What's your name?"

"Hurricane is my nickname," he offered calmly. "My real name is Kane."

She raised her eyebrows. "I don't think I want to know why."

He gave her a flat smile. "No, you don't."

She asked, "You can whip up energy, can't you?"

"Well, that's one word for it," he said, with a wide grin. He looked over at Gage and tilted his chin up in a silent greeting. "Now, Skylar, I believe you have something for me to pick up."

She still hesitated, until Stefan spoke in her mind.

Did Hurricane arrive?

"Yeah. That's a hell of a name."

He laughed. *And he has some crazy-ass skills to go with it,* he added. *So he's the one you want. He'll protect that set of cards and take them to the museum.*

"He's not taking them to you?"

No, stuff like that goes straight to lockup. It'll be catalogued, identified, and studied to a certain extent, but never free to harm anybody again.

"Fine. I just thought they were tarot cards."

And let's hope that that's all they are. Now, do you want to go get them for him?

She looked over at Gage and asked him, "Can you stay here?"

He nodded. "As long as you're only going straight upstairs."

She nodded. "I am."

And, with Hurricane, she headed upstairs. She looked at him and quietly asked, "How long have you been close to Stefan?"

"Is anybody close to Stefan?" he asked.

"We're all close in some way," she noted, "just because of what and who we are."

He laughed. "Isn't that the truth."

"Do you have something to put these in?" He nodded and pulled out a small steel box. She frowned. "You're really serious about these being dangerous, aren't you?"

"Well, let's just say, I don't want to take a chance."

She nodded, let herself into her apartment, then opened the door wide enough for him to step in with her. She walked quickly to her bedroom, opened up the safe, and pulled out the cards. Just as he opened up the box and she dropped the deck inside, a man at the door spoke.

"Now that's what I'm talking about."

And, sure enough, there was her gunman, with the same snub-nosed revolver.

Hurricane looked at him, with an expression of boredom. "And who are you?"

"The man who'll take those cards off you."

"Yeah, you and what army?" Kane asked.

The gunman turned to him. "What are you talking about? I'm the one here with the weapon."

"Yeah? Well, I really don't care to have guns pulled on me," Hurricane told him. "And I really get pissed when people ruin my clothing with bullets."

Skylar shot Kane a sideways glance and then noted Gage climbing the stairs. She just barely saw a slight indication of his presence. She wished he wouldn't show up because that would just add to this craziness.

The gunman glared at Hurricane. "This is bullshit, you know that."

"Sure it's all bullshit, including these cards."

"Then hand them over and be done with it."

Hurricane shrugged, pulled out the cards from the box, and handed them over.

The gunman immediately pounced with glee. "Well, thank God for that."

"But this was just the means to an end," she reminded her gunman.

"Yeah, to keep somebody quiet and out of my life hopefully," he muttered.

Gage stepped up behind the gunman and asked, "Yeah, and just who would that be, Terrence?"

The gunman froze. "Shit." He turned toward Gage. "What the hell? You weren't supposed to be here. You were downstairs and out of the way."

"Did you really think attacking Skylar was something I would let go on right under my nose?"

"Why not?" He gave his brother a negligent shrug. "It's been working so far."

"Only because you had something in your mouth last time to disguise your voice. Just what the hell is this all about?" Gage asked, looking at the tarot cards in his brother's hand.

Skylar stepped forward, but immediately the gun was turned in her direction.

"Stop. No more bravado."

"I think you've got yourself in quite a pickle here, *Terrence*," Hurricane noted.

Terrence glared at him. "Not really. All you guys have to do is stay quiet and calm, and this will all be over in no time."

"Except for one thing," Gage said. "I already know who you are and that you're trying to hurt Skylar."

"No, I'm not. I don't give a shit about her. I just want these damn cards."

"And why is that again? You're willing to do armed robbery for cards? You're about to get five million dollars from the company deal."

"Sure, five million, but it could have been fifty if you hadn't sold it," he yelled, in outrage. "Besides, this isn't for me." And then he abruptly slammed his lips together, clearly wishing he hadn't said that.

Gage stared at him in shock. "Good God. Are you doing all this for Mom?"

Terrence's shoulders slumped ever-so-slightly, and then, as if realizing that he felt much more powerful with the gun in his hand, he stiffened and waved the gun around in Gage's face. "Shut up. You know something? If you were to die right now," he threatened, "I would inherit it all."

"Except for one thing," Gage said. "I already changed my will."

His brother stared at him. "What do you mean, you changed your will?"

"Skylar here inherits everything."

Terrence turned and stared at Skylar in shock, as she stared at Gage in horror.

"Why would you do that to me?" she cried out in dismay.

He looked at her, and he started to laugh. "I thought you'd be happy."

"Hell no," she replied. "I don't want that kind of responsibility, that kind of ugliness. Look at it already, with your own damn brother. Look at what this kind of greed does."

Gage nodded. "You're right," he said apologetically. "I just figured that maybe, in our new life, we wouldn't have assholes like this to deal with."

"What do you mean, *new life?*" Terrence squawked. "She's nothing like the women you go out with. What the hell do you want with her?"

"You know something? You're right about that," Gage told Terrence. "She's nothing like the women I used to go out with. Skylar's a hell of a lot better. She's real and strong and amazing."

His brother snorted and rolled his eyes. "Whatever."

"I guess now you'll pick up Mom, and I won't have to worry about giving her any lump sum payout for an allowance then, will I?"

"It's because of the stupid allowance that she conned me into this."

"Conned you?"

"She promised me that she'd never bother me again with her incessant requests for money and would leave me alone forever, if I could get this for her. She wants the half-million dollars."

"Because my one-time payout wouldn't be enough? She didn't even know how much it was."

"She figured you would cheat her on that too, so I would have to give her some of my money, but that was it. This was the last straw, and she even signed a document agreeing to it."

"You do know that anything she signs isn't worth the paper it's written on, right?"

"You don't understand. She hounds me constantly," he cried out in pain. "If it isn't a new dress, it's new bedding, new curtains, new something or other. I can't keep up with it."

"You shouldn't have to," Gage agreed, studying him. "She'll have to deal with this on her own."

"But she doesn't deal with it on her own. You walked away and told her that you were cutting her off, and now she's making my life miserable."

"How do you think life will be for you now?" Gage asked him in astonishment. "Do you really think this is going away?" And he pointed to the gun and the tarot cards in his hands.

"I just need to give them to Mom," he explained, "and then I'll forget all about this."

"And you expect me to forget about it?" Gage asked, his voice hardening.

"Or me?" Skylar added from the sidelines.

"Hey, don't forget me," Hurricane muttered. "I'm here too. You can't kill us all."

And it looked like, for a long moment, Terrence considered it; then his shoulders dropped even more.

Just then another voice, a strident female one, coming from behind Gage, rang out. "You're such a fucking loser, Terrence. You can't even get anything right."

Terrence immediately turned defensive. "Look. I tried. I'm not cut out for this kind of stuff."

"No, you're really not," Gage confirmed, his hands in the air now, as he was prodded forward. He stepped forward, looked over at Skylar, and said, "Sorry, we're about to have a family meeting that I had hoped to avoid. Family dinners at my house are a bitch."

Skylar stared at him in shock. "Don't tell me that your mother is behind all this?"

"Why not?" the woman asked, with a sneer. And in stepped a woman who Skylar had seen in her shop the other day.

"You were in my store," she noted in surprise.

"Yeah, and, God, what a nasty piece of shit that is."

Immediately Skylar stood straighter and opened her mouth, but Gage calmed her down with his touch. "Forget about it. That's just who she is."

"Wow, nice family. *Not*. At least I don't have to worry

about doing any family dinners."

"Exactly. Remember that part about starting anew?"

She nodded. "Yeah, I understand completely." Then she remembered the threatening letter that had sent Gage to her store in the first place. She turned on the woman. "You sent Gage that threatening letter, didn't you? To force him to find Jonesy and to get the damn cards—didn't you?"

She glared at the two of them. Gage's mother sniffed, as if she hadn't expected anyone to figure that out, and Terrence looked a little ashamed, but not by much.

Skylar looked over at Hurricane. "See what I mean?"

"Yep, that's part of what the cards are all about."

She frowned. "What do you mean?"

"They're storm cards. A lot of tarot cards have a specialty. This set is *storms*. Like Mother Nature. Builds up strong negative energy that brews a tempest that usually only cries out through an act of violence."

The woman glared at him. "Shut up. Unless you have somebody who's willing to buy these for big money, I don't want to hear your voice."

"I could buy them," Gage offered. "Skylar here was offered a lot of money, but we haven't settled on a price."

"She's not getting them. They're not hers," wailed his mother.

"Actually they are," Gage corrected her.

"No, no, no." Mom's wails got louder.

Terrence looked at Gage and shook his head. "Hell no, those cards are part of Uncle's estate."

"Yes, maybe they were intended to be," Gage acknowledged, "but no way to know that Jonesy actually had them. This deck was found in her shop recently, so the cards belong to her."

"No way," Terrence yelled, "that's BS."

"The other thing to remember, Terrence," Gage added, "is that you don't inherit anything from Jonesy's estate."

His brother looked at him in shock. "What do you mean, I'm not inheriting anything? Of course I am. It's being split evenly between the two of us."

"Well, it would have been originally, until you started dissing Jonesy on his collection, and then he cut you out of the collection recently, and he didn't have much else. By the time the charities are paid out first, there's not likely to be anything at all—but for the collection," he added quietly, knowing his brother would think terribly of Jonesy for doing this, but Jonesy's instruction letter had been clear. "So, if the cards are part of his estate, they become mine, and I give the deck to Skylar."

"No fucking way," his mother roared at Gage. She snatched the tarot cards from Terrence's hand. "Terrence, kill Gage," she screamed. "It's the only way we'll clean this up, and then we'll have all his money as well."

Terrence stared at her. "Jesus, Mom. Don't say that shit!"

She ripped the gun from him and replied, "He has always been a piece of crap, just like his father."

Skylar stared at them in shock. "Are you kidding me? You people will seriously commit mass murder?"

Immediately the gun turned on her. Gage's mom nodded. "You know something? We'll start with you."

"Well, you could," Hurricane admitted, "but you could also just take the cards, which are really beautiful, and sell them to me."

"Yes, yes," she readily agreed. "How much will you pay for them?"

"One-half million, *if* you take them out and let me see them in your hands."

She frowned. "For one-half-million dollars? Jesus, yes." She juggled the card box ever-so-slightly with the gun, then pulled them out, so they sat in her hand. "See? Take a look at them. Don't touch them. They're too expensive for you to touch."

"No, of course not," Hurricane agreed, as he glanced at Skylar. "We can take a look without touching, can't we?"

She nodded slowly, not sure what he was up to. Then she watched, as he reached out a gentle finger and wafted some energy toward it. But it wasn't any nice clean energy; it was dark and stormy. As she stared, Kane's energy hit the tarot cards, and the explosion came from inside the cards themselves.

The woman gasped and stepped back. "Oh my, these cards really are powerful, aren't they?"

Terrence puffed up and nodded. "I told you, Mom."

"Well, in that case, you'll pay a hell of a lot more," Gage's mom demanded of Kane.

Kane gave her a genial lazy smile. "Not so sure about that. Half a million is about right."

She hesitated and then decided, "Fine, half a million, but I want it now."

"I don't have it on me obviously," Kane noted, and he kept feeding a little bit of energy into the cards.

By now, Mom had to put the cards in her other hand, as they were getting hot and crackly.

Skylar watched, fascinated, as Kane fed more and more energy into the deck. She shook her head. "That's amazing."

Kane smiled at her. "They're pretty cool, aren't they?"

She nodded. "Can they do positive things?"

Kane shrugged. "It depends. Sometimes, if you've got a lot of anger, it can help dissipate it. Sometimes, depending on how you plan to use them," Kane added, with a little bit of emphasis, "you can up the charge."

And Skylar realized what he meant. "Ah." And she immediately sent a stream of energy into the cards.

Gage's mother shrieked, tossing them in the air. "Good God, they're hot." They dropped to the floor with a heavy *thud*. She snatched them back up, only to drop them again. She tried to put them in the pocket of her jacket, then into her purse, but they were getting hotter and hotter.

Skylar saw sparks on them now. "It would be interesting to try this with someone else." She looked up and then smiled. "Like *definitely* someone else."

"What do you mean?" Hurricane asked, curious.

She tilted her head toward the door. "Do you see somebody beside Gage?"

Everybody turned to look at Gage, and even he looked at her in surprise.

She nodded. "Yeah, your angry friend is here."

Gage frowned. "Right now?"

"Yes, because that kind of energy pulls in that kind of sympathetic energy," Skylar explained. "Rage begets rage."

"What are you talking about?" his mother cried out.

Gage replied, "Linden is here."

She stared at him. "You've lost your senses. He's dead."

But then, just like that, the tarot cards were picked up into the air and then dropped again.

She stared at Gage and asked, "Did you do that? What the hell? Did you do that?" And she stepped back, freaked out.

"I wouldn't go any farther than that," Gage suggested,

studying her intently. "That railing doesn't look like it's very secure.'

"Did you do that?" she shrieked.

Gage shook his head. "No, I've been trying to contact Linden because I know he's really upset."

"Oh, good God," Gage's mom replied, "that's the biggest load of bullshit I've ever heard." But then a form began to take shape before her. She stared at it in horror. "Is that him? Is that him?"

"Yes, I would imagine it is," Gage stated. "I'm hoping he has calmed down somewhat."

Skylar shook her head. "He's still angry. And I think the energy of the cards is making him angrier."

Gage looked at her and winced. "Anything we can do to help Linden? An awful lot of energy is flying around here."

Skylar checked his brother, who stared at Gage in shock. "Is Linden really here?" he whispered.

"Yes, he's really here," Gage confirmed.

"Not that you'll be able to see him of course," Skylar murmured.

"I don't get it. I mean, how much of this stuff is real?" Terrence kept shaking his head in denial.

"It's all real," Skylar admitted. "By the way, why did you contact Stefan and Dr. Maddy over your brother's condition, when you actually wanted him dead?"

"I didn't," he whined. "I never wanted him dead. I just wanted her to stop," he cried out in frustration, pointing at his mother. "It just seemed like every time Gage did something, she would turn on me and make my life so miserable. And I was also trying to save my brother because he is an incredible businessman. He creates things out of nothing, and I don't know how he does it. I've never been able to reproduce it, so I've always been kind of linked with him for my income."

"And yet you have more than enough coming to you out of this company sale."

"Maybe, if I knew what to do with it," he whined.

"Well, you don't," his mother snapped. "You're useless when it comes to making money. Only Gage makes money, and that just pisses me off because he won't share."

"Won't share?" Gage stared at her. "I've given you millions."

"And you have hundreds of millions," she complained, with a wave of her hand in disgust. "And I'm damn tired of it."

"Damn tired of what?" Skylar asked, as she studied the woman, seeing her energy was fragmented between anger and envy, as it came off her in little nasty spits. Just then she realized that the tarot cards were almost beelining a triangle of energy toward her. "*Uh-oh,*" she said and instinctively took a step back.

Hurricane reached out a hand and held her fast. "We'll need to protect the others."

She stared up at him and then saw Gage's friend standing there, glaring at her. She shrugged. "All that hatred and energy is right there," she said, pointing toward the mother. "If you want a target, use her. She's the one who created Gage."

Linden immediately turned his energy on Gage's mother. His mom couldn't see Linden, but Linden could see Gage's mom. And this combustion was about to converge.

Skylar looked at Hurricane. "Please tell me that we won't level the building."

"No, we shouldn't," he admitted, "but we'll have to do

some damage control."

And just like that, the tarot cards started to hiss and sizzle. She heard Hurricane whisper, "Three, two, one."

At *one*, he threw a massive energy blanket out and around, but he was using Skylar's energy at the same time. Realizing what he was doing, she quickly poured energy into this blanket that went around the mother and around Linden, keeping Gage and Terrence outside. Then came the implosion.

As they watched, the mother shrieked and collapsed, while the supposed friend blew up. The blanket sank back down, covering the tarot cards.

Terrence raced to his mother, who lay on the ground, completely unconscious. He put a hand to her neck, stared at Gage, and whispered, "She's dead. She's almost cold, she's so dead." And he stared at the three of them in horror. "Good God," he said, backing up. "Good God."

"Yeah," Skylar directed at Terrence. "You might want to mind your *P*s and *Q*s from this moment on."

He stared at her in shock, and then he ran, as far and as fast as he could. She saw the fear rocking him. "Go after him, Gage," she urged. "He's liable to run into the street like that and get hit."

He hesitated, looked at his mother, and asked, "What about Linden?"

"His energy, his rage, seems to have burned itself out," she shared, studying the pale collapsed spirit, now a small shimmering ball, low at Gage's feet.

He looked in the same direction she pointed to. "I can't see him."

"I'm not surprised," she noted quietly. "And it's fine that you can't. He doesn't appear to be anything like what he was before."

Gage looked at her with hope. "Do you think he'll be okay?"

"Why don't we give Linden a little time to adjust?" she suggested, "and then we'll see if we can get him to cross over."

He smiled and gave her a warm glance. "I'd like that." He looked down at the tarot cards that appeared to be completely untouched and whispered, "Do you think that's what killed Jonesy?"

"Quite possibly," Hurricane agreed. "Whether because of monetary greed or the evil power associated with this deck, there's absolutely no joy for anybody who'll use the tarot cards for purposes other than good. It'll return and kill whoever it is who's trying to use them for evil."

Hurricane walked forward, carefully scooped up the cards, and put them in the steel box in his hand, then immediately closed the lid. He turned and looked at Skylar, grinned, and waved. "It's been a slice. If you don't mind, I'll get these back to safety."

She watched as he disappeared in the opposite direction of Terrence. She stepped closer to Gage. "We need to call the police this time."

"Yeah." He nodded, as he stared down at his mother. "I should feel grief, … shouldn't I? I should feel something."

"Not right now you shouldn't. Too much happening, too much to sort out, too much to get your mind wrapped around," she murmured. "So I wouldn't worry about it. All that emotional part will come later."

He wrapped his arms around Skylar, pulled her close, and whispered, "Good God, I still don't understand all that happened. How worthless and evil can my family get?"

"It doesn't matter," she reassured him. "Later, much later, we can sort it all out." He held her tighter, and she whispered, "I burned a lot of energy again."

He tilted his head, so he could look down at her face. "Meaning?"

She gave him a quick frown. "Meaning, I'm hungry."

He shook his head and then started to laugh. He scooped her up into his arms, swung her around in a big circle, then put her down, whispering, "And that's fine. I have absolutely no problem getting more food."

"Well, I'm going down to my store," she shared. "You left it open."

"I did," he admitted, "but I left Thomas in charge."

She rolled her eyes at that. "You can stay here and deal with the cops."

And, with that, she raced downstairs and stepped into her store, not at all surprised to find it completely full of people. She smiled as she noted the loving energy Thomas had used on her customers, linking them to the objects they had chosen to purchase. They seemed frozen to their spots, until she stepped behind the counter. Afterward they all came up to make purchases. By the time she'd finished ringing them all up, she looked over at Thomas. "Thanks, buddy."

He laughed. "Hey, no problem. That's what family is all about."

And she had to admit the family that she had created for herself was the best damn family she could ever have hoped for. As Gage popped into her mind, she smiled and added, "Definitely, that's what family is for."

This concludes Book 21 of Psychic Visions: Talking Bones.

Read an excerpt from String of Tears: Psychic Visions, Book 22

String of Tears: Psychic Visions (Book #22)

HURRICANE STEPPED OUT onto the deck of his Maine coastal home and watched as the Atlantic Ocean crashed over the beach. He loved it here; something about the storms electrified him. But then it was his specialty; it's what he did. That he was a climatologist was something else again. He hadn't fully utilized his education very much in the last ten years. He needed to help put out too many other electrical storms or energetic storms instead. And this last one had been a prime example—tarot cards that could kill. "What the hell?" he muttered. He shook his head.

He lifted his face into the wind and let it pour over him. When he heard Stefan's voice in the back of his head, he smiled. "That was a hell of a journey you sent me on."

But I knew you could handle it, he stated. *Besides, you were already in New Orleans.*

"Yep, and I was hoping to spend a couple days there," he muttered. "Not turn around and bolt."

You still can. I'm sure they would like to see you again.

"That Skylar is pretty amazing," he noted.

You have no idea, Stefan muttered. *The things she can do with the dead are some I've never seen before.*

"Okay, now you've got me fascinated."

Well, I might have, he agreed, *but we have another problem.*

"What the hell is that?" he asked, with an eye roll. "You know that I thought all this stuff would help, but instead it seems like the energy just keeps getting crazier and crazier."

You're right. It does, and I'm not sure what's going on with this one though.

"In what way?"

I think it concerns all your trips, collecting all these items and putting them in the museum.

"Yeah. What are you getting at?"

I have a jeweler, who has been putting a lot of emotions into the designs she makes, and, of course, that's making her products very attractive.

"That's smart of her. So what about it?"

She contacted me.

"About what?"

A string of pearls she's trying to repair.

"*Uh-oh.* Don't tell me. Teardrops?"

A whole string of them. Pearls are known to be the tears of the ocean.

"Sure, and?"

Every time she goes to repair this necklace, she gets visions of murders. One for every pearl.

He sucked in his breath. "Good God, are you serious?"

Yes, very serious, and I've done just enough surface digging to understand that an awful lot of energy is infused into these gems. The problem is, she seems to think that maybe whoever created this necklace had a matching bracelet, and he wasn't quite done with the job.

"Well, who is this person, the jeweler who you're talking to?"

She lives in Maine, which is another reason for contacting you, since you're right there. … Her name is Jewel.

"Jewel. Jewel. Jewel. I don't think I know anybody by that name."

No, but you're likely to.

"Why is that?"

Because she just resurrected from the dead.

JEWEL OPENED HER eyes, the same panic choking her, as she bolted upright, swinging her arm against a bed rail. Machines beeped at her side, and a nurse came running.

"You're fine. You're fine," she reassured her, "and we're more than happy to have you awake."

Jewel stared at the nurse in shock. "What happened?" she murmured.

"We don't know everything," she began, "but basically you died and came back."

"I died?" Jewel asked in shock.

The nurse smiled. "Yes, but it's fine. You'll be just fine." The nurse stared at her with a big grin and added, "You've been very, very lucky."

Jewel nodded slowly, waited while the nurse checked

everything, and then withdrew. Jewel wanted to ask a million questions, but, at the same time, she didn't want to ask any. She had no idea what had happened. Whatever had put her in the hospital was a complete blank. Did she have an accident? Was she having surgery? She didn't know.

She heard a man's voice in the background, somewhere in the dark recesses of her brain, telling her, *You better not say anything. You* better *not say anything. Or else.*

She didn't know what the "or else" meant, but she knew it was important. Her fingers went to her throat, reaching for something that belonged there, something that was always there, a necklace. But not now. She looked around for it, but, of course, no personal belongings were allowed in the hospital. She kept clawing at her throat, prodding her memory to return. When the nurse returned, Jewel asked her, "My necklace, do you know where it is?"

The woman looked at her in surprise. "Sorry, you didn't have on a necklace." She stopped and then calmly explained, "Honestly, you didn't have a stitch on. We don't have ID for you. You didn't have any clothing, nothing. Nobody knows what happened or how you came to be found at the front of the hospital, completely nude but not a mark on you."

She stared at the nurse in shock. "My name is Jewel," she stated. "And I really need to get back that necklace."

The woman shook her head. "The doctor is on his way," she said gently. "You can talk to him about it." She held out a glass of water. "Here. Take a sip."

Jewel immediately took one swallow of water, and then, as if her body suddenly realized what water was, she sucked back the entire glass.

The woman looked at her in surprise. "Well, that's a good sign."

Jewel nodded. "Did you say I didn't have any clothes on?"

"You didn't have anything on, but, at the same time," she repeated, "you also didn't have a mark on you, so we don't know what happened."

"Good God," she murmured. She stared down at the hospital gown that covered her, and then she looked at her arms and the bruises all over her wrists and higher up. "If I didn't have a mark on me," she asked, "where did these come from?"

"Well, that's just it," the nurse added. "Bruises show up after any trauma but later on. We're still trying to figure out what happened though. So, if you remember anything at all, it would be a really good thing," she noted.

But Jewel looked at her, shook her head, and said, "I can't remember anything."

Find Book 22 here!

To find out more visit Dale Mayer's website.

https://geni.us/DMTearsUniversal

Simon Says... Hide: Kate Morgan (Book #1)

Welcome to a new thriller series from *USA Today* Best-Selling Author Dale Mayer. Set in Vancouver, BC, the team of Detective Kate Morgan and Simon St. Laurant, an unwilling psychic, marries all the elements of Dale's work that you've come to love, plus so much more.

Detective Kate Morgan, newly promoted to the Vancouver PD Homicide Department, stands for the victims in her world. She was once a victim herself, just as her mother had been a victim, and then her brother—an unsolved missing child's case—was yet another victim. She can't stand those who take advantage of others, and the worst ones are those who prey on the hopes of desperate people to line their own pockets.

So, when she finds a connection between more than a half-dozen cold cases to a current case, where a child's life hangs in the balance, Kate would make a deal with the devil himself to find the culprit and to save the child.

Simon St. Laurant's grandmother had the Sight and had warned him that, once he used it, he could never walk away. Until now, her caution had made it easy to avoid that first step. But, when nightmares of his own past are triggered, Simon can't stand back and watch child after child be abused. Not without offering his help to those chasing the monsters.

Even if it means dealing with the cranky and critical Detective Kate Morgan …

Find Simon Says… Hide here!
To find out more visit Dale Mayer's website.
https://geni.us/DMSSHideUniversal

Author's Note

Thank you for reading Talking Bones: Psychic Visions, Book 21! If you enjoyed the book, please take a moment and leave a short review.

Dear reader,

I love to hear from readers, and you can contact me at my website: www.dalemayer.com or at my Facebook author page. To be informed of new releases and special offers, sign up for my newsletter or follow me on BookBub. And if you are interested in joining Dale Mayer's Reader Group, here is the Facebook sign up page.
http://geni.us/DaleMayerFBGroup

Cheers,
Dale Mayer

About the Author

Dale Mayer is a *USA Today* best-selling author, best known for her SEALs military romances, her Psychic Visions series, and her Lovely Lethal Garden cozy series. Her contemporary romances are raw and full of passion and emotion (Broken But … Mending, Hathaway House series). Her thrillers will keep you guessing (Kate Morgan, By Death series), and her romantic comedies will keep you giggling (*It's a Dog's Life*, a stand-alone novella; and the Broken Protocols series, starring Charming Marvin, the cat).

Dale honors the stories that come to her—and some of them are crazy, break all the rules and cross multiple genres!

To go with her fiction, she also writes nonfiction in many different fields, with books available on résumé writing, companion gardening, and the US mortgage system. All her books are available in print and ebook format.

Connect with Dale Mayer Online

Dale's Website – www.dalemayer.com
Twitter – @DaleMayer
Facebook Page – geni.us/DaleMayerFBFanPage
Facebook Group – geni.us/DaleMayerFBGroup
BookBub – geni.us/DaleMayerBookbub
Instagram – geni.us/DaleMayerInstagram
Goodreads – geni.us/DaleMayerGoodreads
Newsletter – geni.us/DaleNews

Also by Dale Mayer

Published Adult Books:

Shadow Recon

Magnus, Book 1

Bullard's Battle

Ryland's Reach, Book 1

Cain's Cross, Book 2

Eton's Escape, Book 3

Garret's Gambit, Book 4

Kano's Keep, Book 5

Fallon's Flaw, Book 6

Quinn's Quest, Book 7

Bullard's Beauty, Book 8

Bullard's Best, Book 9

Bullard's Battle, Books 1–2

Bullard's Battle, Books 3–4

Bullard's Battle, Books 5–6

Bullard's Battle, Books 7–8

Terkel's Team

Damon's Deal, Book 1

Wade's War, Book 2

Gage's Goal, Book 3

Calum's Contact, Book 4
Rick's Road, Book 5

Kate Morgan

Simon Says… Hide, Book 1
Simon Says… Jump, Book 2
Simon Says… Ride, Book 3
Simon Says… Scream, Book 4
Simon Says… Run, Book 5

Hathaway House

Aaron, Book 1
Brock, Book 2
Cole, Book 3
Denton, Book 4
Elliot, Book 5
Finn, Book 6
Gregory, Book 7
Heath, Book 8
Iain, Book 9
Jaden, Book 10
Keith, Book 11
Lance, Book 12
Melissa, Book 13
Nash, Book 14
Owen, Book 15
Percy, Book 16
Quinton, Book 17
Hathaway House, Books 1–3

Hathaway House, Books 4–6

Hathaway House, Books 7–9

The K9 Files

Ethan, Book 1

Pierce, Book 2

Zane, Book 3

Blaze, Book 4

Lucas, Book 5

Parker, Book 6

Carter, Book 7

Weston, Book 8

Greyson, Book 9

Rowan, Book 10

Caleb, Book 11

Kurt, Book 12

Tucker, Book 13

Harley, Book 14

Kyron, Book 15

Jenner, Book 16

The K9 Files, Books 1–2

The K9 Files, Books 3–4

The K9 Files, Books 5–6

The K9 Files, Books 7–8

The K9 Files, Books 9–10

The K9 Files, Books 11–12

Lovely Lethal Gardens

Arsenic in the Azaleas, Book 1

Bones in the Begonias, Book 2

Corpse in the Carnations, Book 3

Daggers in the Dahlias, Book 4

Evidence in the Echinacea, Book 5

Footprints in the Ferns, Book 6

Gun in the Gardenias, Book 7

Handcuffs in the Heather, Book 8

Ice Pick in the Ivy, Book 9

Jewels in the Juniper, Book 10

Killer in the Kiwis, Book 11

Lifeless in the Lilies, Book 12

Murder in the Marigolds, Book 13

Nabbed in the Nasturtiums, Book 14

Offed in the Orchids, Book 15

Poison in the Pansies, Book 16

Quarry in the Quince, Book 17

Revenge in the Roses, Book 18

Lovely Lethal Gardens, Books 1–2

Lovely Lethal Gardens, Books 3–4

Lovely Lethal Gardens, Books 5–6

Lovely Lethal Gardens, Books 7–8

Lovely Lethal Gardens, Books 9–10

Psychic Vision Series

Tuesday's Child

Hide 'n Go Seek

Maddy's Floor

Garden of Sorrow

Knock Knock…

Rare Find

Eyes to the Soul

Now You See Her

Shattered

Into the Abyss

Seeds of Malice

Eye of the Falcon

Itsy-Bitsy Spider

Unmasked

Deep Beneath

From the Ashes

Stroke of Death

Ice Maiden

Snap, Crackle…

What If…

Talking Bones

String of Tears

Psychic Visions Books 1–3

Psychic Visions Books 4–6

Psychic Visions Books 7–9

By Death Series

Touched by Death

Haunted by Death

Chilled by Death

By Death Books 1–3

Broken Protocols – Romantic Comedy Series

Cat's Meow

Cat's Pajamas

Cat's Cradle

Cat's Claus

Broken Protocols 1-4

Broken and... Mending

Skin

Scars

Scales (of Justice)

Broken but... Mending 1-3

Glory

Genesis

Tori

Celeste

Glory Trilogy

Biker Blues

Morgan: Biker Blues, Volume 1

Cash: Biker Blues, Volume 2

SEALs of Honor

Mason: SEALs of Honor, Book 1

Hawk: SEALs of Honor, Book 2

Dane: SEALs of Honor, Book 3

Swede: SEALs of Honor, Book 4

Shadow: SEALs of Honor, Book 5

Cooper: SEALs of Honor, Book 6

Markus: SEALs of Honor, Book 7

Evan: SEALs of Honor, Book 8

Heroes for Hire

Heroes for Hire, Books 4–6

Heroes for Hire, Books 7–9

Heroes for Hire, Books 10–12

Heroes for Hire, Books 13–15

Heroes for Hire, Books 16–18

Heroes for Hire, Books 19–21

Heroes for Hire, Books 22–24

SEALs of Steel

Badger: SEALs of Steel, Book 1

Erick: SEALs of Steel, Book 2

Cade: SEALs of Steel, Book 3

Talon: SEALs of Steel, Book 4

Laszlo: SEALs of Steel, Book 5

Geir: SEALs of Steel, Book 6

Jager: SEALs of Steel, Book 7

The Final Reveal: SEALs of Steel, Book 8

SEALs of Steel, Books 1–4

SEALs of Steel, Books 5–8

SEALs of Steel, Books 1–8

The Mavericks

Kerrick, Book 1

Griffin, Book 2

Jax, Book 3

Beau, Book 4

Asher, Book 5

Ryker, Book 6

Miles, Book 7

Nico, Book 8

Keane, Book 9

Lennox, Book 10

Gavin, Book 11

Shane, Book 12

Diesel, Book 13

Jerricho, Book 14

Killian, Book 15

Hatch, Book 16

Corbin, Book 17

Aiden, Book 18

The Mavericks, Books 1–2

The Mavericks, Books 3–4

The Mavericks, Books 5–6

The Mavericks, Books 7–8

The Mavericks, Books 9–10

The Mavericks, Books 11–12

Collections

Dare to Be You…

Dare to Love…

Dare to be Strong…

RomanceX3

Standalone Novellas

It's a Dog's Life

Riana's Revenge

Second Chances

Published Young Adult Books:

Family Blood Ties Series

Vampire in Denial

Vampire in Distress

Vampire in Design

Vampire in Deceit

Vampire in Defiance

Vampire in Conflict

Vampire in Chaos

Vampire in Crisis

Vampire in Control

Vampire in Charge

Family Blood Ties Set 1–3

Family Blood Ties Set 1–5

Family Blood Ties Set 4–6

Family Blood Ties Set 7–9

Sian's Solution, A Family Blood Ties Series Prequel
Novelette

Design series

Dangerous Designs

Deadly Designs

Darkest Designs

Design Series Trilogy

Standalone

In Cassie's Corner

Gem Stone (a Gemma Stone Mystery)

Published Non-Fiction Books:

Career Essentials

Career Essentials: The Résumé

Career Essentials: The Cover Letter

Career Essentials: The Interview

Career Essentials: 3 in 1